Paul lived most of his life in Central Massachusetts, where he ran his own architectural design company for 23 years. He is a two term past president of the MA Society of the American Institute of Building Design. In 2013, he and his wife moved to Florida, where they currently live. Paul began writing in the fall of 2018. Since then, he has written two short stories each month, and has won, "The People's Choice Award" for two of them at public reading events. He has been involved with reading to the elderly at rest homes and other similar locations. Paul's first book, *The Odd Life of No One in Particular,* published by Austin Macauley Publishers, of London, England, is currently available online. Paul continues to write fiction and non-fiction novels and is slowly working on getting them published. He is an excellent marksman with both handguns and rifles, and he and his wife occasionally still visit the gun range. In the past, he has been involved in a weekly NASCAR racing series and go-kart racing.

This book is dedicated to my beautiful wife, Diann who has given me her support through good times and bad. She has always been my biggest critic, as well as my biggest fan. She is my muse in everything I do.

Paul Woodis

## The Signature Killer

Austin Macauley Publishers™
LONDON · CAMBRIDGE · NEW YORK · SHARJAH

Copyright © Paul Woodis 2022

The right of Paul Woodis to be identified as author of this work has been asserted by the author in accordance with section 77 and 78 of the Copyright, Designs and Patents Act 1988.

All rights reserved. No part of this publication may be reproduced, stored in a retrieval system, or transmitted in any form or by any means, electronic, mechanical, photocopying, recording, or otherwise, without the prior permission of the publishers.

Any person who commits any unauthorised act in relation to this publication may be liable to criminal prosecution and civil claims for damages.

This is a work of fiction. Names, characters, businesses, places, events, locales, and incidents are either the products of the author's imagination or used in a fictitious manner. Any resemblance to actual persons, living or dead, or actual events is purely coincidental.

A CIP catalogue record for this title is available from the British Library.

ISBN 9781398453852 (Paperback)
ISBN 9781398453869 (ePub e-book)

www.austinmacauley.com

First Published 2022
Austin Macauley Publishers Ltd®
1 Canada Square
Canary Wharf
London
E14 5AA

Thank you to, Susanne Whelan, without whose help and support this book would not have been finished.

# Prologue

## An Antonio De Luca Adventure

The FBI seems to have a problem. They have a man, Tony, setting up a legitimate business in Boston, but he has no background. They have a file on another man, Stephen, which is wanted in Belfast for two murders and is thought to have fled to the United States but can't make the connection between the two men. Tony unknowingly hires an undercover agent to run his office in Boston. While she is busy digging through his files and records, he is running another agent on a global hunt. She is hunting a man she calls 'The Signature Killer'. She has named him that for the use of a specific item used in each of his assassinations. She believes Tony and Stephen are the same man but hasn't got the proof. The undercover agent also believes they are the same man, and she thinks she has the proof. Her information, however, is never going to be seen by the people that need to see it. Something happens after about five years of running Tony's Boston office that causes him to reveal himself to his office manager, losing his ghost-like quality. The story takes several twists and turns from there and ends with someone very close to Tony being killed. The killer turns out to be an as yet unknown character, but someone that Tony knows very well, and is close to.

# Episode One
## Three Tacos in a Bell Tower

Antonio De Luca was a legitimate businessman. He was also a ghost. While he was the owner of an international Telecommunications and IT company, with seven employees, only one of them had ever had any direct contact with him, and yet had never met him. His company occupied a small office suite on the north-east corner of a glass tower, at the edge of the financial district in Boston. The suite had one small corner office that looked out over a small section of the city to Boston Harbour, Long Wharf, Faneuil Hall, and the North End beyond that. The corner office may not have been large, but it could have passed for any high-end attorney's office in the city. It also had a private bath with a large walk-in shower. The rest of the suite was one large open room of about 800 square feet, also containing one bathroom, which backed up to the private bath. In the open office space there were six desks, no cubicles, Antonio did not like cubicles, just open space. The six desks were occupied by both male and female employees. With just the one bathroom, it was not uncommon for a man to be standing at a urinal, and a woman to walk in to use one of the stalls. As you might imagine, some interesting conversations had taken place in there. The door leading to the main office had a name plate on it that read simply, Annie. The person that occupied the desk in that office was Antoinette Spalding. She did not like to be called Antoinette; she preferred to be called Annie…Antonio had never been in that office and has never met the young lady that was the manager of the office.

Antonio, Tony as he preferred to be called, was never there because he had another international business that he ran out of his pocket on burner phones, from dozens of different locations all over the world. Not only have none of his employees ever met him, but none of his clients from either business have ever met him. While his IT business served the average corporate client with computer issues all over the world, his other business, though not listed anywhere on paper, served high-powered, political and military clients from around the world. He also worked with a few very high-powered corporate clients, and even the occasional drug lord from time to time. None of them knew his real name, or where he was at any given time. None of his clients from his legitimate company could contact him directly. The IT clients just called the corner office in Boston and Annie would take the call and switch it to whichever employee she thought was best able to handle their issue. Only his most important and repeat clients of the other business could call him directly. All others had to call the same office, and if they had used Tony's services before, they would have a code number to give Annie. She simply told them that Tony would return their call as soon as possible. If the client was a new client, they were told to give the code number of whomever they got Tony's information from and leave a contact number and Tony would get back to them. Tony was a ghost because he had to be. He was one of the world's most sought-after professional assassin. He was sought after not only for his services, but because of them.

While Tony was a very gifted marksman, he was also very gifted in the IT and engineering world as well. He developed a small portable frequency scrambler that could allow him to listen in on every call that came into his Boston office, from anywhere in the world, on any cheap burner cell phone. Tony could listen to all of the calls, but because of the scrambler, no other device of any kind could pick up the signals. He could also make outgoing calls using the same scrambler. That was how he, Annie, and his not so legitimate clients were able to get in touch with each other, with no one, not the FBI, not the CIA, not the ATF, not anyone being able to find him. The use of the code numbers along with the scrambled signals also made it impossible to trace who Tony made calls to, so his clients were as protected as he was.

Tony trusted very few people in this world, and even those that he trusted, he had never met face to face. He made his own guns, he made his own bullets, and while he had to have it built somewhere else, and trust the people that built it, he flew his own jet. The barrels, silencers, and all parts of the firing mechanisms of the guns were made of very high-quality carbon fibre. All other parts of the guns were made of high impact plastics. He built his guns that way to keep them light weight more than anything else. Tony built his rifles and scopes with such precision that he could shoot the eye out of a grasshopper at one hundred and fifty yards. Well, at least that was what he told his clients. Tony was very proud of the technology he used in creating all of his tools of the trade. He would often think about them and say out loud, to nobody, "If the world only knew of the things I can create."

Since the only employee that had any possible direct contact with Tony was his office manager, Annie, he had made a gun for her to have as protection. He made the gun for her almost five years ago, just after he hired her. To his knowledge, she had never used it. The gun was a very compact .9mm semi-automatic handgun. The gun was very small, and again very high-quality carbon fibre and plastic. He also supplied a holster of sorts with the gun. It wasn't really a holster so much as a garter belt with a small fabric cup for the tip of the barrel to fit into. There was a narrow strap that attached to the garter belt at the back side of her leg and came over the gun covering the trigger with a flat plastic guard and then attached to the garter belt in the front of the leg with a small piece of Velcro.

The gun and holster were placed (at night, with no one in the office) in a hidden floor safe in the large walk-in shower, called 'The tropical Vacation'. Tony left a note for Annie to check the safe when she came in the following morning. Because the gun was so small, Annie was able to carry it very high on the inside of her left thigh. No one would ever know the gun was there. Well, typically no one would know. But today she was having a particularly stressful day. She had decided to stop at a local pub for a drink or two on her way home. She didn't do that very often, but when she did, she always wore a wig and sometimes a pair of fake eyeglasses. While she was at the bar enjoying a drink, a very handsome and rugged-looking man approached her.

"Hi, is this seat taken?" he asked with a smile that lit up his whole face.

Annie found herself looking into the most beautiful green eyes she had ever seen.

"Not until you take it," she replied.

"Well...hi again, my name is Matt," he said as he sat down next to her.

"I'm Annie, nice to meet you. So, what do you do, and do you come here often?"

"Well, I work for an investigations' firm, and no I don't come here very often. In fact, this is the first time I have ever been in here."

She looked at him for several seconds thinking about what he just said.

"Really, this is my first time in here too. So, what do you investigate?" she asked, still thinking about the word.

"I just do what I'm told. Sometimes I check out people, and sometimes they have me looking into businesses," he said.

He was looking at her face as if trying to read something in it. Then, sounding almost too cautious she asked, "And what brought you in here tonight?"

He told her that he had been having a hard day and just felt like having a beer. He then asked her the same question. She gave him the same answer that he had just given to her. With the conversation continuing she found herself thinking of all the fun and nasty things she would like to do with him. She began to think that by the way he was looking at her he probably was thinking the same thing. Then, getting a little flustered, she excused herself and went into the ladies' room to think about what she was doing. She knew she couldn't go home with this guy. Did she really want to go to a hotel with him?

As she was standing talking to herself in the mirror, the man suddenly burst into the room. Surprised she said, "What are you doing in here?"

He just grabbed her by the shoulders and pushed her up against the wall. He pressed himself tightly against her, and started to kiss, and then grope her. She could feel his hardness and knew he meant business. Before she could stop him, his hand had gone up her skirt and between her legs. As the man's hand cupped the sensual silky thin fabric that lined her vagina, he felt her heat, and he felt her wetness. He also felt…the handle of a gun? While he was hoping and expecting that he would find that she was hot, he found her vagina packing much more heat than he was bargaining for. He backed away a step or two in shock.

"What the fuck is that?" he asked, almost yelling the words.

He started to reach for the bottom of her skirt to lift it up to see if what he thought he felt was what he did feel.

Realising that she was going to have a problem on her hands, she knew she had to take care of the situation. Annie gave the man a hard punch to the throat. As he backed off, with both hands clutching his throat, gasping for every bit of air he could get, she grabbed him by the shoulders and pushed him into a stall and onto the toilet. She then closed and locked the stall door. As she turned to face him again, she already had her 'Lady-9', as she named her gun, in her hand. Pushing the gun tightly into the man's abdomen, and then folding him over at the waist, she then covered his back with her body and gave him three shots to the stomach. With each shot, she gave a loud fake sneeze. Those three sneezes along with the gun being tightly folded inside the body covered the sound of the shots very nicely.

After taking care of the problem, Annie looked under the stalls to be sure nobody had come into the room. With the room still appearing to be empty, she left the door locked, and slid out under the stall door. As she was leaving the ladies' room, she knew she had bigger problems coming. Security cameras would most certainly show her talking to the man at the bar and may even show him follow her into the ladies' room. She had to get out of the pub and find a dark alley quickly. After leaving the bar, she found an area that was fairly concealed and didn't appear to have any security cameras covering it. She hid in there and very quickly removed the wig, and took off her skirt and jacket, and turned them inside out to reveal a completely different colour and pattern. After putting the reversed clothes back on, she then very calmly made her way back to her car, and then home for the night. She thought about calling Tony, to tell him about the incident, but she could only do that from the office phone.

Earlier that day a call had come into the office from client number 63741. She didn't know anything about the client other than the fact that he spoke with a very heavy Spanish accent, and that he had made calls to the office on four or five other occasions. She didn't have to do anything about the call. She knew her boss would have heard the call and was probably already dealing with whatever the issue was this time. Tony had indeed received the call and he knew that when that client called it meant business, urgent and high paying business. He was, however, at that very moment, a little busy with a very hot, very wet young lady of his own. While she was very hot, she was packing a little less heat between her legs than Annie. After finishing up with her, Tony left her alone to make a private call to number 63741. He was one of his more frequent Mexican drug lord clients, and Tony knew that whatever he wanted, it was going to have to be done quickly.

Making the call, Tony found that the job was going to take place in Mexico, in a little town called San Carlos. The town, in the Eastern part of Mexico, was in a mountain region. That was going to be a bit of a problem and add to the price of the job. The town being located where it was, meant that there were no air strips close by to land his jet. He was going to have to land somewhere else and make other arrangements to get to the site. As he explained that to the client and told him what the job was going to cost, he was good with that. He just wanted the job done within the next few days.

The first thing Annie did when she got to the office the following morning, was call Tony. She had to tell him about the investigator and what happened the previous night. When Tony answered the phone she said, "Tony, I think we may have a small problem coming."

Tony asked why she thought that, and she continued, "I stopped at a bar last night, one that I have never been to before, and a guy came up to me and started talking to me. He said he had never been in that bar before either. And that he worked for some kind of investigations' company."

"What kind of investigations?" Tony asked.

"He didn't say. He just said that sometimes he investigates people and sometimes businesses."

Then she told him that she went into the ladies' room to try to get away from him, but he followed her in there.

"So, I had to fix it," she said.

"What happened in the ladies' room, Annie?" he asked.

"Well...he came in and started to get really touchy, and before I could stop him, he found Lady-9, so...well...um, I had to kill him."

Then she added very quickly, "But it's okay. Nobody saw us, and I had a wig and eyeglasses on, and I left him in a locked stall."

After thinking about it for a minute or two Tony said, "Alright, but make sure you keep a very close watch on the situation and keep me posted."

Annie said that she would do that and hung up the phone. After checking his maps, Tony found that there was an airport that had a runway he could use in the town of Burgos, just north-east of San Carlos. Tony's jet was a custom built all electric jet, completely designed by him. The jet was just a bit smaller than a typical corporate jet might be, but it had three electric turbines and made almost no noise at all. The jet had 'variable-sweep wings' to allow for greater speed and performance. There were no exterior ridges, bumps, knobs, or anything that a radar beam could reflect off. For a couple of well-played favours, Tony was able to acquire enough of the same material that the US Military used to paint their Stealth aircraft, to paint his.

Since his jet needed no cargo or passenger space, the fuselage contained a large electric generator that while it didn't make as much electricity as the jet used, it made very close to it. For that reason, the jet had a very long flight capacity. He designed the jet to have a maximum altitude of fifty-two thousand feet, with a maximum air speed of Mach 1.7 miles per hour. With extra-large, heavy-duty brakes and extra-large wing flaps, the jet could land on a surprisingly short runway. Tony was especially proud of his jet and often said to nobody, "If the world only knew of the things I can create." He made the flight from a small private airport somewhere in the upper mid-west to the private airport in Burgos in very short order. Not being the type of person that would rent a car at the airport, Tony had his client provide a stolen car left near the airport for his convenience.

The only luggage he carried was his briefcase. That too was custom made by him. The case, while looking like a standard briefcase, had three compartments in it. As you open the case the first compartment had several files, papers, and other normal things you would expect to find in there. If you flip the briefcase over and open it, you will see the back side of all of the same things, in the exact same position as the things you saw in the front of the case. If you were to lift the rear compartment, which was lined on the front and back sides with a thin layer of a lead like alloy, also developed by Tony, you would find a high-powered sniper rifle, disassembled and neatly packed in the foam insert made for it, along with a very high-powered scope, and very high-quality silencer, also made by Tony. He was very proud of all of the things he had developed for his second little job, and wished that he could tell people about them, but he knew that could never happen.

You would also find a pair of coveralls, and gloves. The rifle made the same way he made Annie's 'Lady-9', was a bolt action model. He did that so he could collect all of the bullet casings and not worry about leaving one behind. The bullets Tony made and used were very special. The casings were supplied by a legitimate manufacturer that would skim twenty or so off an order of thousands and call them defective and sell them to Tony. The cordite was purchased in the same manner. He cast his own bullets in copper and drilled out the centre of them. After drilling them out, he would fill the centres with dozens of very small lead pellets, and then cap the bullet. When one of his bullets hit its intended mark, it simply exploded and sent all of the lead pellets swirling around inside the brain. His intended mark was definitely going to be dead, and there was no bullet left to trace.

Having arrived at the airport in Burgos, he found the stolen car and made his way to San Carlos. The centre of the town was very small, and it reminded Tony of one of those towns you saw in old western movies. Just out of the centre of town was the church. From the bell tower, Tony could see all of the centre of town. The bell tower was going to be the best spot for him to set up. Not knowing how long he was going to be there, he stopped at the little Cantina in the centre and got three tacos, each one different, to go. While he waited for the tacos, he made a little small talk with the girl behind the counter.

"Sure, is hot here. Is this normal for this time of the year?" he asked.

The girl looked at him and replied in very broken English,

"Is warm but gets hotter."

"Does this place get busy around lunch time?" he asked.

She just nodded at him and gave him the tacos. Tony paid for them, and left the building, heading for the church. His job was simple. There would be a man wearing black cowboy boots, blue jeans, a white shirt with a red vest over it, and a black cowboy hat. He went to the Cantina for lunch almost every day. When he shows up, Tony was to take him out. The man, Tony was told, stole a lot of drugs from number 63741 and a great deal of money, and he was also fucking his wife. She was going to have to disappear too, but that was going to have to happen a little differently and it was going to have wait. The grounds around the church were roughly landscaped and didn't look as if anyone did much with them. He found a nice thick bush on the side of the church that was away from the Cantina to leave his briefcase in. After removing the coveralls and gloves, he assembled the rifle and mounted the scope.

Making his way to the bell tower without being seen was easy. There was nobody around. Once up there, he put on the coveralls and gloves, and pulled a length of rope out of a pocket in the coveralls and attached it to a beam in the tower. He checked his scope, to make sure he was good with the distance. He was about two hundred yards from the Cantina. That was a little close he thought, but he would make it work. Now he could settle in and eat his three tacos in the bell tower. As Tony ate his tacos, he gave number 63741 a call to make sure the job was still on. The reply he got was,

"Of course, the job is still on. I want you to blow his fucking head off right there on the street. I want people to know that they can't fuck with me and get away with it."

"Okay...same payment plan as always. You still have the numbers?" Tony asked.

Number 63741 replied that half had already been sent, and the rest would be sent when the job was done.

"Okay, I haven't seen any kind of police around. Does the town have anything like that?" Tony asked.

"Yeah, but try not to kill them if you can help it. I don't think they will bother you too much," said number 63471.

He was pretty sure that when the police saw who got shot, their investigation would be moving very slowly. The man apparently was not liked by many people in the town. After being in the bell tower from mid-afternoon of the first day, and all night, it was now approaching lunch time on the second day. Tony had been thinking about two things in all of that time. The first was the odd coincidence of the investigator at the bar with Annie, and the second was if he wanted to shoot mister red vest going in or coming out of the Cantina.

At about 12:15 on the second day, Tony saw mister red vest approaching the Cantina. Watching him through his rifle scope, Tony thought that the man didn't look like your average drug running thief but was good looking enough to probably be sleeping with any man's wife. He decided to let the man go in and have his last meal. As Tony sat and waited for the man to come back out, he ate the last of the three tacos he bought yesterday. He decided that day old tacos were not as good as fresh ones. Then his phone buzzed. It is Annie, his office manager. She never called him unless there was some kind of problem.

"What's up, Annie?" he asked.

Annie sounded a little uneasy.

"The police were here this morning with a security camera photo of the dead guy and the girl he was talking to last night. Even with the wig and glasses on, the girl looked a lot like me."

"What did they say to you?"

Annie told him that they asked if she knew the woman in the photo. After telling them that she had never seen her before, she said one of the officers held the picture up next to her face.

"Really, because it looks like the two of you could be twins," the cop said.

Tony told her to get rid of the wig, and glasses. She told him she already had.

"I'm a little concerned about this. Keep me very up to date about it over the next couple of days."

Mister red vest is back out on the street.

"I gotta go right now," Tony said and got off the phone.

He picked up the rifle and focused the scope on the side of the man's head. He was standing talking to another man. Tony wanted to wait for them to split up, but it didn't look as if that was going to happen any time soon. With the high quality of the silencer Tony made for the rifle, no one would hear the shot. He decided to take his shot and did. Through the scope he saw a small hole appear in the side of mister red vest's head. He saw both of the man's eyes blow out of his head, followed by what was probably brain matter reduced to soup. The man fell to the ground before the other man he was talking to could react.

As Tony was getting ready to repel down the back side of the church to make his getaway, his phone buzzed. When he got to the ground, he looked at the phone. It was number 63741. Tony answered the phone as he was taking off the coveralls. Before he could say anything, the voice he knew as number 63741 was already saying, rather loudly into the phone,

"That was incredible, I was right there beside him when he went down. I was telling him that I knew about him and my wife, and what I was going to do to her because of him. He said that he was going to kill me. I guess that's not going to happen. The rest of your money is on the way."

He was laughing very loudly as he hung up the phone. Tony took his rifle apart, put it and the coveralls and gloves back in the briefcase. He put the suit coat that he left with the briefcase back on, picked up the case and headed for the side of the street to go back to his stolen car. He looked like any other normal businessman would walking along the street.

Tony was thinking about that thing with Annie, the police, and the investigator. Something was bothering him about it. He decided to spend a little time in Mexico as long as he was already there. He knew he could drive to Cancun from where he was without much trouble, and he had a number of different passports with him if he needed one. A little rest and relaxation was what he needed while he waited for the next job to come up, and maybe get his mind off the problem Annie had created at the office. Tony didn't know it at the time, but Annie was busy creating more of a problem than he could have imagined.

To Be Continued

# Episode Two

## A Call from Svetlana

As she sat in her office on Monday morning, Annie was thinking about the problem she was having. She knew that the police were pretty sure that she was the one that killed the agent in the ladies' room. One question that kept coming up was, if that was true, why haven't they arrested her? But then, the bigger question was, what was that agent doing there in the first place? The more she thought about her meeting the man, the less she thought it was a coincidence. Is she, or Tony, or both, being investigated, and if so…by whom? And was that the reason she hasn't been arrested yet? Just thinking about it, she was beginning to spook herself.

She knew one thing for sure, before it goes any further, her beloved 'Lady-9' was going to have to take a vacation. She got up from the desk and removed the gun. She then made sure that the windows in her office were shaded, and the door locked. She took the gun and went to the hidden safe in the bathroom. Opening the safe, she removed the false bottom and carefully placed 'Lady-9' in and replaced the bottom. After closing the safe she went back out to the office and opened the door and cleared the windows. She knew that she was then going to have to talk to Tony about the situation. She hadn't heard from him since last week and wasn't sure where he was, or what he was up to. But she had to get his feeling about the whole thing now that he has had time to think about it. As she sat at her desk and was reaching for the phone, it started to ring. Already being a little spooked, it scared the shit out of her, and she jumped right out of the seat.

"Hello, Telecomm International, how may I help you?" She said after picking up the phone.

The person on the other end, a man, spoke with what she thought sounded like a Russian accent.

"Hello, I need speak to Tony, please. I need speak with him very fast, please."

Trying hard to understand him, she said, "Tony isn't here. If you leave your contact information, and your code number, or your associates code number, Tony will get back to you."

"I have no such number of persons; I don't know what you are meaning to me." He continues with, "I just need to speak with Tony, very important I talk with him soon, okay?"

Then he gave Annie a phone number to reach him and hung up. She knew that Tony heard the call, and was probably thinking the same thing she was, he would be calling her any time now. After about five minutes, Tony was on the phone with Annie.

"Do you think that call could have anything to do with what happened last week?" he asked.

"I don't know," Annie replied, "I'm a little concerned about the whole thing. If you think about it, that agent being at that bar doesn't really seem like a coincidence, and I have a strong feeling that the police think I killed him. But I don't understand why they haven't arrested me yet."

Tony is more concerned now than he has been.

"Why do you think that?" he asked.

"Well, the agent came up to me at the bar almost as if he had followed me in, specifically to talk to me. I saw him hanging around for a few minutes while I was sitting at the bar, and then he just came straight to me."

And then she reminded him about the visit from the police.

"And the police came to the office with that picture, and they were really sure they were looking at the same girl. The wig and eyeglasses didn't really fool anybody."

"Okay…has anyone contacted you since then?" Tony asked.

"Not yet," she replied.

But they both knew that calls like the one from the Russian, with no code numbers was not a new tactic used by some law enforcement agencies to try to down track Tony.

"Where is lady-9?" Tony asked.

"She's good, she's on vacation in the tropics," she told him.

Tony told her he would get back to her after he has time to think about the Russian call.

Around four o'clock that same afternoon another call came into the office from a Russian number. When Annie picked up the phone, the person on the other end this time was a woman. She spoke slightly better English than the man from the previous call did.

"Hello, Telecomm. International, how may I help you?"

"This is friend of Tony. Please have Tony call me as soon as possible."

As soon as she said that Tony cut into the call.

"It's okay, Annie, I've got the call."

After Annie hung up and there was a slight pause, Tony came back on the line.

"How have you been Svetlana? It's been a long time."

"Yes, Tony. It's good to hear your voice. I have to ask for your help once again, my friend." She paused for a moment and then continued, "My brother is in trouble. He is the one that called for you earlier."

"How can I help you? What kind of trouble is your brother in?"

"Do you remember that my brother has 'a business' that he has been running for the last few years?" Svetlana started to explain.

Tony did remember about her brother's business. He had in fact used the services provided on more than one occasion.

"Yes, I remember. He has some very nice young ladies' working for him. Some are very talented. What seems to be the problem?"

"Well," she replied, "there are some men that are trying to take it away from him. They are demanding large payments of money, and they have already kidnapped three of his best girls."

"How are they getting to the girls to kidnap them?"

Tony was a little confused about how that could happen.

"My brother said that they would have three or four men make appointments at the same time, and they will pay the men to go in and grab one of the girls and leave with her. Then they demand very large payment to get her back, sometimes more money than my brother has."

She was starting to cry and was having a very hard time with all of it.

"They tell him if he does not pay, they will sell her in Asia as a common whore, where she will be forced to do many bad things every day for no money, until she is completely ruined, and then they will kill her and bring her back to him. I need you please to help my brother with this problem."

Tony told Svetlana that he would certainly help her brother. Tony and Svetlana had been friends for many years, she didn't have, or need a code number. The issue of the number of people to be dealt with was the next thing to be discussed. Svetlana told him that as far as she knew, there were four men Tony was going to have to deal with. Tony said that might be a problem because after hitting the first one or two, the others may go deep into hiding.

"Well, either that, or the others will get the message and move to Siberia," she replied.

"That's possible, but as long as they're still around, they will be a problem," Tony told her. He then said that before hitting the first one, he was going to try to have a plan that would put them all in the same place at the same time and hit them all at once. They then discussed the issue of payment. Svetlana said that she would be the one sending the money, and after agreeing on the amount, she would send one half to which ever numbers Tony wanted to use this time. The job was going to be a very difficult one, but a very high paying one. Tony was going to have to put some real thought into it.

The first problem was that the job was in Russia. For some reason, Tony had always had trouble moving around in Russia as quietly and easily as he did in most other countries. The next problem would be trying to get all four of the men in the same place at the same time, without them getting suspicious. Tony had some thinking to do. He also still had some thinking to do about Annie and the little problem that was going on at the office. Were both of them being investigated? If they were, how did that happen? Someone, a client, if possible, must have tipped off someone. Tony called Annie and told her to go out to a bar after work, but without any type of disguise. He said that he wanted to see if any undercover cops, or another agent from the investigations' company would approach her. She would have to be very careful about how she handled herself.

Annie decided she would go out Tuesday night, but to another bar she had never been to. Before leaving the office on Tuesday, she went into the bathroom and checked her makeup and hair. Satisfied, she headed out. She knew of a place down near Quincy Market that was big, busy, and noisy. She had never been in there, but she felt as if that would be a good time to check it out. As she was walking from the office building to the pub, she was trying to see if she was being followed. There were a lot of people on the streets at that time of the day, and it was making it difficult for her to spot any one in particular. But she thought she may have picked up on one. He doesn't look like a cop. He does, however, have that 'I'm an investigator' look about him. She was going to have to keep a close eye on him. Annie went into the pub, and it was exactly what she had heard it was; big, busy, and very noisy. She just walked around in the bar area for a while, looking at the people. The man that she thought was following her had also come into the bar. Trying not to stand out, he went up to the bar, sat down and ordered a drink.

Annie was wondering what he would do if she suddenly left. She toyed with the idea for a minute, but she was too curious about the man. She had to see if he would make contact with her. She went to the opposite end of the bar and took up a seat. After ordering a drink and looking at the menu, she looked back at the seat the man was sitting in, to find it was now empty. At first, she started to panic just a bit, but then calmed down. So maybe she wasn't being followed. That's not a bad thing. And then, the same man pulled up a seat right next to her. Suddenly a real momentary rush of panic ran through her body. The man smiled and asked, "Is this seat taken? Are you waiting for someone?"

"The seat's not taken, and no, I'm here alone. How about you, are you here alone, or are you looking for someone?" Annie asked back.

He said he was there alone and had just stopped in for a quick drink on his way home.

"What a coincidence. Me too," Annie replied.

"Well then, I'm a very lucky man to have your company for a drink," he said.

"So, what do you do?" Annie asked.

"Oh, I don't do anything in particular. I'm what they call a problem solver, I work for several different companies. When a company has a problem that they can't fix on their own, they call me."

"And what kind of problems do you solve for these companies?" she asked.

"Well, I guess I solve lots of different kinds of problems, but mostly missing persons and that sort of thing."

Annie, started to wonder, and was pretty sure the man was playing with her.

"You mean like, if someone goes missing from one of the companies?"

"Yes, that sort of thing," the man told her.

Tony had a plan, but he was going to need Svetlana's brother's help. He was already on his way to Russia, to a small, private airstrip he had used on her behalf before. He called and told Svetlana to meet him there and told her about what time he would be landing. This particular job was going to call for something other than Tony's favourite bolt action sniper rifle. He was going to have to use an automatic assault weapon, and he was going to have to get it from outside Russia. He didn't like doing that, even using sources previously used and mostly trusted. On his way to Russia, he made a quick stop in Belarus. There, he made the purchase of the assault weapon he was going to use. Arriving at the airstrip in Russia, Svetlana was there waiting for him. The two of them quickly got into a car and left the area. After they drove around for a while to make sure they were not being followed, they went to Svetlana's house. Once there, they started to talk about the problem her brother was having. Svetlana told Tony that since Padlov, Svetlana's brother, called Tony's office, he had lost one more of his best girls.

Tony got right to it. He told her to tell Padlov to arrange a meeting with the four men.

"Tell him to say he has all of the money they want, but he wants to meet with all of them to make sure that everybody is in agreement about leaving the girls alone. Have him tell them he will meet them at the Marx memorial, at 9:30 p.m. on Thursday."

Tony had her give Padlov those instructions so he could have time to set up a solid escape plan for both Padlov and him. He then told her to make sure to tell Padlov, that when he's there, do not look up, and wear a hat that will keep his face covered from any security cameras in the area.

"He should get a stolen car to drive to the meeting. After we are done there, we won't need the car anymore, so he can just leave it, and tell him to be sure to wear gloves."

Svetlana said she would pass on the instructions and begged Tony to please not let her brother get hurt. Tony told her that he knew the area of the memorial quite well, and he was very confident in his plan.

As Annie was sitting at the bar with yet another investigator, probably from the same company, or at least hired by them, she started to get a bad feeling. She didn't feel comfortable without Lady-9 between her legs. Suddenly, the man then turned in his seat and, looked at her and announced,

"Annie…My name is Juan, and the man sitting on the other side of you, well that's Paco, and the two men at the table right here behind us, well I guess you don't really need to know everyone's name. All you need to know is that the 'agent' you killed the other night was working for us. By 'us' I mean the Menaloa Cartel. Now the five of us are going to take a very calm and quiet walk back to your office. You're going to call your boss on that magic phone you have there, and you're going to tell him that you are going to be spending some time with us."

Seeing the devastated look on Annie's face he asked if she knew who the Menaloa Cartel was?

"Yes, they are one of the three deadliest drug Cartels in Mexico," she replied.

"We are not just one of them, we are the meanest, strongest, one," he told her.

The five of them left the bar together and headed for the office. Annie was trying to think of something she could do to help herself, but the four men have her surrounded. At the office, Annie called Tony. Once on the line with him, she started to explain the situation to him. Juan took the phone from her, to let Tony know that this was no joke, and that they meant business. They did not like the fact that Annie killed one of their people, and that retribution had been ordered and they were there to carry it out. Juan told him Annie would be with them until noon time on Friday. After that, he would be happy to send back whatever remained of his girl, Annie.

The new development was going to change things just a bit. Tony called Svetlana and told her to have her brother tell the four men to meet him on Wednesday evening, at the same time. He was afraid that might make them suspicious, but there was nothing else he could do. Svetlana called Tony back and said that the meeting was set for Wednesday night. Tony told her he needed a photo of her brother so he would know which one not to shoot. At about 8:30 Wednesday night, Tony was in position just a few yards from the Marx Memorial. He was well hidden by the unkept landscaping around the area. At about 9:30, a man that Tony could identify as Padlov came to the Memorial and sat on a bench nearby. As the time began to push ten o'clock, Tony can see that Padlov was starting to get nervous and a little antsy.

Then, four men came out of the dark, no more than five feet from Tony. They walked up to Padlov and demanded to see the money. Padlov did have a large bag with him, but it was full of his dirty laundry. As he handed the bag to the closest man, Tony took all four of them out with one very short burst of gun shots. He dropped the gun, ran out of the bushes, told Padlov to pick up his laundry, and they were both off between two buildings to another stolen car, with a driver waiting on a street behind the buildings. Svetlana's brother was taken to her house. Tony only went in to say goodbye to her and that he had to get back to Boston to help Annie. After talking to Tony from his office on Tuesday night, Juan and his entourage took Annie to a secluded safe house in Canton, MA where she would be kept until Friday at noon.

They had orders to do whatever they wanted to do to Annie, as long as they didn't kill her. They decided they could use some entertainment, and she certainly looked like she could entertain them. Annie was about five feet tall, with almost jet-black hair, and deep olive skin. She was a little heavy for her height, but she carried it very well, and dresses to accentuate her features. She was taken to a bedroom, stripped naked, and tied to a bed. The four of them, over the next few days, would be enjoying her company a great deal.

Tony was back in Boston now. It was very early Thursday morning. He had to come up with some sort of plan to help Annie. He had been thinking about it while he was on his way back from Russia but wasn't able to really come up with anything solid. He had to know where they were holding her. He decided that he only had one option. It would, unfortunately, start a war that Tony really didn't want, but felt he had no choice. On his cell phone, he punched in number 007. The digital display on the phone lit up like a GPS map. On the map was a small red dot. That was the exact location of Annie. When he hired her, he had a small microchip implanted in her skin for just this kind of occasion.

Now that he knew where she was, the problem would be getting in, and both of them back out alive. He didn't want to have to kill all four men, that was going to start a war with the Menaloa Cartel. He wanted to come up with a plan to get her out, without killing anyone. Tony made a call to Mexico. He called code number 60269. He was able to talk to him because 60269 had used his services a few times in the past. When he came on the line Tony says,

"I have the location where your boys are holding Annie. If they let her go, unharmed, I will forget any of this ever happened. If they fail to do that, in any way, I will kill all four of them, and then I will make a visit to one of your under bosses and take out his entire operation. You won't know until after it happens. So, are we good?" Tony then asked.

"I don't like that your girl killed that man in the ladies' room; that was disrespectful. He was working for me at the time. What I really don't like is that you killed one of my personal runners in San Carlos," Number 60269 replied.

Surprised, Tony took a few seconds to answer back,

"He was stealing drugs and money from one of your under bosses, and he was fucking the man's wife." He paused for a second and then continued, "it was your under boss that called for the hit."

"Well, the hit was never cleared with me, and you know how this works. I was not made aware of that situation before the hit was called for. Some retribution will have to be made. Your end of it is being taken care of as we speak. You leave that situation alone until Friday at noon and you and I will be good. As for retribution being taken in Mexico, be very careful my friend as to how you handle that, or we may not be so good after that," Number 60269 warned Tony.

Number 60269 cut the phone connection before Tony could say anything else. By Tony's end of the retribution being taken care of, he knew that Annie was being abused and hurt in ways that he didn't want to think about. He also knew that if he went in there and tried to do anything about it, 60269 would come after his entire Boston office, just to get back at him. Tony was going to have to come up with a plan to make his former client pay very heavily for whatever his men were doing to Annie. When Tony found out that Annie had been take on Tuesday night, he called his Boston office first thing Wednesday morning and had one of the other girls, Libby, fill in for Annie, telling them that she was sick. Knowing there is nothing he could do to help Annie at this point, Tony was going to make people pay with their lives. He would have to be very careful and put a lot of thought into that before acting on it, though.

Tony finally came up with a plan that he felt was good and would work. On Friday morning, at around ten o'clock, Tony took up a position outside the safe house where Annie was being held. He wanted to be sure that he was there when the four men left the building. At about 11:45 they came out of the house and walked calmly to the van they were driving. As they did, Tony was taking several high definition, colour, very close up, photos of each of them. He wanted to be sure he had very good pictures of them. He was going to need them later. While he was taking the pictures, and waiting for the men to leave, his phone buzzed. When he looked at it, he saw that it was Svetlana. He answered the call quickly, to hear her crying on the other end. Tony asked her what was wrong, and he heard her say,

"He's dead, Tony! My brother Padlov, he has been killed and left naked at the Marx Memorial."

Tony thought about that for a few seconds. It was obviously a message, but from whom?

"Who else was involved with the group that was trying to take over your brother's business?" he asked her.

She told Tony that she didn't know, but that she got a note that morning telling her not to try to interfere with them again, or next time it would be her, dead and naked, at the Memorial. Tony said that he had to take care of the thing with Annie before he could come back to help her, but that as soon as he could, he would be there for her.

Now back to concentrating on Annie! Tony realised he was going to have another small issue on his hands. The ghost of Tony was going to have to be revealed, at least to Annie. He was going to have to go into the house and free her from whatever bonds the four men had used. They were going to meet each other for the first time in the almost five years that Annie had worked for him. Tony sat outside the house for a few minutes trying to think of another way around it, but there really wasn't anything else he could do that made any sense to him. He went into the house as quietly as he possible, with his .40 cal. handgun drawn, just in case there were more men still in the house.

After looking around most of the house first, he finally went to the bedroom where he knew Annie was. The door had been left partially open, almost wide enough for him to walk through. Looking in through the open door, he saw Annie lying naked, tied spread-eagle to the bed. She was blind folded and had what looked like dried semen all over her face, and all over her breasts, stomach, and vagina. She also had what looked like a small river of semen still running out of her vagina, down her ass to a very large wet sport at the base of her ass. Those men had abused and humiliated her to a point that infuriated Tony and seeing her that way hurt him terribly. As he took a few tentative, quiet, steps into the room, even with the blind fold on, Annie still knew someone was there. She started to plead and beg with the unseen person.

"Please stop. Don't do it anymore, I can't take any more of this." She started to cry.

Tony moved to the side of the bed and covered her body with a sheet. Without taking the blind fold off he said, "Annie, it's me, Tony. I'm here to take you home, you're safe now."

Hearing the words, but not really comprehending them at first, after a pause she says, "Tony, my Tony, my boss Tony?"

"Yes, that's right, it's me, your Tony."

As he was telling her that, he was untying her hands from the bed. She started to cry inconsolably as she was trying to tell him what the men did to her and how they hurt her. Taking the blind fold off, he scooped his arms around her back and held her tight. He told her that they were going to take care of the men that did all those things to her, and that he was going to let her be a part of it, and that she was going to enjoy what he had in mind for not just the four men, but a few more, just to be sure retribution was paid in full.

To Be Continued

# Episode Three
## The Mexican Retribution Begins

As Tony and Annie sat on the side of the bed holding each other very tightly, Annie was still not really able to tell Tony what happened to her. She just couldn't stop crying enough to talk yet. Tony, seeing the condition she was in, began wondering just what those men did to her, besides the obvious. As he held her, he couldn't help noticing how firm and toned her body felt. *She must visit a gym on a regular basis,* he thought. After a while, she began to calm down enough to talk. Without letting go of him she asked again,

"Are you really Tony, my boss?"

"Yes, Annie it's me, and I'm here to bring you home now," he said. "But first, let's get you cleaned up a bit."

With the sheet still covering her body he laid her back down on the bed and began to untie her feet. She started to cry again, and he scooped her up in his arms and held her tightly. She started to try to talk about what they did to her.

"Tony, those men all did horrible things to me, but they made me do things to them, and to myself, unbelievably humiliating, and degrading things with all of them in the room, calling me names and telling me to do things. They were making me do things I can't even talk about, I just feel so dirty, I don't think I will ever be able to get my mind to forget those things."

"Try not to think about it. You stay here and I will go draw you a nice hot bath. Maybe after you soak for a bit, and get yourself cleaned up, you'll feel better," he told her.

Tony left her lying covered on the bed and went into the bathroom to draw the bath for her. When he came back to get her, she said, "I don't think I can walk. My pussy is very swollen and sore."

Tony bent down and picked her up, keeping her covered with the sheet. He brought her into the bathroom and put her and the sheet into the tub.

"You can adjust the water to however you like. Just sit and soak for a bit, and then you can clean up. I think that will help."

Tony had put out soap, a washcloth, and shampoo next to the tub, along with a couple of towels on a chair beside the tub.

"While you do that, and take all the time you need, I will go back out and look for your clothes."

As he headed out of the room, he heard Annie say in a very soft and hurt sounding voice,

"What if I'm pregnant?"

He turned back to her and said, "Don't worry about that now. You will be very well taken care of no matter what you need."

Tony left the bathroom and closed the door. Once he was out of the room, Annie balled up the wet sheet and threw it on the floor next to the tub, and just started to soak in the hot water. As he was walking around the house looking for Annie's clothes, while trying very hard not to, he couldn't help thinking how beautiful and sexy she was. He was thinking about seeing her through the partially open door to the bedroom for the first time. He thought about her very smooth, deep olive complexion, her ample breasts, that even with her hands tied above her head stood straight up. When he held her, he could tell just how firm her breasts were. And that smooth belly; it was just perfect. Her legs he thought looked firm and powerful, and he of course found himself thinking about that perfectly groomed, tiny black triangle of carpet, that those beautiful legs lead up to. And there was that ever so faint tan line that indicated the very small bikini that she must wear when sunbathing. He was beginning to hate himself for thinking about her that way and was trying to concentrate on finding her clothes.

As he walked around the house, he was starting to realise that her clothes were not there. The men must have taken them as souvenirs. Tony wondered which one walked away with her panties. He was going to have to treat him with a very special kind of disrespect, before killing him. As he was headed back to the bathroom to tell Annie that her clothes were gone, she came out with a bath towel wrapped around her. It was just large enough to cover all the vital parts. Tony stood looking at her and was again taken by her beauty. He told her that all of her clothes were gone, even her shoes, and that he was sure the men had taken them. Even though her vagina was still quite sore and swollen, Annie was at least able to walk on her on now. Tony found a clean blanket in a closet and wrapped it around her. Knowing she was able to walk, he still picked her up and carried her out to the car. She noticed right away that it was her car that Tony was driving. When she brought that to his attention, he said, "Well, I needed a car in a hurry, and yours was left at the office so I just hot-wired it. I will repair any damage I caused, or just get you a new one."

Tony brought Annie back to her house in Brookline, a small bedroom community of Boston. After bringing her into the house, she asked him to stay while she got dressed. While tony waited for Annie to brush her teeth and get dressed, he called code number 60269. When he got the man on the phone, Tony first asked about the police and Annie not being arrested.

"You have no worries there my friend. That situation has been taken care of," the man from Mexico told him.

Then Tony started in. He was very upset with how Annie was treated, but he knew he had to stay calm.

"The retribution given at my end was not deserved by Annie and was incredibly disrespectful. You should have called me if you had a problem and dealt directly with me."

"I have seen the video of what was done. I agree that it may have been a little more than I called for, but no one was hurt, and the message has been sent," 60269 replied. The answer only served to make Tony even more mad about what was done.

Keeping himself as calm as possible he said, "Your message has been received. I have no desire to start a war with you, so can we just say that we are both good with each other?"

"I would like to be able to say that my friend. You understand how this business is run, and I respect you for that, we are good," Number 60269 replied.

When Annie came back into the room, she was dressed in a casual button up shirt that was not tucked into the very short mini skirt she was wearing. Tony could see that besides all of the other beautiful features he had seen, he could now see that she had very large beautiful brown eyes, and shoulder length black slightly wavy hair. As he stood looking at her, he realised that she was looking at him in much the same way.

Just as he was thinking that she said, "You're not at all what I had pictured you to be."

Tony is about six feet tall and weighs about two hundred pounds, all of it muscle. He doesn't have a once of fat on him. Without asking her she volunteered,

"You're much younger and definitely much more handsome and rugged than I expected."

She had him pictured as mid-forties, and not someone that she would find attractive. He was actually 37, and quite attractive.

Tony suddenly found himself saying, "You're a bit younger than I expected, and far more beautiful and sexier than I had imagined you to be."

He didn't intend to say all of that, but it just came out. Annie is very attractive and just 26 years old. Then the reality of the situation began to creep into Tony's mind. Annie must have picked up on the change in what he was thinking.

"I guess were going to have to talk about the elephant in the room," she said.

"Yes, we have some important things that we have to talk about. You know that you are the only person associated with me that can identify me. That puts both of us in a somewhat dangerous position," he told her.

"I know," she said, "but after almost five years, you have to know that I would never betray you to anyone…ever."

"Yes, but through those five years you never knew what I looked like."

Tony had a problem. He knew the ghost was gone and he was either going to have to trust her with his life or eliminate her. He wanted desperately to be able to trust her with his life.

"So…what are we going to do to the men that hurt me? I want to be there and be a part of that," Annie asked.

Tony decided that if she was willing to kill for him, he would be able to trust her.

"We are going to Mexico, and we will start with some random members of the Menaloa Cartel. They are going to start having some very unfortunate and deadly accidents. We will work our way to the four men that hurt you. All of the hits are going to have to look like accidents so they can't come back on us."

"Okay, as long as I get to hurt those bastards that hurt me before they die," she replied.

"I think you're going to enjoy some of the things I have in mind for them in particular." Tony had already given it some thought.

But then she told him that she wasn't sure that she could identify all of them from memory. He gave her a file with dozens of photos of each of the four men, taken close up and at several different angles.

"Oh yes, these are the bastards," she told him.

"Alright, I have a little more planning to do for this before we can get started on it, but in the meantime, I have to go back to Russia for a couple of days. When I get back, I think I'll be ready to get started on our Mexican friends."

Tony told Annie to take all the time she needed before going back to work, and then he was gone and headed for Russia. He called Svetlana to let her know he was on his way and about what time to meet him. After landing, and being picked up by Svetlana, Tony told her that he only had a couple of days before he was due on another job. She knew he was almost always on call for something, so she wasn't surprised. She told Tony about the note she received and what happened to Padlov. Tony asked if she was sure that she couldn't think of any other people that were involved with the takeover attempt of his business. She told him as far as she knew, it was just the four men that he had already killed.

Tony decided that there must have been someone else waiting to make a move on Padlov, and they must have felt with the other four men taken out, that was the right time. Knowing that he didn't have a lot of time to play with, Tony had to get right to it. He asked Svetlana if Padlov had security cameras inside and outside of the building. She said that he did, but she didn't know where the security room was. This was not good news for Tony. He was going to have to figure out how to take care of the cameras before going too far with any kind of attack plan. Tony took a ride around the building that afternoon. He was able to pick out several exterior cameras and note their positions. This would at least help get him close to the building later that night.

At about 1:30 a.m., Tony approached the building on foot. He was trying to stay to the blind side of the cameras as much as possible. Armed only with his .40 cal. semi-automatic handgun and silencer, he was going to have to be very careful. The gun had a ten-round clip, and he had four extra clips with him, but that only gave him fifty shots. He did have a ten-inch knife with him if it came down to that, but he hoped that it wasn't going to.

The first obstacle was the guard at the front door. Tony knew there was a camera above him, so he was going to try to draw the guard away from the view of the camera. As the guard heard Tony in the bushes beside the building he went to investigate: One shot, one man down. Tony then went out to the street and walked up the front walk to the door as if he was a long-time patron and just walked in. Next, he was met by two men inside that were checking everyone coming in for weapons. Tony gladly showed them his handgun, and then used it, two more shots, and two more men down. He knew that cameras were now the biggest issue, he was on them and there was no way he was going to be able to avoid them. He decided the only thing he could do now was to walk through the building and take out anyone with a weapon. This was going to be a very risky little stroll.

As he began his march, men started to come at him from all sides in the main lounge area. As guns started firing from several different directions, he kept close to the floor and wound in between the furniture and the patrons and girls. He was very difficult for the armed men to find by doing that. At the same time, he had clear shots at most of the armed men and was able to take them out without too much trouble, or too many wasted shots. Next, he headed up the stairs to the halls leading to the private rooms. Each hall would have at least one or two guards in them. Having heard the gun shots coming from the lounge, the hall guards were most certainly going to be headed in that direction and very alert. Approaching the top of the stairs, Tony crouched down to make himself as small a target as possible. He saw the guards running toward the stairs and he was able to shoot both of them before either one got a shot off.

At the top of the stairs, Tony laid down on the last few steps and using the floor as a gun rest, waited for the guards to come from the other two halls at the end of the main hall he was in. As four men came around the corners, two from each side, with guns drawn, Tony was able to shoot two before the other two started shooting at him. With nothing but his gun and a very small part of Tony's head sticking up above the floor, the guards had very little to aim at and were shot before they could focus on Tony's head.

Next on Tony's list was going room to room, to find any guards waiting to trap him in the middle of a hallway. Most of what he found were patrons and naked women huddled behind beds or other furniture. In a room four or five doors from the end of the main hall, he opened the door and found three armed men standing at a table. It looked as if they were trying to make a plan of some sort to trap him at the end of the hall. Three shots, three more men down. Finding them like that meant to Tony that he was going to find more men in one or more of the rooms just around the corner planning the same thing. He was going to have to be very careful with the doors in the other two halls. Before leaving the room he was in, he picked up a couple of shoes and took them with him.

At the corner of the hall, he stood and looked around the corner and down the hall; it was empty. He threw one of the shoes part ways down the hall and against a wall. The noise brought two men with guns already firing in the direction of the noise, out of the room. Tony shot both of them before they realised it was a trick. He then turned to the corner on the other side of the hall and did the same thing with the other shoe. He got the same results and was able to kill both of those guards before they realised the trick. Tony was pretty sure that took care of the roaming guards. He now had to find the security room, kill the men in there and destroy the security tapes. There were two problems: He didn't know where the room was located, and he didn't know how many people would be in it. What he was sure of was they knew he was there, and they were probably watching him.

Looking down the hall that the last two guards were in, he saw a door marked 'private'. He had to assume that was the office and probably the security room. Looking up to the top of the walls in both directions of the hall, he saw the cameras that were watching him. There were five cameras, he shot all of them before moving into that hall. As he carefully made his way down the hall, he took a shoe off one of the dead guards. He was going to try to draw them out of the room with the same trick he used on the other guards. He threw the shoe against the wall just opposite the door and without the door opening, several shots were fired from inside the room threw the door. Tony made his way down the hall very quickly and quietly. He stood next to the door and made a thump as if a body had just fallen to the floor. After about a minute, the door opened just enough for him to ambush the room and he was able to kill the only person in the room. Tony was very surprised to find just one person in there, but he was also happy about that. He quickly destroyed all of the security tapes and the recording devices.

Having fired as many shots as he had from his .40 cal. handgun, Tony found that the barrel and firing mechanism were getting a little soft. He had never fired that many rounds so fast before from any of his guns and didn't know how the carbon fibre would hold up. He was going to have to make some adjustments with the next guns he makes. Tony left the building and made his way back to Svetlana's house. He told her all of the men were dead, and she should go in and take over the business. Tony told her he would be happy to run full background checks on anybody she wanted to hire. They hugged each other and gave each other a long and very passionate kiss. Then she asked him to spend the night. Tony told her that he really would like to, but he had a very important job he had to get to, and then he was gone.

Back in Boston on Tuesday afternoon, Tony went to Annie's house. Once he was there, he found that she had gone back to work, so he called her and told her to come home. He said to put the same girl in charge that was in charge while she wasn't there. When Annie got home, she found Tony inside her house having a drink and relaxing.

"How the fuck did you get into my house?" she asked.

"If you're going to work with me in the field, you have to learn that locks are only meant to be temporary delays. Why don't you get yourself a drink, and we'll talk about what we're going to do in Mexico," he told her. Annie grabbed a bottle of scotch and poured some in a glass for herself, and then refilled Tony's glass. Annie sat in a chair near Tony. She wanted to be sitting in his lap hugging and kissing him. She knew for something like that to happen, she was going to have to wait for him to make the first move. Looking at her and trying to fight his own very strong attraction to her, he started to talk about the first part of the plan.

"Okay…The Menaloa gang have a meth lab that puts out meth that looks like little chunks of coal. They call it 'Black Diamond'. A lot of their money comes from that. We're going to find it and cause it to blow up."

"Sounds like fun to me," Annie cut in.

"It's either in Los Indios, or Matamoros. It has to be near a shipping port, I think."

"Okay, so how are we going to find it without them knowing about it?" Annie asked.

"Keep those pictures of the men handy. I've changed my mind about who I want to start with. I want the leader of the guy's that took you."

"Oh, that's easy. It was this one," she said holding up one of the pictures.

"He said his name was Juan, and I think he was one of the worst ones to me at the house." Annie started to cry a little as she told Tony that.

"Then that's where we start. I have to make a small adjustment in the plane, and then we leave for Mexico tonight. I will see you in a couple hours. I think you should get some rest. And oh, by the way, how is Lady-9?" Tony asked.

"She is home, hot, and ready." Meaning that Annie already had the gun loaded and strapped in its proper place on her leg.

"I'll see you in a bit," Tony said and then left.

The adjustment Tony had to make in the jet was just to add a small jump seat that fit just behind the pilot seat. Annie, being as small as she is, should be quite comfy back there for the trip. When Tony got back to Annie's house, he saw that she had a suitcase packed and set by the door. He looked at it and then at her and explained,

"You can bring your pocketbook with you. If you feel that you want to bring a clean pair of panties, put them in that, but the suitcase is not coming with us."

"Oh…I just thought you brought stuff with you on the trips," she replied.

"Nope, not enough room," he told her.

Annie had never seen the jet. Now seeing it for the first time, she was quite impressed with it. Getting into the cockpit, she told Tony how impressed she was.

"Thanks, I designed it myself. I think you're going to like riding in it."

As she was getting into the jump seat, she noticed a clear plastic box under it. The box was about twenty inches long, twelve inches wide, and about eight inches high, and had one large compartment and one small one, both with sliding doors at the ends of them.

"What's this box for back here?" she asked.

"Oh, that's a box for pet snakes. I picked it up on the way over to your house. You're going to get a pet rattlesnake when we get to Mexico."

"I really don't like snakes, Tony."

"Well, I have a feeling that Juan isn't going to like them either."

From past dealings with number 60269, Tony had a rough idea where he would find the head of the Cartel and most of its people. He got Annie strapped into her seat, gave her a helmet with an oxygen mask and radio. As they approached fifty thousand feet, and Mach 1.5 mph, Annie said into the radio, "Wow, this really is fun."

"I told you I thought you would like it," Tony answered.

When they arrived in Mexico, Tony took Annie to a house that he used several time in the past on jobs in the area. He couldn't let Annie come with him as he looked for the men because they knew her, but they had never seen him before. After several hours of snooping around in a few different places, Tony found the man he was looking for. Being very patient, he was able to follow the man to his house. He then spent a little time checking out the man's house and found that he lived alone. *This was perfect,* he thought. He went back and got Annie, and they spent a little time finding a suitable pet rattlesnake for Annie. With the snake safely in the clear plastic box, they went to pay Juan a visit.

Spending some time looking through cracks in the window shades and curtains they were able to find Juan sitting in a chair watching the television.

Very quietly going to the front door, they found it was not locked. So once inside the house, knowing that Juan probably had a gun with him, Tony told Annie to go into the room and stand between Juan and the television.

"Hello Juan, remember me? I'm quite sure you do," Annie said as she went into the room and stood in front of Juan.

For Juan, seeing Annie was so shocking that all he could do was sit there and say, "What the fuck?"

By the time he got that out, Tony was behind him with his gun pressed firmly against Juan's head. He told Juan to put his hands out in front of him with nothing in them. Then he told him to get up and go into the dining room, where he had Juan sit in one of the armchairs at the table. Tony already had the chair pulled out well away from the table. When Juan sat in it, Tony held the gun on him while Annie duck taped his arms and legs to the chair. Tony started the conversation,

"Well Juan…don't you have anything you want to say to Annie? She came a long way to see you."

Juan just looked at Tony and said, "I don't know who you are but fuck you and your little bitch girl here. By the way, she has an incredible pussy, but you probably already know that."

Staying as calm as possible, as Annie was about to punch Juan in the face, Tony told her not to do that, but to go and get the plastic box they brought with them. Annie looked at Tony and smiled, then hurried into the other room to get the box. When she came back with the box, she stood in front of Juan with it so he could see what was in it. He sat looking at the large rattlesnake in the larger section of the box, and nothing in the small section.

"What are you going to do with that?" he asked without taking his eyes off the snake.

"We're going to play a little game. I understand that you like it when Annie does things with your pecker. So, Annie is going to put these gloves on, and she's going to open your pants, reach in and take your pecker in her hand and pull it out of your pants. From what Annie has told me about you, I'm thinking you're already liking this game," Tony told Juan.

He then told Annie to give the box a good shaking, just to make sure Mr. snake was awake and ready to play.

After shaking the box, the snake was awake and very angry.

"Now," Tony told Annie. "Take the sliding cover off the end of the box, and slide Juan's pecker inside the small compartment. Then I want you to push the box against Juan as hard as you can."

Juan, now afraid of what was about to happen, started to yell,

"Wait, wait, please don't do this! I'll do anything. I'll tell you anything but please don't do this."

"Oh...I see you know this game. Okay then, you know that Annie is going to ask you some questions, give her the answers she wants, and you win; don't answer, or give her the wrong answer, and you lose. If you lose, Annie gets to give you her pet snake," Tony explained to Juan, smiling as he said that to him.

Annie started to ask her questions.

"Okay, let's start with some easy ones, are you one of the men that kept cleaning yourself off in my hair after you fucked me?"

"Yes, yes I'm sorry," Juan replied.

"Are you the one that took my panties?"

"Yes, I still have them, and you can have them back," he said.

"No thanks, now where is the black diamond meth lab?"

Juan didn't say anything for a few seconds.

"I don't know that's not part of my job."

"Give that box another little shake, Annie," Tony cut in. After shaking the box and making the snake very angry again she asked, "Are you sure you don't want to rethink that?"

Juan was still quiet. Annie reached over and unhooked the latch on the sliding door to the large compartment containing the snake.

"No, please don't do that. I'll tell you. It's in a container yard in Los Indios. There are three shipping containers put together and stacked three high. The first level is just storage, the lab is on the second level, and the third level has packing and security guards. Now please take that snake away from me," Juan begged Annie.

Annie, with a mock sad look on her face said, "Okay, you win...ooops!"

To be Continued

# Episode Four

## Annie's Pet Snake and Party Games

Juan screamed in surprise and fear, as much as in the excruciating pain he felt as the very angry snake struck his penis. Sinking its fangs into him, and injecting its venom as it did, Annie just looked at Juan and smiled. She was almost laughing at what she was watching. She knew that the fear he was feeling had to be making the pain feel worse than it was. Although, she was also pretty sure the pain in itself must be almost unbearable. After biting him once and drawing back, the snake then struck with a second bite. Again, sinking those large sharp fangs deeply into Juan's penis; injecting its venom yet again. Juan began screaming and yelling things in Spanish that Annie and Tony only wished they could have understood. He was trying very hard to rip and pull himself free from the tape that held him in that chair. He, unfortunately, wasn't going anywhere. After the second bite, and the snake withdrawing back completely into the large compartment of the snake box, Annie closed the door to keep the snake confined in the box. Tony then told her to put the box on the table, next to Juan.

"All this fun is making me hungry and thirsty," Tony told Annie.

"Okay, I guess I could use something to eat. I know I could use a beer to go with the entertainment."

They both headed for the kitchen to see what they could find. Juan must have done some shopping recently. They found lots of good stuff to make sandwiches, and the fridge was well stocked with beer. After making themselves each a sandwich, and grabbing a beer, they made their way back to the dining room and sat at the table next to Juan. As they sat eating, they could see Juan's penis was swelling dramatically, and turning a very deep red. The areas of the bite marks were now starting to turn almost a purple-black colour, with a pus-like liquid coming out of the fang holes.

When they were just about done with their meals, Tony got up and went into the front room. He came back into the dining room with a small duffel bag he brought to the house with him. Setting it on the table close to Juan, Tony saw the excruciating pain he was in, was really quite obvious. Juan was moaning and had large tears streaming down his face. But seeing the bag Tony set on the table, he took time out from the moaning to ask what was in the bag.

"Oh, I brought something along to help you, after all, I'm not a monster."

After telling Juan that, Tony reached into the bag and pulled out a 1.75ml bottle of tequila. Looking down at his penis, now about three times its normal size and turning an even more ghastly colour, Juan said, "But I need a doctor, quickly!"

"Yeah, yeah, I know. But first we'll give you a couple of shots of tequila to help you feel a little better," Tony told him.

Annie then asked Juan, "You do like tequila don't you Juan?"

Through his pain and tears he looked at the bottle and said, "I like tequila. That shit you got there is cheap piss, I don't want it."

As Juan was talking, Tony was pulling more stuff out of the bag. A pair of very heavy leather gloves, more tape, a piece of clear plastic tubing, about ¾ inches in diameter, and twelve inches long, and a small plastic funnel, and a shot glass.

After giving Annie the gloves and looking at Juan's penis, Tony told her,

"That thing looks like it's going to explode. Why don't you put these gloves on and maybe if you give it a good squeeze, it'll shrink back down a bit. Just don't stand in front of him when you do that."

Annie smiled and watched as what little colour was left in Juan's face drain away, Annie put on the gloves. Juan immediately started crying again and begging her not to do that.

As Annie grabbed Juan's now enormous swollen, blackish penis, she squeezed as hard as she could. She also decided it might be fun to give it a little pull and a bit of a twist, all at the same time. Juan screamed and fought against the chair for a few seconds, and then he passed out from the pain. Letting go of his penis, Annie and Tony saw that the skin had split between the bite marks, now connecting them with a large, jagged gash. His penis was now bleeding quite freely, so Tony grabbed a small towel and stuffed it between Juan's legs to collect the blood. While Juan was still out, Tony cut off a length of tape from the new roll. In the centre of the tape he made a small slit and stuck the clear plastic tube through it. He was careful to be sure that the tube extended about two inches beyond the inside of the tape. He then stuck the tube in Juan's mouth, pressing his tongue down with the tube. Tony stuck the tape to Juan's mouth, keeping it closed, and the tube in it. He then had Annie hold the tube up, while he taped it to Juan's forehead. He stuck the funnel into the end of the tube and told Annie,

"I think you should go get us each a couple of beers so we can be ready when Juan is."

She ran to the kitchen and came back with a couple of beers for each of them. Juan was coming back around as they sat and looked at him. You could see the pain reclaiming Juan's face as he became more alert. Looking at Annie, Tony said, "I think our little friend deserves a drink after what he's been through, go ahead and give him two shots of that fine tequila he's been looking forward to."

Annie got up and filled the shot glass.

"I'm only doing this because Tony wants to help you with your pain," she told Juan.

Then she poured the first shot into the funnel, and down his throat. She then filled the glass again and gave Juan the second shot.

An hour later and along with ten shots of tequila, Juan was ready for his 'accident'. Juan's penis no longer looked like a penis. The swelling had caused it to become deformed, and it was oozing blood and a yellowish, foaming pus like liquid from the gash, the bite marks, and the tip. The deep purple-red colour was now moving to his entire groin area. Tony cut the tape holding him in the chair and removed the funnel and tubing from his mouth. Juan was too drunk now to put up much of a fight. He was, however, still vaguely aware of what was going on. Tony and Annie carried him into the bedroom. They threw him on the bed, removed all of his clothes, pulled the bed covers down, and arranged him in the centre of the bed on his back, with his legs slightly spread.

"Go and get your pet snake, and don't be afraid to give him a good shake on your way back here," Tony told Annie.

She did as she was told, and when she came back into the room, Tony was sitting on Juan's chest, facing his feet. He told Annie to remove the door at the outer end of the smaller compartment in the box. Now with one of the heavy gloves on, Tony held Juan's penis up out of the way, and told Annie,

"Put the other glove on, and grab Juan's balls. Hold them both together and stick them inside the little compartment in the box."

Tony knew that this didn't have to be done, but he wanted to give Annie one last shot at giving Juan as much pain in the same area that he gave her. With Juan's balls held tightly together and in the small compartment, Tony said, "Okay, give him your pet one more time."

Knowing what was about to happen, Juan started to scream and fight as much as he was capable. Annie smiled and removed the door in the larger compartment. The snake sprang at Juan's defenceless balls and sank one fang in each of them, injecting more venom into Juan's genitals. As the snake pulled back Annie locked it back in its compartment. Tony got down off Juan and he and Annie both stood and watched as he tried to grab his extremely painful testicles, and roll into a fatal position crying in excruciating pain.

Satisfied that Annie had gotten her revenge on Juan, they pulled the bed covers up over him, and at the bottom of the bed, released the snake under the covers. They watched as the snake made its way up the bed, biting Juan several more times as it went. Finally, the snake came out from under the covers, and onto the floor. Making its way toward the front of the house, Tony and Annie let it go. After a few minutes, Juan went into anaphylactic shock from the multiple snake bites. Knowing that he was going to die within minutes, they placed Juan on the floor, face down, with one leg still on the bed. Tony took Juan's cell phone and dialled the first number of the emergency services and placed the phone on the floor about a foot from Juan's outstretched arm. As Tony and Annie looked at the scene, it looked like a snake had gotten into Juan's bed and attacked him while he was passed out drunk, and that was how he died.

Now it was off to the meth lab. As they were leaving the house, Tony got a call from Boston. It was Libby, the new girl in charge of the office. She said that she was holding a call from someone using a code number 77910. Tony heard the call but chose not to pick it up. He knew the number; it was a client from Colombia. But with Libby calling him on it, he had to take the call. Tony had a job to do in Colombia, and his client didn't want to wait too long for it to be done. The job was a political one, and it was going to cause a lot of heat in the area, he was going to have to plan this one very carefully. The drive from their current location to Los Indios would take several hours. Not wanting to waste so much time on the road, Tony's map showed a small airstrip not too far from the shipping yard. They would go back to the jet and fly. The airstrip put them within walking distance of the container yard with the meth lab. Using very strong binoculars, Tony found the meth lab among the other containers. He was also able to spot four cameras placed around the lab. Tony needed a plan, and it was going to have to involve those cameras.

Getting up on top of a stack of containers close to the lab, Tony used a small calibre handgun to take out three of the cameras. Meanwhile, he had Annie placed between two stacks of containers, with a clear view of the door to the storage compartment of the lab. He gave her one of his high-powered sniper rifles, with a scope on it. Anyone coming out of that door would not be able to see either Tony or Annie, but Annie would have a clear shot at him. Within minutes of the three cameras getting shot, two very large men came out of the door, both carrying automatic assault weapons. Annie immediately shot one of them. Since the rifle was a bolt action weapon, it took Annie a few seconds to chamber another round. In that time, the other guard pulled back and hid just inside the container, next to the door. As he just tried to peek around the edge of the door, Annie shot him, taking off much of the right side of his head.

With Annie holding her position, Tony got down off the other containers and approached the lab from the now blind side. As Tony covered the door, Annie joined him. Tony was now using a higher calibre handgun. They both very cautiously entered the storage part of the lab. Not finding anyone else in that part, they headed up the stairs to the lab area. Not wanting to be seen, Tony just peeked above the top of the stairs to see if he could tell how many people were in there. He was able to count seven people, all working in the lab. Apparently, there were no more security people to worry about. None of the people in the lab matched the pictures of the men that took Annie.

This was just going to be an attack against the Menaloa Cartel, and number 60269 in particular for the order against Annie. They went back down and brought the two dead men inside. They placed both of them near the door, as if they were trying to get out. Tony told Annie to wait outside while he went back up the stairs and with the small calibre handgun, shot a large flask of very volatile pseudo-liquid being heated in the drug making process. The entire lab was suddenly one big fire ball. Tony slid down the stairs and out the door. Once he was out, they blocked the door with an iron bar. The lab would be destroyed, all of the people inside the containers would be burned to death, and all of the stock would be burned. The Menaloa meth lab was going to be out of business.

Tony knew he still had three more of the Mexicans to deal with, but he had to get to Colombia. He didn't really want to take Annie with him, but he didn't see any other choice. The job was in Cartagena, and it was going to be a very dangerous one. Number 77910 was a very high-ranking military officer, and the target was a very prominent political figure. Tony would normally spend two or three days on a job like this. It would take a lot of planning and the timing would have to be perfect. He wasn't going to be able to do that with Annie along. He would have to come up with some kind of plan on the way. Leaving Mexico, and heading to Colombia, Annie was not happy. She wanted the other three men that hurt her to pay, and she wanted them to pay with the same kind of pain that Juan paid. Tony explained that he had to do the job in Colombia right now, and then they would get back to Mexico. Annie wanted her end done quicker, but she knew she was going to have to wait.

Having done work for number 77910 before, Tony knew of an airstrip in a small town just South-West of Cartagena that he could safely use. Once they had landed, the next thing they needed was a car. Looking around the area, Tony found a car parked on the side of a dirt road with a flat tire that was being fixed by the driver, however, the driver had been shot and was dead. He finished changing the tire and they took the car to the city. When 77910 called, he told Tony that his target, the Minister of the Central Government Law Enforcement Agency, would be having a late-night dinner at an open-air restaurant. He gave Tony the address of the restaurant and the approximate time the Minister would be there. The first thing Tony had to do in the city would be to drive around the area of the restaurant. He needed to find a location with a clear view of all of the tables, and easy access for him to get out. He decided that as long as Annie was with him, he would use her as his driver to leave the area after the hit. He told Annie to pay very close attention to the street layout as they made several passes through the area.

At about 10:00 that night, Annie pulled the car into a small alley next to an abandoned warehouse. They were about two hundred and twenty yards from the small group of outdoor tables at the restaurant. From the third floor of the warehouse, Tony focused the crosshairs of his rifle scope on the man who had been described to him as the Minister. He panned the table and saw a woman sitting next to him, and another couple also at the table. They were enjoying a late-night dinner together. Tony placed the silencer on the end of the rifle barrel and then re-focused on the Minister. As he waited patiently, the Minister finally looked directly at him, and Tony squeezed the trigger. A small hole appeared in his forehead, and his left eye shot completely out of his head and onto the table. His right eye was left hanging by the optic nerve on his cheek. He did not move, his body just sat there as if frozen in time. As he sat there, brain soup created by the lead pellets of Tony's bullet spinning around in his head, began to flow from his nose, eye sockets, and ears. And then he slumped over onto the table.

Not hearing a gunshot, no one knew what was happening when they heard the screams coming from the Minister's table, and then saw what had happened to his face. Tony got up and ran down the stairs to the car waiting in the alley. As he got into the car he said, "Okay, now drive as if you're coming home from the grocery store and follow the route we practiced earlier."

As Annie drove the car; Tony pulled the back seat up and hid the rifle under it and replaced the seat. He then took out a .45 cal. handgun and moved around into the chamber. The ride to the jet was going to take about an hour, and he knew anything could happen in that time. Killing the Minister of the Central Government Law Enforcement Agency was a very big deal, and every cop in the country was going to be looking for someone to hang that on. Getting to the jet without any problems, Tony retrieved his rifle and leaving the car on the side of the runway, they headed back to Mexico.

As Tony was getting the jet up to fifty thousand feet, he heard Annie come on the radio. "So…Is that what you do every day? You go around killing people for the people that are just numbers?"

"That's what I do sometimes," he answered.

"And you never meet these number people?"

"Almost never it keeps things cleaner that way," he said.

"Well, how do you get paid then?" she asked.

"I have accounts they send the money to." Tony was starting to think Annie was asking too many questions.

Back in Mexico, Tony landed at the same airstrip where he had left the jet before. The problem now was how were they going to find the three men that they needed to find. He knew where most of the Menaloa Cartel members were centred, but that didn't necessarily mean those guys would be there. Not wanting to spend a lot of time looking for them, he decided to start by looking in the local bars and whore houses. Annie again had to stay at the safe house she was at before. She couldn't be seen looking for them. After looking in four or five bars, Tony found two of the men he needed. Again, waiting patiently, he was able to trap both of them together in one of their pick-up trucks. With the two of them drunk and tied up in the back of the truck, Tony brought them to Annie. Now the question was, what can she do to them and still make their death's look like an accident. After thinking about it for a while, Annie had the answer.

She told Tony,

"Let's tie each of them to chairs, and then I want to pour a small amount of gas on their peckers and balls, and then light them on fire. After their stuff is all burned up, we can take them out in the truck and let it drive off a cliff or into some trees and burn the truck with them in it."

Tony agreed and actually cringed at the thought of what she was going to do to these guys. Getting them out of the truck and tying them to the chairs, they then sat having a couple of beers and waited for them to sober up. Annie wanted them to be fully aware of what was happening to them, and by whom.

A few hours later, both of them seemed to be fully aware of the situation. It was time for the fun to begin. Annie had the chairs set so both men were looking at each other. She stood between them and began the fun.

"Do you guys remember me? Well, do you?" she asked.

"We know who you are," one of them said.

"Good, then you know why you're here, right? You know it's my turn to have some fun with you?" she said as she held up a small can of gas.

"What are you going to do with that?" one of the men asked.

"Well," she said, "I'm going to pour some of this on your peckers, and then I'm going to light them on fire. How does that sound?"

Both men began to plead with her.

"Please don't do that, we'll do whatever you want to make it up to you, but please don't do that."

She waited for them to stop talking, and then she started to pour a small amount of gas on them. With both of them crying and pleading desperately, she smiled at both of them, and then turned to one and put a match to his crotch.

Annie watched as the man's pants went up in flames. And when he was screaming, she could tell the fire had made its way to his flesh. As she was watching the man's genitals burn, she went to the other man and whispered into his ear, "That's going to be you in a few minutes."

With the first man screaming and trying to tear himself out of the chair, Annie and the other man could see his genitals being burned into a blackened lump of charred meat. Once there wasn't anything left to burn, Tony put out the small fire. You could then see that there was nothing left but a small charred, lump, between the man's legs. Annie turned to the second man, who was screaming and trying to tear himself out of the chair. She smiled and then lit him up. The screaming and crying continued until there was nothing left but the same small lump of charred meat, between his legs, and the fire was put out. Both men sat crying and close to losing consciousness.

As Annie and Tony sat and had another beer, they watched the men and decided to let them enjoy the last few moments they had to live. After finishing their drinks, they untied the two men from the chairs. Being unable to walk, just barely conscious, and in excruciating pain, the two were pretty easy to handle. Tying them up and throwing them in the back of the pick-up truck, they noticed that along with their genitals, their assholes and a small portion of their asses had been completely charred. Annie chuckled and said, "Oh look, bonus burns!" Tony and Annie headed out in search of the perfect cliff to run the truck off. Not too far from the safe house, they found just such a cliff. As the road led from the desert floor, up the side of a small plateau, the open side of the road became an open cliff with just a flimsy guard rail on it. At the top of the plateau, they untied the men and put them inside the truck cab. Both men were still too far from knowing what was going on to put up any kind of fight. Annie splashed some gas around inside the truck cab, and all over the men. Then Tony opened the hood of the truck and threw a little gas on the motor, which immediately started to burn. He then removed the gas cap from the filler to allow the fumes out. He felt that would help the truck burn quicker. Then they gave the truck a good push, and watched as it rolled down the road, and at the first corner, went through the guard rail and over the cliff. When the truck hit the desert floor, they heard the crash and then the loud eruption of the fuel tank. Tony knew there wouldn't be much left of the men or the truck. Just another tragic accident!

With the two men that they had, now gone, that left just one more of the Mexicans, the man called Paco. Annie said that he was another one of the really nasty men and had some special ideas for him. Tony wasn't sure how they were going to find him. He had looked all over the normal area he would have expected to find members of the Menaloa gang. He thought maybe they should move a little to the north, maybe up closer to the Nogales Cartel region. He thought if they found him up there, that would make life so much easier. His death wouldn't have to look so much like an accident as the others did. Maybe they could make it look like a hit from a rival Cartel. They found him in Nacozari, very close to the Nogales Cartel territory. Tony had never done any work in that area, so he wasn't familiar with it, and didn't know of any safe houses to secure

Annie. He decided again that as long as she was with him, he may as well use her.

They watched Paco for a few hours to see if he was with anybody and to try to figure out why he was up in that area to begin with. It seemed a little odd to Tony to find a Menaloa man so close to the Nogales territory on his own. This was either a very dangerous and stupid place for him to be, or his being there involved one or more of the Nogales men. The easiest thing for Tony to do would be to call number 60269 and tell him that while on a job in that area, he saw one of the Menaloa men meeting with some of the Nogales men. That would take care of Paco without Tony getting involved. But he knew he had to let Annie make things right with all of the men that hurt her, and Paco was the last one.

Later that night, Paco headed back for the Menaloa territory. He was alone, and this was no doubt going to be the best time for Tony to grab him. At the edge of town, in the middle of a very busy area, Paco stopped for gas. As he was filling his tank, Annie walked up to him. Shocked, he just stood there looking at her. Finally, she reached out to touch his arm and said, "Hi, you know I kinda liked you. I've been looking all over for you. How would you like to go somewhere and fuck some more? Nice and hard like you did it before."

Softening a little he asked, "Really?"

"Sure, you know a place where we can be alone? A place that's nice and quiet, nobody will bother us at?" she asked him.

Paco, now feeling a bit excited, told Annie to wait in the truck while he went in to pay for the gas, and to pick up some beer. As Annie waited, and Paco went in and paid, Tony hopped into the back of the truck and covered himself with a tarp. When Paco came back out and got into the truck, he and Annie headed off for what he believed to be a night of fun and nasty sex games, with a girl that he played with for a few days and thought he would now only see in his dreams. Annie and Tony had other party plans of their own for Paco.

To be Continued

# Episode Five
## Tony Has a Problem

Paco headed back through town and out toward the open desert. Annie was trying to keep Paco talking and interested in having sex with her, she wanted him to believe her story. After going a few miles outside of the town, without seeing any buildings around, she was starting to get a little nervous. Tony was feeling the same way. He knew they were headed back toward Nogales territory. Both Tony and Annie were wondering the same thing. Was Paco playing Annie? Was he really bringing her back to some of his Nogales friends as a gift of good faith? Annie began to cuddle up to Paco, and she started to rub his crotch. Realising that he already had an erection, and having gone deeper into the desert, she decided to take action. She whispered into Paco's ear, "Why don't we stop right here, and I will give you a quick little preview of what I want to do with you later tonight?"

As he started to pull the truck over to the side of the road, Annie opened the front of his pants. With her left hand, she reached in and grabbed Paco's erect penis, and pulled it out of his pants. While she was starting to bend over as if to take it in her mouth, her right hand slid up her skirt to find the comfort of 'Lady-9' waiting there for her.

As she pulls the gun out, she also slammed Paco's penis down on the seat of his truck. Paco got the words, 'but what the…' out, and then there was the loud crack of the .9mm handgun issuing one bullet to the end of his penis. The soft copper bullet filled with lead pellets exploded going through Paco's penis. The result was as if she held a shotgun to it. Looking down, not really feeling the pain completely just yet, he saw about the last two inches of his penis were now missing. As it all came together in his mind, Paco threw open the door, jumped out and fell to his knees holding himself, crying, screaming, and yelling more of that Spanish that Annie and Tony only wished they could understand.

With all of that going on, Tony came out from under the tarp. When Paco saw him, he tried to reach for a gun that he had tucked in the small of his back. Annie got there first and removed the gun. As Tony and Annie stood looking at Paco, trying to decide what to do with him now, several very unpleasant ideas were thrown around. Most of the worst by Annie. Tony decided that since they were so close to Nogales territory, there was no point in trying to make his death look like an accident. This could just be a rival Cartel murder. Paco wasn't saying much. He was still on his knees holding his penis, trying to stop the profuse bleeding that was going on. Tony looked at Annie and suggested that maybe she help him with that. After all, she was the one that caused it. After climbing into the back of the truck she looked in a tool chest. Tony heard her say, with a bit of glee in her voice,

"I can most certainly help him with that." When she got down off the back of the truck, she was holding a propane torch.

Paco, not seeing Annie yet, was yelling, "Yes, yes, please help me, I'm going to bleed to death."

Annie came around in front of Paco, with the torch lit. She was telling him,

"Don't you worry, Paco, my friend, I have no intensions of letting you bleed to death. That would be way too easy for you."

When he saw the torch, Paco tried to get to his feet to run, but Tony was behind him and gave him a solid whack on the head. Paco went down immediately and fell unconscious. Knowing they were going to have to secure Paco somehow, they dragged him closer to the door of the truck. While Annie held both of his hands at the bottom of the door, Tony slammed it as hard as he could. Both of Paco's hands were now severely broken and crushed, but they were also being held firmly in place by the door.

Tony gave Paco a few slaps on the face, and he began to come around. As reality started to re-visit him, he wasn't sure from where the most pain was coming, hands or penis? With Tony holding his feet, Annie set the torch to his penis to cauterise the end of it and stop the bleeding. It was just about then that Paco decided where the most pain was. More screaming and crying started again, and that unintelligible Spanish, that at that point probably weren't even real words. With the bleeding stopped, and Paco held firmly in place by his own truck door, Annie now had some thinking to do. What would Nogales men do to a Menaloa man that wandered too close to their territory? This had to be good; it had to be satisfying for her, but it had to look right. Because he was more familiar with the customs of these people, she decided to consult with Tony. He had some ideas, but she wanted slower, longer lasting pain than the things he was suggesting.

When she was in the tool chest looking for the torch, Annie remembered seeing a five-pound hammer in there. She was going to need that. She also remembered seeing several short pieces of fence posts in the back of the truck. She was going to need one of those as well. Annie told Tony what her plan was, and he began to wonder who this young lady really was.

Getting the hammer and the piece of fence post, they got to work. With Paco still in a pain induced fog, but also somewhat aware of what was going on, Annie placed the fence post between his ankles. As Tony held a foot against Paco's right ankle, Annie stood on Paco's left leg to hold it in place. Making sure Paco saw the hammer as she raised it above her head, he began to issue a long drawn-out, 'Nooooooo'. The sound of bones being crushed and splintered as the hammer hit Paco's left ankle was gruesome. The screaming cry that followed was both ear piercing and pitiful at the same time. Annie and Tony then switched sides and repeated the act. Paco, at that point, was again very nearly unconscious.

As Paco laid there, hands crushed in the truck door, both ankles crushed, and his feet now flopped to some angle not proper for feet to be in, Annie was happy. But Annie was not done. With Tony holding up both of Paco's legs, she placed the fence post under his knees. Just being able to hold on to reality at this point, Paco could offer nothing to his defence. He felt the hammer come down on his right kneecap, and then somehow amid all of that excruciating pain, the world simply faded away for him. When he began to recognise the ugly reality of his world as it now was, he could feel the unimaginable pain equally in both knees. He also realised that while he had no feeling beyond his wrists, his hands were no longer stuck in the truck door.

As the fog started to lift a bit more, he began to pick up on other small details. He was naked. He was lying on his stomach in the dirt. And oddly, his left arm felt a little different than his right arm. Turning his head to look at that arm, he saw the fence post under his elbow, and then the hammer came down at it. Paco was able to offer no more than a small grunt, and then the world was gone again. When the fog lifted this time, he felt the pain in both elbows. But with all of the major joints in his body having been so savagely crushed, he couldn't distinguish one pain from another. There were, however, two things that he did notice. There was a very large hole in the ground next to him, and he was now sitting on the fence post, as if straddling it. Annie and Tony were standing in front of him, just looking at him. Annie asked Tony, "Do you think he is fully back yet?"

"I don't know. If we had some water left, we could splash it on his face, maybe that would help," he said.

"Well, we don't have any water left, but I really have to pee." Removing her panties, she straddled Paco's face and peed on him.

As Tony watched her, he said, "Yeah you know, I think that helped."

Once Annie was finished, she picked up the hammer, and standing in front of Paco told him she had one more little party favour for him. Squatting down in front of him, she grabbed what was left of his penis and lined it up on the centre of the fence post. She then smashed it with the hammer. Feeling the pain, but no longer really able to register it, he saw nothing left now but a flattened, exploded, bloody piece of flesh, which used to be his penis.

Annie was now done. With the help of a couple of the pieces of fence posts from the truck, they placed Paco in the hole, in a vertical position. The two pieces of fence were placed under each arm pit to sort of hang him in that position. As they were filling in the hole, Paco appeared to be crying, but he wasn't making any sound. Packing the dirt as they went, getting up above his waist, they removed the fence posts from his arm pits. Paco slumped forward slightly, but as they continued to fill the hole, they made some adjustments along the way. With the hole filled to Paco's neck, Tony held his head back so Annie could get enough dirt under his chin to hold his face up facing the sky. Annie then took a hunting knife, also found in Paco's tool chest, and gave most of his head a nice shave. Well...she may have missed a clump of hair here and there, and maybe dug in a little too deep with the knife. His head was a bloody mess with a few clumps of hair left on it. The only question now was, do they leave him still alive, or kill him before they go?

Annie had another idea. She went back into the tool chest. She came out with a cordless drill, and a 1'wood auger bit. After having Tony set up the drill for her, she then drilled a 1'hole in Paco's forehead, all the way into the brain. Paco was fully aware of what was happening at that point. His screams and cries of what must have been a pain never felt before were short lived. As the drill bit entered the brain, he fell silent. He would be dead very soon.

Their Mexican retribution being complete, they could now head home. On the flight back to the little private airstrip somewhere near Boston, Tony had some thinking to do. As far as he knew, Annie was the only person in the world that could identify him, and place him at the scene of one or more killings, depending on how much immunity the feds were going to give her if it came to that. But he also knew that he liked her, very much. This was the worst possible problem for an international assassin to have. And one that he never thought he would ever have to face. Svetlana could identify him, but she couldn't put him at any crime scenes, and she owed him too much to do that anyway.

When they arrived in Boston, they took Annie's car, which had been left in Tony's private hanger, back to Annie's house. Once there, they both went through the house making sure no one was there, and she would be safe for the night. As Tony was saying goodnight, she asked him, in that small, insecure, but very sexy voice she could sometimes use, to stay the night with her. Someplace very deep inside him, Tony wanted her to ask. He knew he shouldn't, but he knew that if she asked, he would. After they each took showers and had a light meal that Annie prepared, they sat and had a couple of glasses of wine. There was very little talk of what happened in Mexico or Colombia. They mostly talked about reflections of life, and then things that two people talk about leading up to them falling into bed, and making very passionate, but soft and gentle love together. Tony couldn't help it, he loved every inch of Annie's body, and he made sure she knew that. He explored her for hours, as did she with him. They both found each other irresistible. Yes…Tony had a problem! He was going to have to figure this out very soon or risk the feds or someone else getting to Annie.

The next morning Tony told her that he had to go to his shop and work on some new guns, and that he didn't want her going out of the house until he came back. He told her not to answer her phone and gave her a burner cell phone so that they could talk. He was going to be gone for a few days, maybe a week. If there was anything that she needed, she was to call him and no one else, period! Not having any other choice, he took Annie's car to his shop. His shop was under the airplane hangar, with hidden access to it from the hanger. Off the end of the shop was a safe room. Access to that room was through a hidden panel under the stairs from the hanger. It was time to rethink the way he was making his guns. They didn't perform as well as he would have liked when being fired multiple times quickly.

Setting out to improve the performance of the gun barrels and firing mechanisms under heavy fire situations, he decided to give up some of the lightness for durability. Still making them out of carbon fibre, he decided to add thin strands of steel embedded in the fibre. To test this idea, he built his first ever automatic assault rifle. In his shop he had a firing range which he used to test all of his weapons when he made them. Testing the assault rifle, he fired several full clips through it. When he was done with the test, the gun was as solid as it was when he started the test. He now had a new formula for his weapons and would start replacing them as he could. He had to get back to the problem of Annie.

On his way back to Annie's house Tony was still trying to figure out what he was going to do. This was a very big problem, and he was fighting with himself over the answer that kept coming up in his mind. As he turned onto her street, he saw what looked like dozens of Brookline police cars along with several unmarked police cars blocking the road ahead. They were all in front of Annie's house. Pulling over to the side, he sat and watched for a while. What he saw was not good. The house had crime scene tape all around the perimeter of the yard. He saw several police officers and suits, come out of the house with clear plastic bags marked 'Evidence'. Using binoculars, he tried to see if Annie was sitting in any of the cars, but he couldn't find her. He wanted to try calling her, but he knew he couldn't risk doing that.

As he sat and watched, he saw an evidence bag come out of the house that really bothered him. Looking closer through the binoculars confirmed what he thought he saw: The police had 'Lady-9'. This was not good at all. If they had the gun, they had bullets, bullets made by him; bullets made by no one else in the world. If they test fired the gun, they were going to see what happens to the bullet when it hits the forensic model. From that he was sure they would be able to link those bullets to dozens of assassinations around the world. That alone wouldn't give them Tony, but it would put evidence in a file somewhere for future use.

While sitting on the side of the road watching the police and FBI work at Annie's house, there were many things going through Tony's mind. Did they have Annie? And if they did, would they be able to get her to talk about what the four Mexicans did to her, and why they did it? Would she talk about what happened in Mexico, and with enough pressure, would she give him up to help herself? Then while thinking about all of that, he realised that his fingerprints were all over the house. He was going to wipe it down when he went back today. And then of course there was most certainly going to be DNA in the bed sheets, lots of it. None of those things were going to lead them to Tony the killer, but they were going to put Tony, Annie's boss at his Boston business, at her house very recently. He knew if they had her or not, they were going to want to talk to him. He wondered if they would tell him if they had her or not. As far as the gun and the bullets went, he was going to have to leave her on her own with those. He decided to turn around and go back to the shop. He would stay in the safe room for now, but he knew the police would be calling him very soon. They were most likely going to want DNA and fingerprints from him. They were obviously going to match much of the forensic information gathered at Annie's house, but all that would tell them is that she was screwing her boss. But then again, if she gave up any information about him, the fingerprints and DNA would certainly help her case. Tony wasn't sure how to handle any of it. He had to know if they had Annie before talking to the police about anything. He got his answer quicker than he expected.

The phone at the Boston office rang, and when Libby picked it up, Special Agent Stephany O'Brian of the FBI identified herself and then asked to speak to Antonio De Luca. Libby put her on hold and then switched to Tony's line.

"I have the call Libby, go ahead and put Agent O'Brian through." Deciding he didn't really have a choice; he was going to try to play this as cool as he could. "Agent O'Brian, this is Tony, how can I help you?"

She sounded young, but already field hardened. "Do you have a young woman by the name of Antoinette Spalding working for you?"

"Yes, I do. Annie has been with us for about five years now. Why is an FBI Agent calling and asking about her?"

"You are aware that she is not in the office today, aren't you?" she asked.

"What is this about Agent?"

"Do you have any idea of Ms. Spalding's whereabouts, Mr. De Luca?"

That was the question he was waiting for.

"Well, I take it if you're asking about her, and don't know where she is, I have to assume that she's not with you. But you still haven't told me what this is about. Why are you looking for Annie?"

"She is a person of interest in an investigation regarding the death of a man at a restaurant a couple of weeks ago. We just want to ask her some questions about that."

Tony had a strong feeling that Agent O'Brian was fishing, or at least not being completely up front with him. The important thing was that the police apparently didn't have Annie. But then again, if they didn't have her, where was she? He still didn't feel safe trying to call her. Annie however knew that as long as she was in a safe place, she could call him, and the call would be secure. Tony told Agent O'Brian that he hadn't heard from Annie, but if he did, he would let the Agent know. He was relieved that the police didn't have Annie, but worried that she hadn't tried to contact him.

The following day a major Boston newspaper ran a banner headline reading 'Local Woman Sought in Connection with Several Murders'. The story was about Annie and the mysterious 'Exploding Bullets' as they were being called, that were now linked to several unsolved murders dating back years. Tony figured they must have run ballistic tests on Annie's gun, and matched the damage caused by her bullets to the damage done to some of his victims. The phone rang. It was Libby holding Agent O'Brian again. Tony took the call.

"What can I do for you today Agent O'Brian?" he asked.

"Well…for starters, how about coming into my office for a little chat?"

"Okay, I think that can be arranged. What time were you thinking about?"

The Agent suggested he plan on 11:00 a.m. and then said, "And as long as you're coming in, would it be possible for you to bring Ms. Spalding's employment records with you?"

Tony agreed that he could do that and started gathering the info she was looking for. That reminded him that once a month all of the employment and payroll records were sent to one of those semi-discrete postal service boxes by Annie. He was going to have to get that information to Libby before the end of the month. Armed with Annie's employment records for as long as she had been working for him, Tony arrived at the Boston FBI Field Office, to see Agent O'Brian.

"Thank you for coming, in Mr. De Luca. Please have a seat."

"Thank you, Agent O'Brian. I have all of Annie's records with me," Tony replied.

"Thank you, that's great! Can I get you anything before we begin, a cup of coffee maybe?" she asked. She seemed softer than she did when they were talking on the phone yesterday.

"Sure, coffee would be good, thanks," he said. After having her assistant get each of them a coffee, they got down to business.

"So, I'm going to be right up front with you Mr. De Luca. A handgun found at Ms. Spalding's house along with bullets loaded in the gun were tested and found to match the same type of ammunition used in several unsolved murders not only in this country but in many others, going back decades."

Tony, trying to look shocked at that news told the Agent,

"Really? I know that Annie has a .9mm handgun that she keeps for protection. Were all of these murders you're looking at committed with a .9mm handgun?"

"I can't really talk about the details of the murders, but I can tell you the one that led us to her in the first place was committed with her gun."

"Maybe she was attacked and felt as if she had to defend herself," Tony suggested to the Agent.

He then handed over the employment records to Agent O'Brian and asked her to try to match any of the murder dates to Annie's attendance records. The Agent took the records and told Tony they were going to need a few days to go thoroughly through them, and he would get them back when they were done with them.

As days started to turn into weeks, Tony still had no contact from Annie. She seemed to have just disappeared. The FBI had taken DNA and fingerprint samples from Tony, and of course matched them to samples taken from many areas of Annie's house. At first, Agent O'Brian tried to make much more of that than it was, but Tony knew it really meant nothing more than the fact that he had been to her house, and they had sex. The employment records were copied by the FBI and the originals returned to Tony. Agent O'Brian called the office to check in with Tony on occasion, which meant that they couldn't find Annie either. So far, she was still a suspect in many of the murders, even though her attendance records indicated that she was at work when just about all of the murders took place. It was those mysterious bullets that they just couldn't seem to get past.

Tony was beginning to feel as if the problem he had regarding Annie had taken care of itself. Libby was doing better at taking over Annie's old position. Tony was back to work assassinating people for the 'number people' as Annie had once called them. He thought about her every day. He thought about her disappearance, and wondered what that meant; did she really get away on her own? Was she being held somewhere as a federal prisoner or witness? He also thought about how beautiful and how very sexy she was, and how much he missed that. But he also knew that he would have had to do something very drastic, something that he really didn't want to do, had she not gone missing. She knows too much about him and his work. She is a very dangerous liability to have wandering around.

Another question that sat at the back of his mind every time he took a new assignment, was the very real question of whether the FBI or other law enforcement agencies were watching him or not? He was trying to be extra careful each time he went out. Most of his work had been out of the country which helped make things a little easier for him. However, on this particular day, he received a call through the Boston office from a person claiming to have gotten his information from code number 00376. That number belonged to a client in the United States. It, in fact, belonged to a high-ranking member of the CIA. Tony decided to let Libby take the call and tell the unknown client that he would get back to him. Tony had started to become a bit paranoid over the past few months since Annie's disappearance, but he felt that he still had good cause to be. After thinking about it for a while, he decided to place a scrambled call to number 00376 to talk about this new client using his code. In talking to number 00376, Tony was told that the new client was a very high-ranking political figure from Texas, and that his call was not a trap, but was a real call for Tony's services. Still a bit leery, Tony returned the call. When he called the contact number left with Libby, as the man answered the phone, before he could say anything, Tony told him not to give his name.

"This is the person you were trying to reach earlier with a call to a Boston number. What can I do for you?"

The man on the other end of the line began his story. "I have someone in my life that has become a very big problem for me, I need to get that situation remedied as quickly as possible."

"Is this person a political figure?" Tony asked.

"No, this is more of a personal issue for me," the man told him.

"Okay, I'm going to give you a number that you can send all of the information about this problem to and include a good photo with the rest of the info."

The call was ended, and within minutes, Tony began to receive the necessary information about the target. As the material was coming in, he sat going through it. Very quickly he realised the target was a woman. "When are these political assholes going to learn?" he said out loud to no one there. The last piece of information was the photo. The photo had two people in it and looked like a wedding picture. The face of the groom had been removed before the picture was sent to Tony. The woman was very pretty, looked to be maybe mid-thirties, and looked as if she took pretty good care of herself. Once he had time to go through all of the materials sent, Tony called the new client.

"Alright, this seems like a pretty normal job. Do you have any problem with when this gets done?" Tony asked.

"No…just not in front of the children if it can be helped," the client replied.

"No children will be involved; I can promise you that. Here are the payment terms and information to make the payments."

After giving the client the terms and information about payment, Tony paused and then went on.

"Payment must be made exactly following those terms. If you fuck it up, you will be the next one on my list."

The client agreed, and then Tony assigned him a code number to be used in all communications. He would be code number 00688. Still being a bit concerned with doing a job inside the country, Tony began to make plans for the hit. He was still using the same mysterious 'Exploding Bullets' as they were being called. And since Annie was missing, and Tony assumed at this point that she was dead, the authorities would credit any use of them to her. Tony set out to do his latest job. This was going to prove to be one of the more difficult and dangerous jobs he had done in a very long time. The target was, after all, a past president's daughter, and a senator's wife.

To Be Continued

# Episode Six
## Stephany Has a Surprise

Looking through the high-powered rifle scope, Tony was watching a man give a speech about the right to life from the moment of conception. The speech was being given on the steps of the Massachusetts State House, in Boston. From his perch approximately 340 yards away, across the common, he could also see his target. She was standing a few steps behind and above the man speaking, and off to his left. What he also saw, standing to the left of his target was FBI Special Agent Stephany O'Brian. She appeared to be very carefully watching the crowd of thousands standing on the common. There was also a full detail of Secret Service Agents around the man speaking, and at the top of the steps of the State House. Many of the Agents were using binoculars as they scanned the common and surrounding areas. Tony recognised the man speaking as a senior senator from Texas. What Tony couldn't see from his vantage point, was the right hand of his target holding the hand of her nine-year-old daughter, who was holding the hand of her six-year-old brother.

Tony was on the roof of a building on the North side of West Street, halfway down the street. From there, he had a very clear shot at his target, and should be able to vacate the area quite quickly after taking the shot. As he was watching the senator speak, he began to notice that Agent O'Brian was talking with what he assumed to be some other Agents. She looked as if she was very much on guard and possibly even as if she had been alerted to some sort of threat or other issue. He started to pan the Agents at the top of the steps, the ones with the binoculars, to see if he could get any indication of what was happening. As he panned across the platform, he saw two agents that appeared to be looking directly at him. He looked back at Agent O'Brian, and she was just stepping down beside the senator, with both hands out, ready to grab him and move him out of any line of fire. Secret Service Agents were also starting to move down the steps toward the senator. Very much unlike Tony, he panicked and took his shot.

Before Agent O'Brian could get to the senator, the bullet grazed his left ear, and struck the target at the bridge of the nose. The impact of the bullet hitting such a spot, caused most of her face to explode. Flesh, bone, parts of her eyes, and brain soup splattered on everyone directly around her, including her children. Tony knew he had been spotted, and that the police would be there in a matter of minutes. He had to get out of there very quickly. He hid the rifle in a hole in the stairwell wall. As he was making his way down to the street, coming out of the building, he was greeted by the first officer on the scene. He shot the officer with his new carbon fibre and steel composite .40cal handgun and then went back into the building. Cutting through the building and going out the back, he crossed the alley and went through the rear entrance of a restaurant. He made his way through the restaurant as casually as he could. Coming out onto Temple Pl. He then headed for the common.

As he made his way to the common, he removed the wig he was wearing, turned his shirt inside out, to reveal a completely different shirt, and added sunglasses to the mix. He would lose himself in the crowd at the common. The steps of the State House were cleared, the senator brought inside the building. What was left of his wife was put into an ambulance and taken to the nearest hospital. The senator would be brought to her shortly. The two children that were standing with his wife, were covered with bits and pieces of their mother. They were, as you could imagine deeply in shock. Now wandering among the people on the common, Tony was still unaware that the children had been there. Boston police officers were everywhere. Men and women wearing FBI and ATF jackets were also everywhere.

Looking back at Temple Pl. Tony saw several police officers coming out of the same restaurant he had gone through to make his escape. They were headed for the common, and more officers and FBI and ATF Agents were starting to stop and question people as they were trying to leave the area. He knew as long as he stayed calm, he would be able to get through this. But then, while talking to someone that had been in the front of the crowd, he found out that the senator's two children were standing behind him when their mother was shot. Tony nearly collapsed at the news. He didn't like doing things that way. No child should ever have to see something like that. He felt as if he broke his promise to number 00688.

Walking around in the crowd, trying to gather his composure before having to talk to any law enforcement people, Tony's arm was grabbed. Turning to see Agent O'Brian holding on to him, he felt the blood rush from his face. "Are you alright?" she asked.

Thinking fast he answered, "Yes...seeing that woman's face explode like that was bad enough, but I just found out that she had her two children with her. I can't imagine what that will do to them."

"So, you were here on the common, up near the front of the crowd?" she asked.

"Yes, I saw the whole thing," he replied.

"Well, we're going to want to be talking to as many people as we can about what they saw, so if you could make yourself available to me later in the week, I would appreciate it."

"Of course, just give me a call," he said. He gave her his contact information, and was allowed to leave the area. The following day, all of the major newspapers carried the story. All of them had said that the intended target was the senator from Texas.

While he was sitting and reading, he was struck by some information he hadn't given any thought to. According to the story he was reading, a news photographer with a telephoto lens, had seen the Secret Service men looking at the building Tony was on. A few pictures of the gunman had been taken by him. The FBI now had all of those pictures, and they were at FBI Headquarters in Quantico, Virginia being run through a computer facial recognition program. Tony tried to think back to when he was lying on the roof waiting to take the shot. How much of his face could have been exposed? It was not usually something he had to worry about, so he couldn't think of what position he might have been in, that would give a clear view at his face. When the FBI revealed to the press that they had the pictures, and were running them through the computer program, there was something they held back. All the recognition programs had to work with was, one ear, the eyes, a partial size and shape of the nose, and a partial overall size and shape of the face. It wasn't much to go on. A few days later, Agent O'Brian called Tony and asked him to come into her office. He told her he would, and an appointment was set up for later that day.

When Tony got to her office, the Agent had a file folder on her desk that was marked indicating that it came from Quantico. At the top of the folder it was marked, 'The Signature Killer'. She asked him to have a seat, and then if she could get him anything before they got started. Tony took the seat and declined the other offer. As the Agent sat down behind her desk, looking directly at Tony's eyes, she opened the folder. In it were several pictures of faces, each had some sort of small file attached to the back of them. The one on top of the pile didn't look anything like Tony. He was very relieved. That was the reaction Agent O'Brian was looking for. But then…she flipped that picture over to reveal the next one. Trying to keep his best poker face, he knew some of the colour was lost from it. He was looking at himself in the picture. The Agent caught the reaction and sat looking at Tony for several seconds without saying anything. As he finally looked up from the picture, and met her eyes, she asked, "Do you know where and when that photo was taken?"

"No, not really, and I'm not sure why you stopped on that particular one. It does look a bit like me, but I see there are several more pictures in the folder." Pulling that picture from the folder, and then closing it, she flipped to the file on the back of the picture.

"Before I read this, I'm just going to say that I believe this to be a picture of you." She then started to read the file. "Stephen Finn, born Belfast, Ireland in June of 1967. Suspected opposition to the IRA. Served in the Irish military for two years. Believed to have moved to the United States in 2014, but there are no records of him or his whereabouts since that time. Looking at your face now, I have to say, you don't look so much like an Antonio De Luca, as you do a Stephen Finn." The information she had was correct, but Tony would give her his own version of his past.

"Well, that's quite a story Agent. I see you've even named him, The Signature Killer. The man does bear a striking resemblance to me, but that's not me," Tony replied. "I have never been to Ireland, I hear it's beautiful," he added.

Without changing her expression, she said, "I'm going to need your passport. Your birth certificate would also be good." After a short pause, she added, "I tried to run a background check on Antonio De Luca. Would you like to hear what I came up with?"

Tony didn't need to hear what she came up with. He knew she didn't find anything further back than 2014. So far, she hadn't mentioned the rifle or the bullets. Not saying anything about the rifle told him they didn't find it. But why hasn't she said anything about the bullets? Still trying to play poker with the Agent, he said, "I don't know what you found in your background check. I have all of my papers at home, I'll be glad to bring them in for you."

"That would be great, and don't forget that passport," she told him.

As Tony left the building, he was wondering if he should have mentioned the bullet used on the senator's wife and suggested maybe the partial face in the picture was actually Annie's. Keeping those bullets connected to Annie would take a lot of heat off him right now. But he still didn't know if Annie was even alive, it had been several months with no contact.

The next day Tony made a call to Agent O'Brian. He was ready to bring all of his paperwork in to prove he was who he said he was. A time was set, and at that time Tony was sitting in her office with a large folder of his own. The first thing he gave her was his birth certificate. According to that, he was born in Worcester, MA at St. Vincent Hospital on Vernon Hill, in 1968. As Agent O'Brian looked at the document she said, "That's funny, we couldn't seem to come up with any such thing in our background search of Antonio De Luca."

After pausing a few seconds, Tony suggested that the problem may be a result of the original hospital no longer existing. While there is a St. Vincent Hospital in Worcester, it is not the one where he was born.

"It may just be a simple case of records being lost in the transfer from the old hospital to the new one," he said, throwing the possibility out there.

The look on her face wasn't giving away any of her thoughts. She may be young and pretty, but she was definitely already field hardened. As Agent O'Brian sat going through the rest of Tony's papers, he wanted to try to distract her a bit.

"You know, I was thinking about all those pictures you have of possible shooting suspects. I know what happened to that woman's face. The bullet used was one of those 'Exploding Bullets' they've been talking about in the papers, wasn't it?"

She looked up from the papers and said, "Yes, unfortunately the press put that out there."

"Well, maybe that partial face was that of a woman, maybe even Annie's face."

Still looking at him the Agent smiled just a bit.

"That's a nice try, but several of the restaurant staff described a man coming in the rear kitchen door and going out the front just after the shooting took place. The description of the man seems to fit you very well."

"I'm a very common looking man, I'll bet you that there are three or four pictures in that folder that come close to looking like me."

The Agent handed him the folder of pictures, there were twenty-three faces in there. Tony went through all of them and pulled out three that were very close to looking like the one she said was him. After getting her to look at the other pictures, she told Tony that she would need a couple of days to verify all of the documents that seem to prove his story. Tony knew she was not convinced yet. After leaving her office, his phone buzzed. When he looked at it, he saw number 00996 on the screen. He obviously couldn't take the call while he was in the FBI building. She was going to have to wait.

Once out of the building, and down the street, Tony was watching to see if he was being tailed. He saw two men that had that FBI look about them that seemed to be following him. He also saw men in typical FBI suits sitting in two cars along the side of the street. He was going to have to lose all of them, quickly! Tony did not like to be followed or watched by anyone. There was a lot of heat generated by his last hit. Being a past President's daughter, every law enforcement agency in the country would be looking for any man that even vaguely fit the description of the man that walked through the rear door of that restaurant that night. Tony began ducking in and out of small stores to be sure he was being followed. He was definitely being followed. So, to try to throw them off his trail, in the next store he went into, he used the men's room. When he came out, he was wearing a completely different suit. He also added sunglasses and a baseball cap.

After going into one more store and coming out without the hat, but with different colour hair, he was pretty sure he had lost them. Tony walked over to the common and sat on a bench. As he sat watching the people milling around, he noticed that the four men tailing him were not among them. He felt a little safer now and decided to return the call from code number 00996. She was the wife of a very wealthy man from Texas. He was an oil man. He owned several active wells in Texas and Oklahoma. His wife, number 00996, had used Tony's services on a few occasions in the past, mostly when she felt like his business was being threatened.

"Hello ma'am, I'm returning the call you made to my office earlier today. What can I do for you?"

After a short pause she said, "Well, I guess I made a mistake, and now I have to fix it."

Looking at the people around him Tony asked, "What kind of mistake are we talking about here?"

Another short pause, "I met a man, we got close, very close. But I told him it was just going to be a small thing, that I'm married and don't want to screw that up."

Tony's attention was caught by a man sitting at a bench about 35 or 40 yards from him.

"And what's been happening with him?" Tony asked. The man got up and move to a bench closer to Tony.

"He has been calling me at all hours. He shows up at the house when my husband is at work. He has even shown up at a black-tie business function that my husband had. I don't know how he was able to get in."

As she was talking, he got up from the bench, and began to walk directly at the other man. As he did that, the other man got up and started to walk away from him.

"What does this man do for work?"

"Well, I'm not really sure, he doesn't talk about his work much. I think he might be some kind of detective or private eye."

Tony was getting a little intrigued. If this guy turned out to be FBI that would be an interesting turn of events for Tony.

"Alright, you know what to do. And give me as much information on him as you can. And make sure the photo is a good one. I'll call you back after I check out what you send me." And the call was done.

Tony remembered that he had to retrieve the rifle he hid in the building on West Street. The police were still crawling all over that building and the entire area surrounding it. He had to get the gun before they found it, but how was he going to do that? There were two things that Tony could not let happen. The first was to have the police find that gun, and the second was to have them find his hanger and jet. He went to look at the building the gun was in and decided there was no way he was going to get in there without the police seeing him. Not being able to get the gun today, he decided to go home and check the information coming in from number 00996. When Tony got back to his hanger, he was shocked, surprised, and then maybe a little frightened, all at the same time. Inside the hanger was the gun he hid in the wall of the building on West Street.

How could that rifle be there? As far as he knew, there were just two people that knew the location of his hanger. The other person beside himself was Annie, and she had been missing for months. He was sure that because she had made no effort to contact him, she was either being held by someone, or dead. And even if Annie did bring the rifle to the hanger, how did she get it without the police seeing her? And how did she even know where the rifle was hidden? He decided it was time to risk trying to contact her. Using the burner cell number he gave her all those months ago, he called hoping for her to be the one to answer it. As he listened to it just ring several times, with no answer, his hopes faded. But beyond that, there was still the matter of the rifle being left in the hanger. Spooked a little now, he grabbed the rifle and hurried down to his shop.

As he set the rifle on a bench, a frightening thought came to mind. What if there was some kind of GPS tracker somewhere in the gun? He very quickly disassembled the rifle and found nothing. Relieved, he cleaned the rifle and put it back together. Adding a new full clip of bullets, he took the rifle up to the plane and placed it in its travel compartment, ready for the new assignment he was about to perform. Going back down to his shop, he made his way into the safe room. All of the information he had asked number 00996 to send was there. Grabbing a beer, he sat and made himself comfortable as he went through all of the papers she sent him. When he got to the picture, there was a short bio with it. The man's name was Peter O'Brian. Could it be? Was Agent Stephany O'Brian married, and was her husband's name Peter?

Just on a hunch, he did an internet search hacking into the FBI personnel files for Special Agent Peter O'Brian, and there he was along with several pictures of him, some that included his wife Agent Stephany O'Brian. He sat back in his chair and thought about that for a while. Tony was well aware that she already considered him one of her prime suspects for the shooting on the MA State House steps. He also knew that she had people trying to follow him. If he went missing for even a day or two, and her husband came up dead, she would lock him up without even asking any questions. And then if he were to be killed by one of those 'Exploding Bullets' while Tony was missing, that would seal his fate if she ever found him.

Tony placed a call to code number 00996. He told her what he had found out about her 'mistake'. He then told her about the situation he had going in Boston. She was very surprised to find that Peter was an FBI Agent, and then began to think back about some of the things she might have told him about her husband, and his business practices. After pausing to reflect on some of those thoughts she said, "Well given some of the things I might have told him about my husband's business, he definitely has to go, and soon."

Tony, knowing that was always the case with these jobs told her,

"I understand your situation, but his wife is also an Agent, here in Boston, and she already has me as one of her prime suspects for the murder of that Texas senator's wife the other day." After a slight pause he added, "I will get your problem fixed very soon, I promise, but it can't be in the next two days. I'm sorry but I will figure this out."

Not thrilled with the conversation, 00996 ended the call. She began thinking that maybe if she got together with Peter, she could try to play him. Maybe find out if he was even looking at her husband or not or get whatever information out of him that she could. She thought that might buy her enough time for the hit to take place.

Tony came up with a plan; he always came up with a plan. He started to look through several counterfeit postal cancellation code markers he had. He found one from Miami, Florida. With that postal stamp he could address a letter from anywhere and stamp it with the Miami postal stamp. He could then take the letter to any post office and tell them the letter was delivered in error and that it should be sent to the correct address. When the letter arrived at the correct address, it would look as if it was sent from Miami. His plan was to go to Texas, do the job for 00996, and get back to Boston as quickly as possible. Agent O'Brian was almost certainly going to want to know where he was during the couple of days he would be gone. To cover himself, he would stamp a postcard with the Miami postal stamp with the same date as the murder of the Texas man; take it to any post office and tell them it was delivered to the wrong address, and have it sent to the correct address. It would of course be addressed to Agent O'Brian in Boston. Tony would have an alibi putting him in Florida at the time of the killing in Texas.

While Tony was preparing for his quick trip to Texas, he had another thought that might throw Agent O'Brian off him. He was going to go to his bullet casing supplier and purchase fifteen complete bullets from them. These would be military issue, full metal jacket bullets. He was only going to use one, but he was going to need the others to recalibrate his rifle and scope for the difference in the weight of the bullets. He thought that by not using his signature bullets, that would throw the investigation of the man's murder into a completely different direction. He was trying to think of anything he could do, to do this job with as little attention on himself as possible. He called number 00996 and told her that he was ready to do the job.

"I have a date with him in a little while, I'm going to try to find out what he knows about my husband's business," she told him.

"Well, that's okay if you want to, but I plan to make the hit tomorrow anyway."

"What about your situation in Boston?" she asked him.

Tony told her not to worry about that; he had it under control. All he needed now was to look through his collection of postcards, for one from Miami. He found what he needed. He used his counterfeit postal stamp and cancelled the card with the following day's date. Having purchased the new bullets, and re-calibrating his rifle and scope, he left the stamped post card on the table and gathered up what he would be needing in Texas. Tony went outside of the hanger just to see if he could find any unwanted prying eyes, before bringing out the jet. Not seeing anything suspicious, he rolled out the jet, closed and locked the hanger, and then headed for Texas. Knowing that number 00996 lived in Lubbock, Texas, Tony knew his mark had to live close by, since he was frequently showing up at her house. He had a very good photo of him, so it should be pretty easy to find him. Once he landed in Texas, he stole another car and drove to Lubbock. He didn't know exactly where his client lived, but he figured he would start by watching the centre of town. He found what looked like an abandoned grain and feed store and set up in there. Early next morning, Tony saw his target going into a diner. When the man came out, Tony followed him to a small horse ranch about five miles outside of town.

As the man got to the ranch, he began going about tending to the horses. *This must be where the man lives,* Tony thought. It didn't really matter; this was where the man was going to die. There were some small hills just to the North of the ranch. Tony set up on one of the hills. He was about three hundred yards from the front of the barn where the man seemed to be spending most of his time. As he watched his target through his rifle scope, he wondered if there were any other people at the ranch. He decided to watch and wait for a little while, just to see if anyone else was around. After watching the area for about an hour and a half, Tony didn't see any other people. His target had been inside the barn for about a half hour now and Tony couldn't see him, but he knew he was in there. Still watching through the rifle scope, he saw his target come out of the barn, carrying a rifle.

Suddenly, the man lifted the rifle and pointed it right at Tony and took a shot at him. Tony immediately returned the shot and hit the man just above his left eye. The armour piercing bullet made a small hole as it entered the man's forehead and blew about half of the back of his head off as it was exiting. He was dead before he hit the ground. The shot his target took at him, was very close. It actually grazed Tony's right leg just enough to draw a small amount of blood. So…his target was dead, but how did he know Tony was there? When he came out of the barn, he didn't even hesitate. He knew exactly where Tony was. Something was not right with this hit. Tony's stomach was turning, and his mind was spinning. Only he and code number 00996 knew about the hit, so how did Peter not only know he was about to be shot at, but from exactly where the shot was going to come from. He began to scan the surrounding area for any sign of someone that might have tipped off Peter. Not seeing anyone in the area, Tony decided he better get out of there and back to the plane. He would try to figure it out on the way back to Boston. Someone definitely gave away Tony and his location to Peter, but who, and how?

On the way back to Boston, Tony was thinking about Agent Stephany O'Brian. He hadn't heard much from her for a few days, and that was her husband that he just killed. He also wondered who code number 00996 was, that Stephany's husband would be having an affair with her. He began to wonder what the backlash was going to be like over the murder, and then his thoughts went to the fact that Peter knew he was there. How was that possible? As he kept running every scenario he could think of, they all came back to the same one. Someone told him he was there, and his exact location. Number 00996 was the only one that knew he would be out there, but how did Peter know his exact location? The only answer Tony was able to come up with that made any sense, was that because both Peter and Stephany were FBI Agents, maybe they had surveillance cameras set up around the perimeter of the ranch. Back in Boston, Tony pulled the jet back into the hanger, got his rifle and other gear out of it and went down to the workshop. Setting his rifle on the bench to be cleaned, as he always did after each use, he went into the safe room to grab a beer and rested for a bit. Something was different in there, but he didn't immediately see it. So subtle was the difference that it was as simple as the postcard being missing from the table. The postcard, the one he stamped with the Miami postal code. It was gone. He was sure that he left it on the table. He was going to take it to the post office in the morning to be delivered to Agent O'Brian's office.

His rifle made its way back to his hanger without him. And while he was in Texas, the postcard was removed from his safe room. In Texas Peter knew he was there and his exact location. Tony knew all of these things had to be connected with the hit he just did, but how, and why? He wasn't feeling very comfortable now, and he wasn't even sure if he was really safe in his safe room. The following day, expecting Agent O'Brian to be in Texas dealing with the death of her husband, Tony got a call that had not come through the Boston office. When he picked up the phone, Agent Stephany O'Brian was on the other end of the line. She started the conversation, "I don't want you to say anything. First, let me tell you that I think you are a remarkable man, Tony. In case you haven't figured it out yet, I am the one that brought your rifle back to you. I knew you would be needing it. Oh…I didn't tell you about the security cameras around the ranch, I thought it would be a little more sporting that way. And the postcard from Miami, yes, I have it, and I thought that was a very nice touch. I know that was you that shot the senator's wife in Boston, I knew she was always the real target. Politicians…they just can't seem to keep it in their pants, can they? Well, anyway, I know that Annie is in Belfast, and I am going to give you 24 hours to get your shit together and go to her. After that, every law person in MA and probably half of the country will be paying your little estate a visit, so if I were you, I would take this opportunity and go live your life with Annie. By the way, this is code number 00996 over and out."

To be Continued

# Episode Seven
## Annie's Little Secret

Tony sat, still with the phone in his hand, thinking about what Agent O'Brian just told him. Had she really been client number 00996? The one that for the past few years had used his services to remove several people that she must have felt were somehow in her way? If that was true, then she knew about him all along, and this whole Boston investigation was just a game. And why did she have him kill her husband? Was he really even having an affair, or did she just want him gone? Maybe there was a lot of insurance money in the deal for her. Maybe she is the one having the affair and wants the money to run away with her new man. And the cameras, yes, that was very sporting of her, she apparently had a bit of a sense of humour. The important thing was, she told him where Annie was, and she suggested he go to her.

After removing anything in the hanger, workshop, and safe room that might lead the police to him, he prepared for the trip to Ireland. He wasn't sure how he was going to find Annie; he didn't know if she had the phone he gave her. Maybe he would try again to call her. He would think of something on the way. He was actually very happy about what he was doing. He was going to find Annie, and the two of them were going to live a quiet life somewhere, very comfortably together, no more business of any kind. Then, he thought, what if Agent O'Brian was setting him up? What if Scotland Yard, or Interpol, or some other, any other law enforcement agency was waiting for him in Belfast? Could he trust her? He didn't really have a choice. This was his one shot to find Annie, and he had to take it.

Tony made the very difficult call to Libby at his Boston office. His orders for her were simple, close the business, shred everything, and then get out of there. Without giving her any more information than that, he was gone. He was really gone! He was on his way to Belfast to find Annie. If Agent O'Brian was right, and he was sure that she was, then it shouldn't be too hard to find her. He had made up his mind that with the many millions of dollars he had spread out in several banks, under several different names, he and Annie could live very comfortable lives anywhere they chose. Somewhere over the Atlantic Ocean, Tony got a call from code number 60269, the head of the Menaloa Cartel. "Hello," Tony answered.

"You did a bad thing, you and that girl of yours. You think for one minute that I don't know that was you?" He didn't sound very happy to Tony.

"What the hell are you talking about?" Tony asked.

"You know I am talking about what you did to the four of my men that had your girl, and to my meth lab. What you did to those four men, especially my son Juan, I cannot forgive that."

After a slight pause Tony said, "I still don't know what you're talking about. What happened to your son, Juan? And I didn't even know you had a meth lab."

"Don't fuck with me. You think what we did to that girl before was bad? That was just play time. This time will be much different, and you're going to watch, and then I'm going to kill you, too." Number 60269 paused and then continued, "I will give you a choice, you and the girl come to me, or I take everyone at your Boston office, and practice on them, and then I come for you." Tony wasn't really paying that much attention at that point.

"I'll tell you what, the Boston office has been closed, both Annie and I have left the country, and if you think you have anyone in your organisation that can take the both of us, and deliver us to you alive, well...happy hunting my friend. Oh...and don't forget, I'm still out there, and with threats like that, I may be looking for you!"

Tony really wanted to find Annie and just go off somewhere and live a comfortable quiet life with her. He was hoping to be finished with his former life. Based on what Agent O'Brian said to him, he was hoping he could trust her about not being pursued by any law enforcement people, especially since she never paid the second payment for the job she had him do. He felt that would be a fair trade off. Coming in over Ireland, Tony decided that since it was still light out, he would do a couple of fly-bys over the city of Belfast. With any luck, maybe Annie would see the jet and know he was there. He had tried to call her again while he was on his way, but the phone never got answered. He thought it could be just that she didn't have it anymore. It had, after all, been a very long time.

Landing at a small private airstrip he had used many times in the past, he had a small building there to hide the jet. He was going to need a car to get to the city, so typically, he found one that was easy to steal and drove into the city. He made arrangements to have several thousand dollars transferred to a bank he was familiar with in Belfast. The first thing he was going to have to do, would be go and withdraw some of that money. After collecting some money, he began making his way around the city looking for any clues for Annie. Stopping in several pubs, he showed her picture to anybody that would look. It seemed nobody had seen her. He began to stop people on the street and show them her picture, but again with no luck. Maybe he had to go further outside the city. Maybe she was living on a small farm and didn't come into the city very often. He decided he would put an ad in the local newspaper. It would be a simple ad, with large lettering saying something like, "In Belfast looking for 007." And he would put his phone number in the ad.

Tony placed the ad and waited a week with no reply. He was starting to think that Annie wasn't in Belfast after all. Tony called Svetlana, and after talking to her for a while, decided to go to her for a short visit. While getting the jet out of the building, he saw Annie standing next to a car by the runway. He was even happier to see her than he thought he would be. She, on the other hand, seemed somewhat less happy. Going to her and hugging her, he noticed that she didn't really hug him back. As he pulled away, upset he asked, "What's wrong? Aren't you glad to see me? I've been looking all over for you."

After a long pause Annie said, "You just left me hanging out there on my own. You didn't even try to help me."

Confused Tony replied, "No…that's not true. When I went back to your house and saw all the police there, I thought they had you. I tried to find out, but I couldn't get any answers. Then after I knew that you got away, I tried to call you, but you didn't answer the phone. I looked everywhere for you." He paused and then asked, "Annie what happened to you? Where did you go?" She didn't say anything for a few minutes.

On the verge of crying she said, "I went to Canada. I have a girlfriend there and she helped me get out of the country, and over here."

"Why didn't you come to the hanger?" Tony asked.

"Because I thought if the police found me, then they must have found you. I didn't know they just had me for that guy I shot in that bathroom. I thought it was for the stuff in Mexico."

Remembering that he told Svetlana that he was on his way to see her, Tony called her to say he found Annie, and was bringing her with him. Hugging Annie, and her hugging him back this time, he told her he had someone he wanted her to meet. As he was getting the plane ready for the trip to Russia, he couldn't help himself. Just being near Annie again made him feel so good he just couldn't stop holding her, and she was coming back around to feel the same way. It wasn't long before they found themselves making love in the hanger. It was wonderful for both of them. They had missed each other more than they each realised.

When they were finally finished, and back to getting the jet ready, they began to hear noises outside the hanger. It was the sounds of people. Looking out one of the small windows, Tony saw three men, perhaps in their early twenties, milling around Annie's car. It looked to Tony as if they were trying to steal it. When he told Annie that, she told him to let them take it. She just stole it a couple of days ago. After the men took the car, and the area was clear, they brought the jet out and headed for Russia. On the way, Tony filled Annie in on all that had been happening with him. When he told her about Agent O'Brian and the fact that she had been using his service for a few years, she said, "That sneaky bitch! Do you think she will come after us at some point?" Tony said he didn't think so, and he believed he was right about that. Anyway, he told Annie that with the money he had, they could go anywhere in the world, and he could afford some very tight privacy. As they were talking about everything that had been happening, Tony asked Annie why she ended up in Belfast. "That's where you were born, isn't it? I was looking for your family. I thought that if you were in trouble too, maybe you would go back there."

It didn't hit him right away. But, as they continued to talk about all the things that had been going on with each of them; it slammed into Tony's head like a sledgehammer. How did Annie know I was born in Belfast, and what my family name really was? How is that possible? There was only one way that could be possible. Annie had access to the same information that Agent O'Brian had! Now the question was, how did that happen? Tony had a very bad feeling about that. He had to think very carefully about how he talked to Annie about her having that information. He wondered if she realised her mistake yet and was hoping that he missed it. "I imagine there must be a lot of families with that same last name in Belfast," he said.

"Yeah, I found about thirty-five of them. But I haven't been to all of them yet, so I don't know if any of them are connected to you." Did she still not realise? How was he going to get into this delicately? And come to think of it, how did Agent O'Brian know that Annie was in Belfast? And if she knew that, why hadn't anybody picked her up on the murder charge? Tony's head was starting to spin again. He didn't want to spook Annie, or alert her to her mistake, but he had to know how she had that information.

The rest of the flight was pretty quiet, Tony had a lot of things to think about. Annie, on the other hand, had realised her mistake, and was doing some thinking of her own. As they were getting close to the airstrip in Russia, Tony called Svetlana to let her know when to pick them up. He decided to talk to her about Annie's mistake to see if she had any ideas on how he could handle it. Annie was being very careful not to give away the fact that she realised her mistake. She had to come up with a cover if Tony started to question her on it.

Svetlana was very happy to see Tony, and glad to finally meet Annie. She had heard lots of very nice things about her form Tony. On the way to Svetlana's house, both Tony and Annie tried to act as calm and natural as they could, given what they were both thinking. Svetlana had taken over her brother's business and was telling them all about how that was going. Tony was glad to hear that she did that, and that it was working out well for her. In the next day or two, they would pay her place of business a visit and he and Annie could check it out for themselves. Once they got to Svetlana's house, she set them up in a bedroom and then while Annie was in the bathroom, she looked at Tony and asked, "Okay, what the hell is wrong?"

"I need to talk to you alone, but it's going to take a while," he said. As Svetlana set about making drinks for everyone, she added a very effective sleeping powder that she sometimes used at her brothel on unruly clients, or guests to Annie's drink. While they all sat comfortably drinking and talking, Tony could see that Annie was starting to get sleepy. Within several minutes, even before finishing her drink, Annie was out. Without having to worry about Annie for the next couple of hours, Tony began telling his story. "Annie was being investigated by the FBI for a murder that she did commit. They raided her house, and I didn't know if she got away or not. There was no contact from her for almost a year. But the FBI Agent assigned to her case told me they didn't have her, and she kept in touch with me off and on through most of that time."

He then told her about the Agent, and how he came to find Annie. "The Agent, Stephany O'Brian, was actually a client of mine for a few years. I didn't know that, but she called as my client and had me do a job in Texas, which turned out to be killing her husband." After pausing and letting that information sink in, he continued. "After killing her husband, Agent O'Brian called and told me she was the client for whom I just did the job. And then she told me that Annie was in Belfast, and she was going to give me some time to get out and go find Annie. When I got to Belfast I couldn't find her, but as I was getting ready to come here, she showed up at the airstrip."

Tony told Svetlana about Stephany knowing that Annie was in Belfast, and then, Annie having information about Tony's real name and family, and being suspicious about how Annie got that information. He was also wondering if the FBI knew Annie was in Belfast, why hadn't she been picked up on the murder charge? There was something very wrong with all of that, and he had to find out what it was. Svetlana told him that she would make arrangements the next day, to take Annie out and show her the town, and maybe do a little shopping. That would give Tony some time alone to work on the computer to see if he could get any answers to his questions. When Annie awoke, she felt as if she must have drifted off, maybe just tired from the long flight from Boston to the little airstrip in Russia. Svetlana told her of her plans to take her out the next day to see the town and do a little shopping. Annie was excited about seeing the area, and maybe even doing some shopping. She asked Tony what his plans for the day were, and he told her he had to work on the plane and take care of some financial issues.

The following morning, after breakfast, Svetlana and Annie headed out for a day on the town. As soon as they left, Tony went to Svetlana's computer. Having hacked his way into the FBI personnel files to find Agent Peter O'Brian, hacking in again was a simple matter for him. He thought the biggest problem was going to be that he didn't know if Annie's name was real or not. With thousands of Agents to go through, he decided to start with the Boston Field Office files. Hoping that he wouldn't find her, he entered 'Antoinette Spalding' into the system and pressed enter. He sat for several minutes staring at the extremely beautiful face of the only woman that he thought he ever wanted to spend the rest of his life with, (well there may be one other). Agent Antoinette Spalding, Boston Field Office. Current assignment, undercover.

Tony didn't read the rest of the information given. He didn't need to; he didn't want to. As he sat looking at her face, he felt his heart being crushed inside his chest. Before getting out of the program, Tony printed the screen page. He folded it up and put it in his pocket. Knowing the reality now of his situation, he had to get to the jet. When both Annie and he were in the jet together, he couldn't see her from his position in the cockpit. She could have been doing anything back there, and he would never know. Now he knew he had to get to the jump seat compartment and check it for tracking devices. Taking one of Svetlana's cars, he went to the jet and began his search of that compartment. Hoping again not to find anything, after looking for about 20 minutes or so, there it was. He found a small GPS transmitter stuck to the bottom of his seat. Without intentionally looking, he never would have found it. Now the question was what to do with it. He couldn't just take it out and throw it off to the side of the airstrip, which would lead them to Svetlana. He couldn't put it on a car; they would know the movement was not that of a jet. He looked at his map. He found a mid-size executive airport about fifty miles east of his location. He took the transmitter off his seat and just left it on the floor. He got in the jet and headed for that airport. Landing at a commercial airport in Russia would have some issues. The two biggest were first, Tony didn't speak Russian, and the second was that his plane was not going to show up on the control tower's radar. He was going to have to work around both of those issues.

About twenty miles west of the airport, Tony dropped his speed to just above stall speed. He dropped his altitude to just above the top of the trees, which would put him below the radar screen, so the control tower wouldn't see him even in a regular plane. Then he sent out an international distress call to the tower. Once the controller had visual sight of his plane coming in, he was cleared to land on whichever runway was best for his position. After landing, he taxied over to a group of corporate jets and parked as close to one of them as he could. While getting out of the plane, the airport security team came to pay him a visit.

Tony was quick to notice the security team consisted of three military jeeps, one with a .50 cal. machine gun mounted in the back of it. Happily, one of the soldiers spoke a little broken English. Tony did his best to try to explain that his jet was all electric and the batteries were in need of being charged. He told them it would only take about half an hour. After giving the jet a thorough inspection, Tony was shown where he could plug in to charge the batteries. The security detail left Tony to work on his jet. With them gone, he got the transmitter and very quickly went to the closest jet. He placed the transmitter up as high as he could reach into the rear landing gear compartment. He was hoping it wouldn't be seen on a pre-flight check.

Back at his jet, he opened the side hatch to the main generator and pretended to do some work on it. After about a half hour he unplugged the jet, got in and called the tower. He didn't know if anyone understood, but he told them he was leaving, and began to taxi out to a runway. Looking around to make sure there were no in-flight planes that might be an issue, he headed down a runway. As he was building speed, getting ready to lift off, he saw the security team headed toward the runway. He noticed they were moving very fast and there was someone at that .50 cal. machine gun. Increasing the thrust value, he lifted off the ground and began a steep climb at 70%, quickly approaching a speed of mach one.

Continuing his assent, he levelled off at 48,000 feet and set a cruising speed of mach 1.4. Leaving the runway, he was heading east. He made a narrow U-turn and headed back toward Svetlana's house and the small private airstrip. Passing over the airport that he just left, he picked up two blips on his radar. There were two jets that were going to try to follow him. They were heading east. They would never be able to find him on their radars, and they were cruising at about 30,000 feet, headed in the wrong direction. Getting back to the little airstrip, he pulled the plane into the little hanger. Tony got Svetlana's car that he left there, and he went back to her house. When he got there, Svetlana and Annie were already home. Annie seemed to be furious with Tony. "Where have you been? Where did you go? We stopped at the airstrip and you, and the plane were gone. Where were you?" Her questions seemed very harsh to Tony.

"Are you interrogating me now?" he asked. "You sound just like Agent Stephany O'Brian."

After he said that, Annie softened a bit and in that cute sexy little voice she sometimes used she said, "I'm sorry, I was just worried about you. I didn't know you would be taking the jet out. And please don't compare me to that FBI bitch." Tony told them that he made some adjustments on the plane and had to test it to be sure everything was working properly. That seemed to satisfy Annie and calm her down. Tony thought maybe she was worried about the transmitter. Then he remembered that when he hired her, he had a GPS chip placed under her skin. Did she have a similar chip from the FBI somewhere under her skin? Was that how Agent O'Brian knew that Annie was in Belfast? If that was the case, then she knew exactly where she and Tony were right now. Tony didn't want to put Svetlana in any danger; they had to leave right away.

While Annie was out of the room, Tony gave the computer printout to Svetlana as he explained that they had to leave. She was very upset, and now worried for Tony's safety. "What are you going to do about Annie?" she asked. Tony didn't answer right away. He couldn't, he had to compose himself first.

"I don't know, I never thought I would have to come to a decision like this," he said.

"I have people that can help you with this Tony. Why don't you just let me take care of it for you?"

"Svetlana, how can I ask you to do something like that for me?"

"It is okay Tony; I know this is very troubling thing for you and I can help you with it. So let me do this for you, please."

Tony agreed to let his friend help him with this one very difficult task. He was sure he could trust that her people would take care of it properly, and completely. After settling that, Tony made plans to leave as quickly as possible. "Where will you go?" Svetlana asked.

"I don't know yet, but I will find that perfect little spot somewhere that no one will find me."

Svetlana just nodded and then asked, "Will you let me know you are okay?" Tony said that he would, but he knew that he would not be able to have any contact with her, ever again. It was for her safety as much as his. He also never asked what would be done with Annie. He really didn't want to know. With Tony ready to leave, he and Svetlana approached Annie as she sat looking at a magazine, enjoying a glass of wine. Tony handed the computer printout to Annie. Very quickly realising what it was, she started to get up. Svetlana was ready with a handgun already pointed at her. Making her lie face down on the floor, her hands were cuffed behind her back, and her feet zip tied together. As she began to cry and protest, telling Tony she could explain, he bent down and kissed her on the side of her face and said, "I'm sorry that it has to be this way." He then got up and walked out of the room and the house, heading for the airport. Getting in his jet, he headed west. Did he know where he was going? Of course, he knew. He had known for the past year and a half exactly where he was going.

As for Annie, she was taken to Croatia, where both Tony's chip and the FBI chip were located under her skin and removed. The chips were destroyed, and Annie was brought back to Svetlana's brothel. There she was placed in a very lavish suite consisting of a small living room, a large bedroom, and a very well-appointed bathroom with a large walk-in shower and large soaking tub. She was given a new wardrobe of the finest, most alluring, and sexy lingerie on the market. That was to be her entire new wardrobe. It was, after all, the only thing she would need to wear from now on. She was given three female assistants to be with her at all times. For those moments when privacy was going to be needed, they would wait in the living room. Annie was to become an attraction that only Svetlana's richest and most powerful patrons could afford. It wasn't every day that a Russian man, or the occasional woman, got to spend one hour, two hours, or even an entire night with an American FBI agent, forcing her to do whatever they wanted of her.

Unfortunately for Annie, her transition was not an easy one. After a few treatments of car batteries and jumper cables placed on various parts of her body, she did finally make the transition. The ever-present threat of more treatments seemed to satisfy her occasional need for rebellion. Annie of course never saw any of the money for her services as the other girls did. Svetlana felt the room, lingerie, and food were payment enough. Tony never knew what became of Annie, and he never really thought about it, he had other things on his mind. And if Annie was expecting help in the form of Agent Stephany O'Brian, well she was going to be waiting for a very long time for something that just wasn't going to happen.

When Tony got to his final destination, he pulled his plane into the newly built hanger. Closing the hanger, he stood outside just looking around at the beauty of his surroundings, and thought out loud, to no one there, "Who says money can't buy you happiness?" He then headed across the yard to his new home, and for a beer and relaxation. He had been looking forward to this moment for a very long time, and now he was going to enjoy the hell out of it. If the FBI, Scotland Yard, or Interpol, or anyone else for that matter were looking for Tony De Luca, they were not going to find him. Tony De Luca no longer existed. And that guy, Stephen Finn, yeah, he no longer existed either.

To Be Continued

# Episode Eight

## A New Life Starts

About a year and a half ago, Tony began to make his plans for the future. He had visited a small medieval town in northwest Belgium, called Bruges. Wandering around the town he fell in love with it. The cobblestone streets, the fourteenth century buildings, the overall quaintness of the village, and even the people there. On the outskirts of town, he was able to find a small 28-acre farm for sale. The farmhouse needed work and some general modernisation but was otherwise sound. He had the cow barn torn down, and a new one built in the same configuration as the original. The horse barn just needed small general repairs. He had a large hill just to the north of the farmhouse dug out, and a new airplane hangar built. He then had the hill replaced over it. From the air it was impossible to find the hanger. The airstrip leading to the hanger was kept as a well-manicured section of the lawn area around the house.

He couldn't tell anyone about it, not Annie, not Svetlana. This was where Jason Bordeaux had planned his retirement all along. Now being there, he acquired a few milking cows, some beef cattle, a few horses, sheep, and several chickens. He also had a small vegetable garden and a 10-acre vineyard. In the vineyard he grew Pinot Blanc, and Pinot Noir grapes. When the grapes were harvested, he aged the wine in small batch oak barrels. Some of the barrels were scorched and some were not. He often liked to experiment with the underlying flavour notes by adding maybe a little citrus peel, and/or a variety of berries or spices to one or two test kegs. He sometimes also played with the aging time to see what difference that made on some of the wines. Each barrel was very carefully marked and dated to be kept track of.

The threats that were made to Tony by that Mexican drug lord were the last thing he had ever heard from his past life as Tony De Luca. That life, along with all contact to it, went away the minute he left Svetlana's house on his way to Bruges. He was very happy playing gentleman farmer and tending to his livestock and vineyard. Tony, now Jason, was now living in peace, and getting to know some of the people of the town. He liked to go to the centre and visit the local pub, where he met many of his new friends. He occasionally invited some of his new friends to his house for dinner or even a small party for one reason or another.

He seemed to be well liked by most of the people he came into contact with. Sometimes he was invited to someone's house for dinner. He always brought them a couple bottles of his wine. Jason studied and worked at his wine making constantly and was getting some very good wine as a result. He had over time, met several young and quite attractive women in town, many of whom were happy to get to know him better. Jason, now in his early forties, often had thoughts of finding women and sometimes even men, interested in having 'private parties' with him. Most were slow to take him up on the idea. Still, he kept his eyes open and made some effort at finding the right people. Most of the girls he met were fine, but just not the right ones. If a man was to be involved, a woman had to be included. So…he spent his time working his farm and having the occasional sleepover, generally a one-or two-nightstand. He just wasn't able to get interested in any of the girls he was seeing, at least not for anything more than quick typical sex.

Jason had been living at his little farm now for about a year and a half. One day there came a knock at his door. When he opened the door, he was looking at the very attractive face of FBI Special Agent Stephany O'Brian. Taken completely off guard, he was speechless. She smiled at him and asked, "Surprised?" Jason still couldn't come up with anything to say. As Stephany pushed him back inside, she took another step into the house, and said, "Don't worry, I'm not FBI anymore. Those days are long gone. I'm just Stephany now."

"How did you find me?" Jason finally asked playing along.

Ignoring his question, she replied, "Don't worry, I'm not wired, and I don't have a chip anymore. And to prove it, I'm going to let you search my entire body, and I mean everywhere." As she said that she pushed Jason further back into the house. She grabbed the front of her blouse, ripped it apart, and let it fall to the floor. She then grabbed the front of Jason's shirt and did the same thing. After that, they fell into each other's arms and kissed very deeply and passionately. While kissing her, Jason skilfully released her skirt and let it fall to the floor. Left standing with nothing but a matching red lace bra and panty set on, with a black garter belt holding light charcoal stockings, Jason picked her up and made his way to the first-floor master suite. He set her down and she immediately removed his pants and pushed him onto the bed.

As she stood looking at Jason naked on the bed, she removed her bra, unhooked the stockings from her garter belt and removed it and her panties and let them both fall to the floor. Looking at her now, Jason couldn't help thinking how remarkably similar Stephany and Annie looked. If it weren't for the striking gold hair, and lighter complexion of Stephany, they could have been twins. Coming to him on the bed, they embraced each other and again kissed very deeply and passionately. As they kissed, he fondled her breasts, and she stroked his penis. He then began to slide down her body, stopping to visit here and there, to kiss, lick, tease, and play as he pleased on his way down. Her moans of pleasure were all he needed, to know he was doing things that she liked. Reaching her vagina, he stopped to manipulate her clitoris with his tongue. Playing and teasing her, she was building up to an explosive orgasm. When she reached her explosive pleasure, she wrapped her legs tightly around his head, crushing his face against her. She let out a cry of pleasure and satisfaction that only a long awaited and extremely pleasurable orgasm could produce.

Continuing, he went lower on the vagina to find that very hot and wet spot he remembered and missed so very much. As he began to play with her, using his tongue and fingers, she grabbed his head and pulled his face up to hers. As his body slid up along hers, his penis slid perfectly into her. With both of them giving small cries of pleasure, he began to stroke his penis inside her. Reaching that wonderful orgasm, they both so very much wanted, he remained inside her for a few minutes afterward. When he rolled off her onto his back, Stephany then began to kiss his face, neck, and worked her way down his chest to his penis. Taking it in her mouth, she began to suck, and lick it, until it was completely clean. At first, he was a little uncomfortable with that, but it felt so very good, and was actually just a bit, well…more than just a bit, sexy.

As Stephany worked her oral magic, Jason was starting to become firm again, not hard, not yet, but firm. When she was finished, she began working her way back up his body, kissing and caressing as she went. Once back to his face, she kissed him again deeply, passionately, and rolled onto her back. As they both laid side by side on the bed, she looked over at him and said, "You know, the polite and correct thing to do at this point would be reciprocation."

After a moment, Jason looked at her and asked, "You mean I do just like you just did?"

"That's right," she told him with a very sexy and sly smile.

"Well, I guess that's not something I have ever given any thought about doing after, well…you know."

Again, with that sexy smile, she said, "Yes, I do know. I think it's time you try it. I'm pretty sure you're going to like it." She clearly had learned some new and interesting after-play techniques in their time apart. Working his way back down her body, again stopping to play here and there, he finally got to the place she wanted him. Stopping to give her clitoris another gentle but thorough tongue lashing, she had another very much appreciated orgasm. As he worked his oral magic there, he manipulated that now very hot and extremely wet area just below with both of his thumbs. It felt wonderful to her, and the orgasm felt incredible, but she still wanted his tongue inside her. She wanted him to play with her at that spot, with his tongue, and experience what she had experienced on other women in the past few years and come to like very much.

As Jason slid his tongue down to that magic hot, wet, spot, it was as if Stephany had another orgasm. The reality was just her excitement of having his tongue inside her, darting in and out, licking and playing with her. She loved it! She knew by the amount of time, and all that activity and playing, he was most definitely enjoying himself. After their extended re-acquaintance ritual, they settled down to fixing something of a meal for themselves: She in panties and stockings, he in undershorts. "So…nice place we have here. What is the name now…Jason Bordeaux?" Looking across the centre island in the kitchen, Jason replied, "Yes, that's right, Mrs. Bordeaux. And you're going to have to learn how to spell it correctly. Oh…and you better work on your French accent a bit, I told all my new friends that you were working a very classified undercover job for the French police." While sitting eating their meal and enjoying some of Jason's wine, Stephany said, "You know, Jason, as an international team of assassins, I think we did pretty well for ourselves."

"I agree. Did they ever get close to you with the investigations of the one's you hit?" he asked.

"No, I was never even close to being a suspect. And you were never really looked at until Annie hit that guy in that ladies' room. It was the bullets that did it."

"Yeah." He agreed. "I knew that was going to be a problem." But then Stephany told him, "But even with that, I had you pretty well covered until you made that silly little romp around Mexico."

"I needed a vacation, and we were just having some fun. I like what you came up with to handle Annie, though. As near as I can figure, she stole about 1.8 million dollars from us while she worked for me." Looking very surprised at the numbers, Stephany replied, "That's a lot of money. I guess you can't even trust an FBI Agent anymore. She needed to be dealt with." On the day that Svetlana took Annie to town, one of the things Jason, (Tony at that time) did, was call Stephany and talk about Annie's fate with her. It was Stephany that came up with the idea of the American FBI Agent in the Russian brothel. Just after Tony left Svetlana for the last time, Stephany called her and gave her very specific instructions on how Annie was to be dealt with.

"Let me ask you something, did she come up with all that shit you did in Mexico, or was that you?"

"Well, let's just say I hope she never gets away from Svetlana and finds us. I hate to think of what she would do to us. That girl can come up with some very nasty ideas," Jason replied.

Jason asked Stephany about the man she had him kill in Texas. (Calling him her husband). She told him that she got to know him 'very well' and had spent time with him and his real wife. They were one of those couples that seemed to think, three was not a crowd when it came to matters in the bedroom. It was, in fact, that couple, she told him, that introduced her to that little after-play, she had just introduced him to. She told Jason how she had the wife leave a note saying she was leaving her husband, because she found that he was having an affair. Stephany then explained how she killed the woman and left her body several miles out in the desert. She then forged all of the important papers she was going to need and had Tony kill Agent Peter O'Brian. The last name was just a very convenient coincidence. She was able to add about two million dollars to their already several million spread out in many different banks. Jason was impressed with her planning and foresight.

*****

Stephany had been living at the farm for a couple of months now, and in that time, Jason had introduced her to a few local women and some men with whom they had been having sex. Some of the women were very flexible and Stephany loved to watch Jason with them. She also loved to treat them to a little oral after-play as well. It was the same for Jason. He loved watching men make his wife feel good and have orgasms. He loved to watch them as they were inside her, and then watch her after-play with them. She always kept the oral after-play to be done on her by Jason, no one else. He had come to enjoy that part very much, and it made her feel incredible.

One day while doing a little shopping in town, Stephany stopped at the pub. Sitting in her regular seat at the bar, Lucy, the young and very attractive barmaid placed Stephany's normal glass of chardonnay in front of her. Lucy was also one of their sexual playmates. After a little small talk with Lucy, Stephany began to scan the room for friendly faces. What she saw, was a table with six Mexican men sitting at it. They were drinking and playing cards. Calling Lucy over she asked, "When did the Mexicans show up?" After thinking for a few seconds Lucy said, "Yesterday is the first time I remember seeing them, why?" Stephany didn't say anything; she just finished her wine and left the pub.

Lucy noticed that very soon after Stephany left, one of the Mexicans got up from the table and also left the pub. As she watched, Lucy noticed that the Mexican followed Stephany's car out of town. Not sure why, but Lucy didn't like the look of that. She called Jason and told him about the six Mexicans, and one of them following Stephany when she left the pub. Jason thanked her and hung up the phone. Six Mexicans in a Belgian pub in Bruges could only mean one thing: Menaloa Cartel boys. He went to the gun cabinet and selected one of his best sniper rifles. The rifle, equipped with a silencer and a very powerful scope, was, of course, one of his own making. He grabbed a clip filled with standard market purchased bullets, which he was more inclined to use now, then he left the house. Driving toward town, about six miles from the farm, there was a fork in the road. Coming from town you could either go to the right, which would take you to the farm, or to the left, which would take you around a small cluster of hills between the two roads. Jason parked his car about fifty yards from the intersection, and with his rifle, ran into the little cluster of hills.

As Stephany approached the fork in the road, she saw Jason's car parked on the side. That was a message telling her to take the left road. She was glad to see Jason's car. She wasn't 100% sure, but she thought she might have been followed. At the intersection, she stopped to make sure the car, about one hundred yards back, saw her go to the left. After making the turn, Jason watched the Mexican follow her to the left of the hills. There was a small section of road that was a blind spot for Jason, but when the Mexican drove out of it, Jason squeezed the trigger. He saw a small hole in the passenger's side window, where a spider web of cracks appeared. He also saw a small hole in the right temple of the driver of the car, and a large splatter of blood, flesh, pieces of bone, and brain tissue cover the window to the driver's left. The car left the road, went into a ditch and stopped. Around the next turn, Stephany had stopped her car and was waiting for Jason beside a very large excavator, with an extended bucket arm.

The excavator was one of the pieces of farm equipment that Jason left in that location in preparation for times like these. Going back to his car, he drove to the excavator, and after checking to be sure Stephany was okay, got in and started it up. He used the bucket to break the back window of the car and hooked the bucket inside the passenger compartment from the back window, he was then able to pick up the car. With the excavator, he carried the car between two of the small hills. There was a large flat area with no vegetation on the ground. He set the car down and began to dig a hole large enough for the car to fit in, and about twelve feet deep. With the hole dug, he placed the car, with the dead body still in it, into the hole. He then used the bucket of the excavator to crush the car as best he could, and then filled in the hole. After filling the hole, he drove over it several times with the excavator to be sure it was well packed and wouldn't show a depression any time soon. He then took a broom that he carried in the cab of the excavator and brushed the earth to help remove the marks made by the heavy machine.

Back at the farmhouse, both Stephany and Jason knew they had trouble coming. Without wanting to, they each knew they had to have a plan. "So…What do you want to do about this?" Stephany started. "They must be pretty sure that you're in the area."

"I don't know how they could have found me. I got rid of every trace of Tony De Luca before coming here. It was one of the reasons you had to stay away so long, so they couldn't tie the two of us together."

"Well, somehow they either just got shit lucky or they actually figured it out," she said. Jason didn't know what to think. How could those Mexican's have figured out where he went? There was absolutely no trace of Tony De Luca anywhere.

"I can't just draw them out and kill them all. That asshole will just send twenty more of his men after me. I'm going to have to lead them somewhere else, and either kill them there, or give them a reason to keep heading in that direction." The look on her face told him that she seemed to agree with him. He could tell she had something on her mind, though.

"Okay, so...if you don't look like Tony De Luca anymore, and nobody around here has ever heard of the man, how can anybody point them to you?" she asked, and then continued, "and I don't think any of them have ever seen me, or really know anything about me."

"Some of that's not entirely true," he said. "I was here about five years ago, before I bought the place. I was still him back then. And they obviously know enough about you to have you followed."

They needed to come up with a plan. They always came up with the plan they needed. Jason went to the hanger, in the back room of it, there was a storage area. In some trunks that he had hidden away, he started to go through some of the old post cards he still had from his De Luca days. When he found the one he wanted, he then started to look through the collection of counterfeit postal cancellation markers. Finding what he wanted, he went back to the house and wrote a short message to Lucy, the bartender. He signed the card, a picture of downtown Belfast, 'Love Tony', and he stamped it with the postal code marker from Belfast. Deciding to kill two birds with one stone, Jason called Lucy and invited her to the house for a night of fun and games. He told her to bring along a friend and it didn't matter if the friend was male or female. Both Jason and Stephany would be happy with either.

When Lucy and her male friend got to the little farmhouse that night, they all sat down to a light meal prepared by both Jason and Stephany. Then after enjoying lots of Jason's wine, they all headed to the bedroom for the first of the two important matters of the evening. A few hours later, with all of the foreplay, sex play, and after-play taken care of, the second important matter of the evening came up. Jason started,

"Lucy, you know those Mexican men that have been hanging around the bar? Well...they're looking for me. They may be calling me by some other name, but it's me they want." He let Lucy think about that for a few moments then he continued, "I need you to help me get rid of them."

"How can I help you? They have been asking lots of questions about a man named Tony something, and not just to me, but to lots of people. Are you in trouble with them for something?" Lucy asked.

"I used to know their boss. We had a bit of a falling out and he thinks I did something to hurt his son."

"Did you hurt his son?" she asked him.

"It was someone that I was associated with at the time, that did it," Jason told her. "What I need you to do is simply put this post card on the end of the bar, with the writing up, so the Mexicans will be sure to see it. When they ask you about it, and I'm sure they will, just tell them that I was here a few months ago and when I left, I told you I was moving to Belfast."

Both Stephany and Jason were sure that would send the Mexicans running to Belfast and keep them in that area for a very long time. He gave the card to Lucy, and she said she would put it on the bar the next day.

"I will call you and let you know what happens after they see the post card," she told Jason. After Lucy and her friend left the farmhouse, Jason and Stephany continued with a little more after-play, which led into more sex play, and back around to the after-play again.

The next day, Lucy put the post card on the bar as she had said she would. When the Mexicans came in, one of them always came up to the bar, to order the round of drinks for the table. As he was standing there, he saw the post card, and as expected, he asked Lucy about the card.

"This Tony from Belfast, what's his last name, and how do you know him?" The man asked Lucy. As she was getting the drinks he ordered, she took her time to answer the man.

"That's my friend Tony De Luca. I didn't tell you about him when you asked me about him before, because I don't think it's any of your business."

"When was he here? Is he in Belfast now?" The man pressed her now for answers.

"He left here a few months ago. He said he was moving somewhere near Belfast. The card came in today's post, so I would assume that he's still there," she replied, acting very annoyed now. The man then asked if his friend that left yesterday ever came back in? She said she hadn't seen him. The man brought the tray of drinks to the table and told the rest of them about the post card. The news seemed to excite the whole group. But they were still concerned that their friend still hadn't come back, after following the woman yesterday. After talking about the situation, they decided that they would go out to look for him. If they didn't find him, they were going to have to call the boss and tell him everything, and then get new orders from him. The men finished their one drink and left the bar, on the hunt for the missing Mexican.

Lucy called Jason and told him about the Mexicans and that they were going to be looking all over the area for the one that went missing, and that he and Stephany should be on the watch for them. He thanked her again for her help, and then turned to Stephany and said, "The Mexicans are going to be coming around looking for the missing one."

"Well," she said, "this will be a very good test of the difference in the way you look now compared to then."

"Yeah, you're going to have to stay out of sight, though. We can't risk them recognising you." She agreed, and so began their day.

Jason made sure there were no items in plain sight that might trigger a memory for one or more of the Mexicans. He really didn't want to have to kill any of them. He wanted his plan for them to work, and he had hoped that it still might.

A couple of hours later, a van pulled up to the little farmhouse. Looking out a window, Jason knew exactly who was there. It was the Mexicans. With Stephany in another room, out of sight, and with an automatic assault rifle at the ready, Jason went to the door. One of the men came to the door with a picture of Tony De Luca. As Jason stood looking at himself in the picture, he wondered if the other man was seeing any resemblance.

"Have you seen this man around here before?" asked the man.

"No, he doesn't look familiar to me, but then I keep around the farm mostly," Jason told him. Putting that picture down and holding up one of the missing Mexican, he asked, "How about this guy? It would have been in the last couple of days that he may have been around?"

"Nope, don't recognise that one either. Seems like I'd remember him if I saw him, he'd be a little out of place here," Jason said with a smile on his face, but the other man wasn't seeing the humour in it. He gave Jason a very hard look, and then turned and walked back to the van. The men sat in the van for a couple of minutes before driving away. The fact that they didn't just leave when the man got in made Jason wonder what they might be talking about. After the van left the yard, Stephany came out to Jason. Seeing the worried look on his face she said, "It's going to be okay, if that man thought for one second that you were Tony, they would have stormed the house by now."

"Yeah, you're probably right." He agreed.

Later that day, the leader of the group placed a call to his boss, the head of the Menaloa Cartel. After explaining the loss of one of the men, and the development of the post card, he was told to take the men and go to Belfast and find that son-of-a-bitch, De Luca. The following day, the five remaining Mexicans came into the bar. The leader of them gave Lucy an envelope marked, 'Pedro', and told her to give it to his friend if he came back in. Lucy took the envelope and told him she would watch for him. She knew, or at least was pretty sure, he would never be back. The group of Mexicans sat and had a couple of drinks, and then left the bar and headed for Belfast, Ireland. They had no idea, how they would be welcomed to the city that had been the home of the RMS Titanic.

After giving Lucy that post card with the Belfast postal stamp, Jason placed a call to an old friend from his days of opposition to the IRA. He explained his situation to his friend, and together they came up with a plan for the Mexicans. Landing in Belfast, the five remaining Menaloa men rented a van and set out for a hotel downtown. They never made it to the hotel. An Irish welcome committee of fifteen men, in three vehicles surrounded their van under a bridge, and took the men into custody. They were brought to a large warehouse where, after singling out the leader, bound him to a chair. The other four men were then hung by their wrists from a large overhead beam. After removing the shoes from the four hanging men, they were beaten with heavy sticks. They were beaten over every part of their bodies, including the tops and bottoms of their feet. The only part not beaten was their heads. Their leader was forced to sit and watch, as this was being done. All four of the men at one point or another, passed out from the pain before the beatings were completed. In the end, nearly every bone in their bodies had been broken.

With all of the bones broken, the hanging bodies took on odd misshapen forms. The four men were brought back to their reality by the use of smelling salts. Once they were at least vaguely aware of their situations, the ropes holding them up were cut. The sound of the broken bodies hitting the concrete floor was so sickening, that it causes their leader to toss whatever food he had in his stomach onto himself. He also seemed to lose a bit of his own grip on reality as well. The four men all passed out at contact with the floor. The Irish leader had been videotaping the entire process with a cell phone. He then told one of his men, "Okay, that's enough for them, now it's his turn." The four men were then shot in the head.

"Okay, big guy, now it's your turn." The Irishman told the Mexican leader.

The man was removed from the chair and brought to a work bench. With two men holding him, his right arm was placed in a vice and secured. With the camera still filming, a pair of very dirty, bloody bolt cutters were brought out from under the bench. The Mexican leader began to scream. He knew all too well what was going to happen, and he knew they were going to take their time to do it. He was right! One by one, and very slowly, the fingers of his right hand were cut off with the bolt cutters. After wrapping his right hand with bandages, the Mexican was released from the vice. His left arm was then secured into it.

The pain the Mexican man was feeling was almost unbearable. Unfortunately, he was not given the mercy of passing out. With the bolt cutters now being waved in front of him, the Irishman looked him in the eyes, while he told him he was now going to remove all of the fingers on his left hand.

"I am only doing this as a message to your boss. When you get back to Mexico, you tell that asshole, if he sends any more of his people here, he will get a visit by an army that he really doesn't want to meet."

After telling him that, the Irishman began cutting off fingers. Finally, the Mexican began to feel a wave of relief and started to pass out. But then, smelling salts were jammed under his nose. There was no relief for his pain.

With his fingerless hands roughly bandaged, the Mexican was taken to a private airport and placed on a jet that was waiting for him. The jet left for Mexico to deliver the Irish message to the Menaloa Cartel boss. The phone with the video of the beating of the other four men was sent along with the fingerless man. After the jet had left, the leader of the group in Ireland called his friend Jason.

"The Mexican job has been done my friend. And we have sent the message to the boss in Mexico."

"Thank you for your help. I hope the message makes its point, I really don't want a war," Jason replied.

"I think we'll be okay, if we get a visit from more Mexicans, we will be ready, and we know how to deal with these sorts of things," his Irish friend tells him.

With months passing by, and no indication of further interruptions in their lives, Stephany and Jason lived in peace on their little farm. Jason spent much of his time tending to the animals, and general farming chores. Stephany learned how to make blankets and quilts from some of the other women in town. They both occasionally went into town and visited with friends at the pub. They also continued their special little parties, with a small group of sex playing friends. One day Stephany turned to Jason and asked, "So…do you think our new lives have really started?"

"Yes, my love, I do believe we have actually begun our new lives."

To Be Continued

# Episode Nine
## The Mexican Alliance

Nestled deep in the forest and jungles of the mountain region of North-East Mexico sat a large Spanish style house. The house had a white stucco exterior, with Spanish clay roofing tiles. There were several exterior porches and second floor balconies, large Doric columns and arches around many areas of the house. The house sat on a large flat area on the side of a large mountain, with no access from the mountain side. There was a high but decorative concrete wall surrounding the rest of a large grassy courtyard. The entrance to the courtyard was gained through a very heavy iron gate. In the centre of the courtyard was a large fountain with a circular drive around it. The drive passed the front entrance to the house. At either side of the entrance there stood a statue of Mary holding the baby Jesus. This was the compound of Juan Carlos Jesus.

As you went into the house past the statues, you entered through a large arched section of building, with heavy wooded gates. These gates were almost always left open. Today, however, they were closed. Past the closed gates, in a room deep inside the house, at a large table sat the heads of the three Menaloa Cartels, headed by Juan Carlos Jesus, just Carlos to those that knew him. Along with the Menaloa Bosses, were the two heads of the Nogales Cartels. Normally enemies of each other, they have all been brought together for one common cause. They were at the home of Carlos to discuss the problem of Tony De Luca, and what he had done to Carlos's son, Juan, and other Menaloa men.

Carlos was explaining to the rest of the group, the horrible way Tony executed his son, Juan, along with several other of his men. He was also telling them what he did to the Menaloa Black Diamond meth lab. He had put a great deal of money on the table to help entice the other bosses to form the alliance that Carlos felt he would need to find and capture Tony. He told everyone at the table he wanted Tony brought back to the compound alive. He, himself, wanted the pleasure of dealing with Tony De Luca. None of the other Cartel bosses had any grievance with Tony, but the money was a big deal for all of them. After a long discussion on how they would find and capture Tony, an agreement was made among all of the bosses, and the money was split up.

After the meeting had taken place, and the other bosses left the compound, the fingerless Mexican is once again brought before Carlos. Again, Carlos asks, "Are you sure that you can't remember any more than you have told me about the men that did this to you?"

"No sir, I have given you all that I can. Most of the information is on the video in the cell phone," the fingerless man said.

"Okay, he is no longer of use to me, Pablo, Jesus, take him to the field." As Carlos gave the two men the order, the fingerless man began to yell, "No, please, I can go with the men to Ireland and help find those men, and maybe even Tony."

"You had your chance at that and look what it got you," Carlos told him. "Take him away," he said to the other men. The fingerless man was grabbed and dragged, kicking and screaming out of the room. He was brought to a field behind the house, at the base of the mountain. There a hole in the ground was waiting for him. He was made to kneel at the end of the hole, and he was shot once in the back of the head. The body fell rather unceremoniously into the hole, and the hole was filled.

On a day, approximately one week after the meeting of all the Cartel bosses, there were forty-two Mexican Cartel men at the compound. All of the men were from the various Cartels. The men were given their final instructions, which included finding the Irish bastards working with Tony. After finding them, they were to be dealt with in the same fashion Carlos's men were dealt with. They, however, were to be left alive to suffer as long as possible. Then they were to find, capture, and bring back Tony De Luca, so Carlos could deal with him personally. Carlos was sure that his army of forty-two men, heavily armed with automatic assault weapons would be enough to do the job.

The men were taken by bus to a secluded airstrip and placed on three private planes, headed for Belfast, Ireland. Their spirits were high. They all felt as if they were going to go over there, find those men right away, and beat them as they beat the other Cartel men, and leave them to die in agony. In the process of the beatings, they were sure they would get the men to tell them where they could find Tony. Those forty-two men, however, have no idea what kind of shit storm they were walking into. But they would soon find out.

As the three Mexican planes were picked up on the radar screen of the airport in Belfast, the controller realised that they were not coming to that airport, but to a small airstrip mostly used by drug runners, and other illicit flights. Rather than call the police, he made a call to the head of the IRA opposition group that the other (unfortunate) Mexicans already met with. He told him about the three planes coming in from Mexico, and how big they were. The information gave the leader of the opposition group a reasonable idea of what to expect when they intercepted the Mexicans. It has been a couple of years since the last visit by the Mexicans. He had hoped it was over. He called Jason to let him know what was about to happen.

When Jason was told of the arrival of the three Mexican planes, he offered to go to Belfast to help with the fight. His friend told him that wasn't going to be necessary; they had the situation well in hand. Shawn, the opposition leader, then called together the rest of the opposition group. There were approximately sixty members that showed up within about ten minutes of his call. They knew that the Mexicans were probably going to start looking in town for them. To do that, they were going to have to pass under the same bridge the other Mexicans did. This time, however, with that many men to deal with, they weren't going to take any chances. As the vans with the Mexicans go under the bridge, all sixty of the Irish opposition members would be waiting off to the sides with automatic assault weapons of their own.

Unaware of what they were driving into, the Mexicans were enjoying tequila, and having a party time. As the first van drove under the bridge, it was allowed to go further under, to allow the other two van's time to also be under the bridge. At that moment, a hail of bullets ripped through the sides of the vans. Hundreds of rounds of bullets were fired into the vans for several minutes. There was no return gun fire from any of the vans. Waiting a few minutes after the gunfire stopped, the Irishmen approached the vans. To their surprise, there were still four or five men alive in each of the vans, and they opened fire on the Irish, as they were out in the open street.

As both groups were now shooting at each other, and the Irish were looking for cover, with the Mexicans still hiding in the vans, the scene takes on a battlefield appearance. Several of the Irishmen went down in the street. Others found some cover at the sides of the street and continued to blast each of the vans. The battle seemed to come down to who brought the most bullets to the party. The Irish won. Finally, after an extended battle, the last of the Mexicans was killed. The Irish lost twenty-five of their men; the Mexicans, all forty-two of them, were dead. Shawn had set up a video camera at the outbound end of the bridge, and it had been recording the entire battle. The Mexicans would be left where they are. The police would be called, and they would have the mess cleaned up. The dead Irish was taken back to their families for proper services.

The police knew what happened, and who was involved, but they would do nothing about it. One copy of the video would be sent to Jason, and another to that son-of-a-bitch, Juan Carlos Jesus. Along with the video to Carlos, another message was sent, explaining that he couldn't win, no matter how many men he sent. When Carlos couldn't contact any of his men on the first day of their arrival in Ireland, he was concerned. He was aware that something like that might happen to his men. He knew the Irish had people watching the skies around Belfast. But he was one step ahead of Shawn.

When he sent his forty-two men from Mexico, he also sent three non-Mexican assassins from two different airports in the United States to Belfast. He also spent a great deal of time and money-making friendly contacts in the Belfast area. As the three assassins arrived, at roughly the same time the forty-two Mexicans arrived, they were picked up by those new friendly contacts. The three assassins were housed, armed, and given transportation by their new friends. They looked like your typical American tourists, but they were all carrying .45 cal. handguns with silencers.

After the battle at the bridge, Shawn called Jason. "That Mexican asshole sent forty-two men here. I guess he thought that was going to be enough to do something. All forty-two are dead; we lost twenty-five of our own in the fight, though."

"Jesus, I'm sorry to hear that. I should have been there to help. I feel terrible," Jason said.

"Don't worry about it. This is what we do, and given our history together, I'm glad to be able to help you any way I can " Shawn told him.

"Well, if there is ever anything I can do to help you, just let me know, and I will be there for you and the opposition," Jason replied.

Two days after the battle at the bridge, Liam, Shawn's 19-year-old brother, went missing. Nobody in the group seemed to be able to find him. The next morning, in the early hours of the day, Liam's body was found hung by the neck, with his entrails hanging from his body to a bloody mess on the street below him. One of the opposition members called Shawn. "Shawn, we found Liam, and I gotta tell you right up front, it isn't good. He's been gutted, and hung from the bridge," the man told him. Shawn told him not to let anyone touch the body. He needed to see it. When Shawn got to the bridge, looking at his younger brother, he knew this was a message. Could it be more Mexicans? Who else would do this?

After removing his brother from the bridge, and taking him home for a proper burial, Shawn called Jason. "My brother Liam is dead, gutted and hung from the bridge where we killed all the Mexicans."

"Shit!" Jason yells into the phone. "Do you think more of them got in without you knowing?" he asked.

"They may have sent some into Dublin. We wouldn't know if they did that," Shawn said. "Or maybe that son-of-a-bitch smartened up and he sent some non-Mexicans on commercial flights."

"Yeah, he might have done something like that, but that would mean he has some contacts in Belfast that helped them when they got there," Jason suggested. The thought of that rang loud and clear in Shawn's head, and he wasn't sure how to handle it. How was he going to draw out those one, five, ten? How many was he even supposed to be looking for, and how was he going to draw them out to find them? Shawn was calling Jason on a cell phone, a typical plan purchased cell phone. Neither Shawn nor Jason were aware that the call was being monitored and traced by the assassins. "I'm going to have some of my men get on this. We can check unfamiliar faces and see what we can turn up in known data bases," Shawn told Jason, and the call was ended.

The call has been traced from Belfast to the little farm outside Bruges, Belgium. The three American assassins were given a private plane, by their contacts in Belfast, to take them to France. From there, they would drive to Belgium. They would do that, to avoid any eyes that might be watching the skies over Belgium. Jason, Stephany, and Shawn were completely unaware that the men were there. They drove to the little town of Bruges and did some sight-seeing, as if they were any other American tourists. What they were really doing was looking for any signs that would point them to Jason. Going into the local pub, they met Lucy the barmaid, and struck up a conversation with her. "So…miss, we are in town on holiday, and we thought we would try to look up an old friend. The last we knew; he was living somewhere in the area. His name is Tony De Luca; do you know him by any chance?" One of them asked her. Hearing the name Tony De Luca rang some very loud bells inside Lucy's head.

"Yeah, I knew Tony, but he left here a couple of years ago to live somewhere near Belfast, last I knew he was still in that area," she told him.

"Well, we heard recently that he was back living around here. Are you sure you haven't seen him?" The man asked.

"I'm quite sure. We were very good friends, and if he were back here, I'm sure I would know about it."

The men decided to take a ride around town. They had a general idea of the location of the farm, so they were going to check it out. When the men left the pub, Lucy called Jason, "Jason, there are three men, American I think, that were just in the bar asking about Tony De Luca."

"Are you sure that's the name they gave you?" he asked.

"Yes, I'm quite sure, they just left, and their headed in the direction of your farm."

"Do you know what kind of car they are driving, or at least the colour of it?"

"I'm not sure what kind it is, maybe a Ford. It's a four-door car, and it's dark blue," she told him.

"Okay, thanks Lucy. I owe you very big for this one, and I know you're going to want to collect on it," he said jokingly.

After hanging up the phone, Jason filled Stephany in on what's happening. "How do you want to handle this one?" She asked. Jason wasn't sure what to do, he needed time to think about it, "I think that if they show up around here today, it most likely will be just a drive by," he told her.

"They might stop in to see if they recognise either of us," she said.

"That's true. I don't think they will just come barging in shooting without being sure who their shooting at," he agreed. "But maybe if a dark blue four door sedan pulls up with three American men in it, we should be ready to take them out, just to be sure," Jason suggested.

"I guess if they come to the door, you can answer it, and I can be off to the side ready with an auto," she told him.

"I don't think that's a bad idea," he said. About 45 minutes later, a dark blue four door sedan stopped in the street, at the end of the drive leading up to the little farmhouse. Nobody got out of the car, and it just sat there for about two or three minutes, then it left. The blue car wasn't seen around town again after that day.

But on a very dark moonless night, two nights later, in the wee hours of the morning a dark blue four door sedan was creeping its way up the drive to the little farmhouse. The car stopped about twenty-five yards from the house, and three American men got out. All were wearing gloves, but now were carrying automatic assault rifles.

The men knew the danger of their target but felt as if they had the advantage of surprise on their side. What they didn't realise was that they were now on a farm, not the city streets where they were used to working. Geese, chickens, sheep, and cows all started to create lots of noise, protesting the stranger's presence on the land. The noise was enough to wake both Jason and Stephany, and they immediately knew what was about to happen. "Okay, it's on," Jason said. Then he told Stephany, "Don't turn on any lights." They both grabbed automatic assault rifles and headed down the stairs. Looking through small peep holes, they could just make out the shapes of the three men as they approached the house.

When the men were about ten yards from the front of the house, Jason flipped a switch, turning on a couple of very bright flood lights. The lights were so bright, that they momentarily blinded the three men. All of them froze in their tracks, and then with no cover around them, they all dropped to the ground. In the fire fight that followed, hundreds of rounds of bullets were exchanged between the five of them. In the end, the three Americans were dead. Jason turned to look at Stephany, she was not there. He called out to her and got no answer. As he ran to the last place he saw her, he found her on the floor, bleeding badly from a gunshot to her left shoulder. She was unconscious and breathing, but very shallowly. The first thing he checked was to see if the bullet went through and through. It did. That was a good sign to Jason. He just had to stop the bleeding until he could get some help for her.

It was now about five in the morning, Jason called a friend, Kelsey. He was the veterinarian they used on the farm, and also one of their sex-party friends. He told Kelsey that Stephany had been shot and needed help right away. "I'll be there in about 15 minutes," Kelsey said. Jason packed the wound with gauze to stop the bleeding, and then headed out to get rid of the three bodies as best he could before Kelsey got there. He knew he was going to have to deal with them in a more permanent way later. His main concern right then, was getting them out of sight, and getting Stephany fixed up.

"She has lost a lot of blood," Kelsey said to Jason. "How long ago did this happen, and how did this happen?"

"It's been about maybe half an hour now, I'm not sure," Jason replied him. Knowing that the vet must have seen the front of the house, which was all shot up and full of bullet holes, Jason tells him, "We had some men try to come in and rob us tonight. There was a bit of a shoot-out. All of the men left, but not before Stephany got hit."

"I saw the front of the house. That must have been some shoot-out. Do you know who the men were?" asked the vet. Jason had the feeling that the vet wasn't buying the whole story.

"No, I don't think I have ever seen them before. They were driving a big, dark blue sedan, I don't think I've ever seen that before either," he told the vet.

After the vet finished up with Stephany, he told Jason, "She is going to be down for a long time with this. She lost too much blood. She may have to go to a hospital for a transfusion." Jason knew he couldn't bring her to a hospital there would be too many questions.

"What if she doesn't get the transfusion? Is she still going to be alright?" he asked. The vet looked at Jason and he knew Jason's concerns about taking her to a hospital. "If you want, I can come with you to the hospital, I can explain the gunshot as an accident. The police will still have to be involved, but I can keep the investigation as an accident for you."

"Okay, that will be great if you can help us like that. I can pay you whatever you need for your help, you know that," Jason replied. The vet called for an ambulance and as it showed up, a police car was with it. Kelsey realised that now that it was light out, the police were going to see all the bullet holes in the front of the house and decided that he had to change the story. "They had three masked men trying to break in early this morning and had a bit of a shoot-out with them," he told the officer. Looking at the house, as Stephany was being loaded into the ambulance, the police officer turned to Jason and asked, "How many men were there? Do you know who they were, and where are they now?" Standing in the front yard, in the light of day, Jason could see all the blood on the ground.

"I don't know who they were, or where they are now. I think one or two may be wounded. You may want to check with the local hospitals. It looks as if someone lost a lot of blood out here," he replied to the officer.

"They all got away, then, did they?" The officer asked.

"Yeah, they were driving a big dark blue four door sedan if that helps you," Jason said.

"Now if you don't mind, I would like to accompany my wife to the hospital." The officer told him to go. They could finish up any loose ends in the investigation later. Jason wasn't sure it was a good idea to leave the vet and the police at the house without him being there, but he didn't really have a choice. He didn't want to raise suspicion by trying to get them to leave before he did. He knew he hadn't hidden the dead men or the car all that well, it was supposed to be just a temporary thing. He didn't expect anybody to be snooping around, especially the police.

Kelsey sensed Jason's concern and told the officer that he should be off looking for the wounded man or men. There really was nothing he could do at the farm. "Thanks, Kelsey. I owe you big for all of your help today," Jason told him as he was getting into the ambulance with Stephany.

"Don't worry about it, I'm here to help you, and will do whatever I can. You know that. Besides, we have to get that wife of yours fixed up and back to good health as fast as we can. We have too much fun with you guys to be without her for very long." Jason smiled as the ambulance doors were closed and he was on his way with Stephany to the hospital. He knew that Kelsey, and probably the police officer, would show up while he was there with her. He hoped that between himself and Kelsey, they could convince the officer of their story. As the doctors worked on Stephany, Jason was told that she was going to be fine. She would be in the hospital for three or four days and would need to be given some blood. The wound looked clean, and nothing vital had been hit.

Later that day, as Jason was leaving the hospital, the police officer that he met at the farm met him in the lobby. "How's your wife doing, Mr. Bordeaux?" he asked.

"She's doing okay. She will be here for a few days, but they tell me she's going to be fine." The police officer just nodded and then pointed to a bench and asked Jason to have a seat. "So, you want to tell me what really happened out there in the wee hours of this morning?"

"Like I said, my wife and I were sleeping, and we heard the geese start to make a ruckus. And then the chickens, sheep, and cows started. We both got up, thinking there must be a wolf or something like that out there. We each grabbed our guns and went downstairs. When I started to open the front door, I heard guns, and the door started to splinter." Taking a short breather Jason went on, "We couldn't see anything out there, so we just stayed behind the house walls.

When the shooting stopped, I flipped on the outside lights and we both started to shoot at the three men standing in the yard."

"Let's talk about the men in the yard," the officer said. "I would have to say by looking at the front of your house, that they were using automatic weapons, right?" Not waiting for an answer, he continued, "So, you're telling me that these three men came to your house in the small hours, with automatic assault weapons…to rob you?" Again, not waiting for an answer, "Tell me, what do you keep in that house that is so valuable that something like this would happen. What were they there to steal?"

"I don't know what they thought they were going to find. We don't have anything of any value that we keep in the house," Jason told him. The officer looked at him for a few moments and then said, "These men didn't just come to your house and start shooting the place up for nothing. So, if it wasn't something, then that tells me it must have been someone they were after." He gave Jason time to think about that, and then asked, "Do you want to tell me about that?" Jason didn't know what to say. Finally, he said to the officer, "Look, I'm tired, and I have the animals to go tend to. Do you mind if we do this some other time? Tomorrow about this time will be good if you want to stop by the farm." The officer agreed to do that, and Jason left the hospital headed to the farm. He knew he had to get rid of those men and their car very quickly, and permanently.

Back at the farm, Jason's big excavator was six miles away, in the little cluster of hills. He did, however, have a backhoe at the farm. He was going to have to make that work. As he was digging a hole large enough to take care of the problem, his heart sank in his chest as he noticed his friend Kelsey standing off to the side watching him. It was clear that Kelsey could see the car Jason had described as the one the men were driving. He wasn't sure if Kelsey could see the dead bodies inside the car or not. When the hole was just about finished, Jason stopped and got out of the backhoe to go talk to Kelsey. Before he even got over to him, Kelsey let him know he was fully aware of what was going on.

"Well, I see you did better than just wound one or two of them. What the hell happened out here this morning?" Kelsey asked. Jason was worried his friend might tell the police about what he was seeing him do and was not sure how to approach it. He decided to tell him some version of the truth.

"Kelsey, these men work for someone I used to know. It was many years ago. We had a falling out, and the man thought that I did something to hurt his son. It was actually an associate of mine that did it, not me. I thought after all this time I was done with him, and he had stopped looking for me. I guess I was wrong." After pausing for a few seconds, he continued, "Please you gotta help me here. Don't tell the cops about this, please."

"I'm not here to spy on you or check up on what goes on out here. You are my friend and have been for a while now. Everybody has a past. It would appear yours may be a little more exciting than most, and maybe we can talk about it just a bit if you wouldn't mind telling me something about it, over a pint or two sometime. Right now, I think the job at hand better get finished before the police come snooping around again. As for the freshly dug hole, as a vet I can tell the cops that you lost one of your cows in the gunfight, and just buried it here."

"Thank you, Kelsey. You're a great friend, and maybe at some point I can take you up on the pint." Jason knew he couldn't really tell his friend anything about his past life, but he would come up with something colourful to talk about that he hoped would satisfy Kelsey's curiosity.

As the dawn was breaking in Mexico, Carlos had not been able to contact any of the men he sent to Belfast. They were instructed to contact him when they arrived, that never happened. He thought the Mexicans might run into trouble, but how could the three Americans have been taken so fast? He had to know what was going on in Belfast. Another meeting of all of the Cartel bosses was called for. That evening as they all sat around the table at Carlos compound, they were told that none of the men that they sent to Belfast had reported back, and Carlos had not been able to reach any of them. Each of the Cartels had probably lost several men.

"I am going to go to the shit hole of a place and see what's going on there myself," he told the rest of the group. A few of the others offered to go with him. "No, I think the fewer Mexicans they see, the better. I am going to take a few more Americans with me. Maybe that way we can find out what's been happening. Maybe I can even find that bastard De Luca."

The group of Mexicans agreed that sending more Americans was probably a better idea. They all had contacts in the United States and would each pick one of theirs to send with Carlos. He was determined to get to the bottom of this, and at the same time put an end to Tony De Luca once and for all.

Jason and Shawn had already figured out that it wasn't over, more would be coming. The trick now was how to find out, how many would be coming, where they would land, and were they going to be Mexican or American. While keeping in close contact with Shawn, Jason was also spending a lot of time at the hospital with Stephany. Kelsey had volunteered to tend to Jason's farm as much as possible to try to help. He had his story about the dead cow all set, should the cops come around again.

As Jason was arriving back at the farm, after spending time with Stephany, Kelsey was there, and so were the police. There are several officers that time, and it didn't look good to Jason. As he walked up to two cops talking to Kelsey, he heard him telling the cops about the freshly dug hole, and the dead cow. They seem to believe his story. With Jason now there, all attention turned to him. The officer he was talking to at the hospital starts. "Well now, son, you ready to tell me what those men were really doing out here, and what really happened? And by the way, I think we need to talk about the guns you have here. I can't seem to find any permits in your name." Jason stood looking at the bloody ground, and the front of the little farmhouse full of bullet wounds, and broken windows, and he looked at Kelsey for help. Unfortunately, there could be no help from anyone, Jason had to handle this one on his own. Looking at the officer he finally said, "I'm not sure, but I think there may be a possibility that those men…"

To Be Continued

# Episode Ten

## Carlos Goes to Belfast

"I'm not sure, but I think there may be a possibility that those men were here by mistake. I think they thought they had someone else's house," Jason told the officer.

"You telling me that you think this was supposed to have been some kind of gangland hit or something like that?"

"Well, I don't really see any reason for them to have been here shooting up my house in the middle of the night."

"Okay, son, so let's go through this. You and your wife are sleeping; the animals wake you up, you both grab guns? Why the guns?"

"We thought from the racket the animals were making, that there might have been wolves or some other wild animals out here."

"Okay, so you go to the door, and someone starts shooting at you. I'm going to go out on a limb here and say these three men were standing in your front yard firing automatic weapons, maybe assault type rifles at you. And you and your wife, what kind of guns did you say you have?"

"They were standing until we started shooting at them. Then they were lying on the ground. My wife has a .38 semi-automatic handgun, and I have a .45 semi-automatic handgun. And the men had some sort of automatic assault rifles with extended clips." Jason was starting to get a little impatient with the officer who was sounding just a little condescending at that point.

"So, you're telling me that you and your wife were able to fight off those men with the automatic rifles. You guys just using handguns. And from the blood pattern here on the ground, I'm going to say you hit all three of them." Then after a slight pause, "And then they just get up, go back to their car, get in it and drive away into the night. Do you see where I might be having some trouble with this story?" He finally asked Jason.

"Look, all I can tell you is that the men were on the ground shooting. After they stopped shooting, to change clips I suppose, Stephany and I started shooting at them. We both emptied our clips on them, then they started to shoot again. We keep extra clips in a desk by the door. We changed clips, and just stuck the guns out a corner of the windows we were at and started shooting. They stopped shooting; we waited for a bit, and then we heard the car doors slam, and the car drove off. I know we hit some of them, I don't know how bad they got hit, but yes, they were able to get up and get into the car and leave." Jason had just about had enough of that cop. If there weren't so many others around that bastard might not be leaving the yard either, he thought to himself.

"Well, I have to say by the amount of blood out here, all three of them were hit pretty bad. I don't see how any of them would have been capable of driving in their conditions."

"Maybe you should be out looking for the big blue sedan then. Maybe they didn't get too far."

"We have been looking for it all day; it seems to have disappeared."

Jason was done with the police. "Is there anything else you need from me? I have a mess in the house to clean up, windows to cover, and animals to tend to, if you don't mind."

"Well, if that's going to be your story, I want you to come down to the station and fill out a formal statement within the next couple of days. And if you wouldn't mind bringing those handguns with you so we can get them registered; that would be a big help." The officer called to the others and told them that they were done there for the time being, and they left. 'For the time being', Jason didn't like the sound of that. After the cops left Jason looked at Kelsey and asked, "So, what do you think?"

"Well, I think the part about you and Stephany beating those guys off with just handguns sounds a bit rough. Do you actually have any handguns that you can bring to the cop to register? I know having seen the car and the rest of the mess, bodies included, you didn't use handguns to do all that."

"No, we were using automatic assault rifles, too. I do have the handguns that I told the cop about, but they don't have regular serial numbers on them, because I made them myself."

"So, what are you going to do about that?" Kelsey asked.

"I don't know yet, I'll think of something, I hope."

Meanwhile, Juan Carlos Jesus, and his five American professional assassins were on a commercial flight to Dublin. Shawn and his family and friend were saying goodbye to Liam. Shawn knew there was more trouble coming. He sent a couple of his soldiers to Dublin to watch for any sign that those bastards were coming in from there. He always had people watching the airports, commercial and private, around Belfast. As the flight with Carlos and his group landed, Shawn's men were studying the faces of everyone getting off. One Mexican, with five Americans, all appearing to be together. That was the group they knew they were looking for. They called Shawn and told him what they saw. He told them to let them go through, but to follow them. If they were headed for Belfast, let them come, but to keep Shawn updated.

Shawn called Jason and told him that they had one Mexican and five Americans on the way. Jason figured that the Mexican had to be Carlos himself this time. If they could get Carlos that would basically put an end to that Cartel. Jason told Shawn he was coming to Belfast to be with him. Stephany was due to be released from the hospital later that day and Jason would have to be there for that. He said that he would be able to come to Belfast within the next few days. There was also that pesky police matter to attend to before he could leave. Kelsey said he might be able to help with the issue of the unregistered guns.

When Jason got back to the farm with Stephany, Kelsey was there waiting for them. He had two handguns with him, a .38 cal. and a .45 cal., both semi-automatics. He gave them to Jason and told him they were unregistered, but clean guns, and he could use them for the serial numbers if he wanted. "Where did these guns come from?" Jason asked.

"I bought them in Italy several years ago. I somehow never got around to registering them here. They are both Beretta's, very nice guns, and never been fired."

"Alright, thanks. Listen, I have to go to Belfast. Tomorrow morning after I go to the police station I will be leaving. Would you mind looking in on Stephany for me while I'm away?"

"Look in on her? Hell, I'll be happy to stay here with her while your away."

"I bet you will. Just remember, she just got out of the hospital with a gunshot wound, she needs a little rest," Jason said with a bit of a smile.

"I'll be okay, Jason. It was my shoulder that got hit, the rest of me works just fine. Besides, I don't want to be here alone, not right now," Stephany told him. Jason knew she should have someone around; and why not Kelsey? Maybe they could get Lucy in for a little visit as well. The following morning Jason made his statement at the police station and registered the two guns Kelsey had given him. Gun laws are tight in Belgium. He was told that the only reason they were allowing him to have the guns, was because he owned a farm, and may from time to time need them to protect his livestock. The fact that they were semi-automatics was also a bit of a problem, but they worked it out. Back at the farm, Jason prepared to head for Belfast.

Shawn called Jason early that afternoon. "Hey Jason, your Mexican friend is here in Belfast, and we know where he is staying, along with his American friends."

"That's good news. Keep a very close watch on them. I don't want them to do anything, or go anywhere, without someone on them, okay?"

"We got it covered. You on your way here?" Shawn asked. Jason said he was leaving the farm in about an hour. He just had a couple of things to take care of first. Kelsey was already at the house. He told Jason that he was going to replace the broken windows while he was in Belfast. Jason told him he thought that would be a fair trade-off for his looking after Stephany. "Oh, I don't need any trade-off for looking after this young lady, you know that," Kelsey said. All of them had a little laugh at that. Everyone knew exactly what Kelsey was implying, and it would be okay with Jason and Stephany. They had, after all, been sex-players for some time now.

While he was loading the jet, Jason grabbed a few automatic assault rifles, several handguns, and his favourite sniper rifle. He was hoping he would get the chance to use it on Carlos. He also grabbed lots of ammunition for each weapon. Getting the jet out of the hanger for the first time in a few years brought back lots of memories for him. Most of them were good, a few were not. He started to think about Annie and wondered how she was handling her role as a star attraction at a Russian whore house. Going back into the house to Stephany and Kelsey, he said, "Well, I guess I'm ready to head out. I won't be calling you while I'm in Belfast, I don't want to run the risk of leading anyone here again. You guys behave yourselves, and don't do anything we wouldn't do if I were here with you." Stephany giggled and hugged him tightly.

"You better be very careful over there. I want you back here in one piece, you hear me?" she said to him.

"I'll be very careful, and be back before you know it," he told her, still hugging her.

"Don't worry about things here. I brought an extra gun with me just in case. And all kidding aside, you know I'll take good care of Stephany," Kelsey told Jason. After a quick hug from Kelsey, Jason was on his way to Belfast. From the jet, high above England, Jason radioed Shawn to let him know when he would be there. Shawn would meet him at the airstrip with a car. He told Jason that his Mexican friend and the Americans had been very busy since arriving in Belfast. They had made contact with the people supplying them with their weapons and had been driving around town. Shawn said he thought maybe they were looking for Jason, or they were just trying to get the lay of the land, so to speak.

Getting into the car with Shawn, Jason asked, "Anything new to report about our little group?"

"Well, I can tell you that they are very well equipped, and I think they may even have some men joining them from Belfast."

"Really, how many do you think we're going to be looking at?" Jason asked.

"I'm not sure yet. I think the best thing to do is attack them soon, before they can get too organised. If we can get that Mexican guy, and take him out right away, I think that's going to take a lot of wind out from under the rest of them."

"Absolutely, that's why I brought my best sniper rifle. Get me within four or five hundred yards of him, with a decent shot, and he's all mine."

"We know where they are and we have been tracking all of their moves, so I think we should be able to do that without too much trouble." Shawn took Jason to his house, where he met a few of the other men in their group. Over a few pints, they came up with a plan to try to get Carlos before his group could really get started. Jason was told that Carlos and his American friends were staying at a farm just outside Belfast. Shawn knew the owner of the farm and was surprised to find that he was helping anyone that was against an opposition member, no matter what the reason. Shawn and a few of his group would pay the man a visit, and deal with that later. In the wee hours of the following morning, when it was still very dark and quiet, thirty-eight opposition members took up positions approximately 100 yards from the farmhouse.

Jason was on a small hill, about 180 yards from the house. Through the scope of his sniper rifle, he was looking directly into the kitchen of the house. At about 6:00 a.m., he started to see movement in the house. He radioed Shawn to let him know the house was coming to life. As people started to enter the kitchen, he was watching for Carlos. He saw Carlos come in and froze. Behind Carlos coming into the kitchen, he saw a young lady that he knew all too well. It was Annie!

"What the fuck?" He said out loud. How? Why? When? Was he even seeing what he thought he was seeing? How could that be? He picked up the radio and keyed Shawn. "Shawn, Annie's in that fucking house."

"How can that be? Are you sure? Maybe it's just someone that looks like her," Shawn said.

"No, there's no mistake. I'm looking at her right now. It's definitely her." Now he not only had to think about taking out Carlos, but Annie was going to have to go as well. But first, he still had to get over the shock of seeing her there. He had to know how that came to be. He was going to have to call Svetlana. As he kept looking around the kitchen at the other people coming into the room, he caught a glimpse of a picture on a wall. Going back to it, he focused his scope on it and was shocked again. The picture was of Svetlana. She was naked and laid out on display at the base of the Marx Memorial. She must have had twenty-five bullet holes in her. Annie was definitely going to have to go! He wasn't sure how, but he knew that bitch had something to do with that.

So here was his dilemma. He was only going to get one shot. Does he take out Annie, or Carlos, with that shot. "Shawn, I'm going to take out Carlos now. I want you guys ready to move when I say go. Is everybody ready?"

"We're just waiting on you to give us the word. What about Annie?" Shawn asked.

"Take her alive if you can; if not, don't worry about it." Jason signed off, and about five seconds later, Carlos's head exploded at the kitchen table. Jason yelled, "Go!" Leaving the sniper rifle there, he picked up an assault rifle and headed for the house with the rest of the group. As they stormed the house, the people inside were caught completely off guard. While they had weapons that they were able to get to, and some, even got a couple of shots off, they were, for the most part, all killed before they realised what was happening. And as for Annie, she too was now finally among the dead.

As Shawn, Jason, and the rest of their group walked around and through the house looking for anyone that may still be hiding, Jason couldn't help the feeling of some loss. While it was true that Annie had betrayed him, he still had some feelings for her. Six more people were found hiding in the barn and were shot by members of the group as they searched the grounds. Jason went back to retrieve his sniper rifle. Later, back at Shawn's house, Jason couldn't help showing his sense of loss, as well as total befuddlement, regarding Annie. He had to know what had happened at the brothel, and how Annie came to be teamed up with

Carlos. After the raid on the farmhouse, Shawn's people took several pictures of the massacre to be sent to Mexico. They were to be delivered to Carlos's compound, with a message telling them to give it up, or that same thing would take place there, at the compound.

Jason told Shawn he was going to have to go to Russia. He just had to find out what happened there. "You know Shawn, it might not be a bad idea to send a few of the boys to Mexico to keep an eye on the activity around Carlos's compound for a little while. Maybe even watch some of the other Cartels for action that we might want to know about."

"Yeah, I was thinking the same thing. I already have some guys picked out for the job," Shawn said. Jason called Stephany, feeling that it was safe to do so now, and told her about Annie. Stephany was as shocked as he was. When he told her that he was going to Russia to try to find out what happened, she said that she wanted to go with him. "I really think you should stay at home for the time being. How are you doing, and how are things on the farm?"

"I'm just fine; the farm is just fine. Kelsey has been staying with me, you know how Kelsey is. That's okay, isn't it?"

"Yes, of course it's okay. Has Lucy been around?"

"Yes, she was here last night, but she didn't stay the night. We did have a little fun, though."

"Well, I'm glad you're not alone, and tell Kelsey I said not to let you get too tired." Yes, he knew how Kelsey was, he would be chasing her around the house naked, trying to fuck her on every surface that he could catch her. He told her that he would be gone for another couple of days at the most. He said he would call her when he was on his way home. Saying goodbye to Shawn and thanking him and his group for their help once again, he left for Russia. He wasn't sure how, but he was going to find out just what happened there, and when.

Arriving in Russia, at the little airstrip he had used so many times for Svetlana, Jason was now on the hunt for a car to steal. Finding what he needed, he decided the best place to start was the brothel. It had been a few years since the last time he was there, and he wasn't sure any of the same girls would still be there. He was hoping that he would recognise one or two of them and get to talk to them. Since having some plastic surgery done on his face; he no longer looked anything like he did the last time he was there, so he wasn't worried about anyone knowing who he really was.

When he got to the brothel, he went in and took a seat at the bar in the main lobby. He got a beer and then just started to look around, checking faces for a familiar one, or two. As he sat there, several young women approached him, none of them familiar to him. After a while, starting to think he was going to be out of luck, a young woman came up to him that he recognised. Buying her a drink, they both headed for a room upstairs. In the room, he sat the girl on the bed, and very quickly began to tell her who he was, and why he was there. At first the girl seemed to get very nervous and scared. But then Jason saw something in her eyes that told him she knew him.

She remembered Annie, she had been at the brothel for about a year, maybe a little longer. Lots of men went to her; she was very popular. Then one day she got a gun from one of the security men. After killing him, she took Svetlana, and left the brothel. She said, "After that, neither one of them ever came back. Then the next day, someone brought a picture of Svetlana, dead, all shot up, to show us. He said that he was taking over the business, and that Annie was free now. That man still runs the brothel; he is Mexican, I think."

Jason figured that Annie must have called Carlos. She must have made some sort of deal with him. That could be the only explanation. He must have sent some men over to get her and take over the business at the same time. She must have told him that she didn't have anything to do with the murders in Mexico, and that she could help him find Tony. She must have thought that he was still in Belfast. Annie was probably the one that put all of those bullets into Svetlana. Jason wanted to go back and do the same to her, but she was already dead. It was over now; no more Russia, on more Mexico, no more Ireland. Could that be? Was he really just a Belgian farmer, now? He was very much hoping that was the case. On his way back to Bruges, he called Stephany to tell her he was coming home.

When Jason arrived back at his farm, after putting the jet back in the hanger, and storing away all of the guns where they belonged, he headed for the house. He found Kelsey had replaced the broken windows and was now repairing the damage done to the masonry on the front of the house by all those bullets. He was a good friend. Jason invited him to come in and have a beer with him, Kelsey readily accepted, and followed Jason into the house. Stephany was in the kitchen preparing dinner for all of them, trying to time it for Jason's return. She had it pretty close, and it was just about ready. She was very happy to see Jason, and he was happy to be home with her. "I think it all might be over now, completely," he told her. Smiling brightly, she gave him a very big, tight, hug, along with one of those very deep passionate kisses that Jason loved from her.

Not wanting to talk too much about what 'it' was, with Kelsey still there, they talked about what had been going on at the farm while Jason was away. Jason was pretty sure that Kelsey had a pretty good idea what 'it' was all about, but still, he didn't want to throw it out there with him around. "Lucy came by a couple of times. She brought a friend, a man, someone new," Stephany told Jason.

"Do you know who this man is, Kelsey?" Jason asked.

"No, I've never met him before. He said his name is Patrick, and he lives on the other side of town. Lucy said that he's only been there a couple of months. I guess he's been going to the pub a lot. He and Lucy seem to be very good friends."

"Has he become a new member of our little party club then?"

"Oh, Jason, I think you're going to like him when you get to meet him, and yes, he has. He has some interesting and new party games that I know you're going to like," Stephany said to Jason. Then Stephany turned the conversation to a more serious note, asking how Shawn was doing with Liam's death. Jason said he was having some trouble with it, but he was pretty sure he was doing better now. Even though he was pretty sure of the answer, Jason asked how Stephany's shoulder was. She told him it was just fine, and really didn't bother her much. After dinner, Jason and Kelsey went back out to do more repairs to the front of the house. It would seem Kelsey was very handy to have around. Jason didn't think he would have been able to replace the windows or repair the masonry without help from someone.

While they were outside working on the house, Jason began to ask Kelsey about the new guy. "So, what do you really think of the new guy Lucy brought over?"

"I like him. He's a lot of fun. I think being the new guy, he tends to try a little too hard, but I guess that's natural. He does seem to talk a lot, and ask a lot of questions, though."

Thinking about that, Jason replied, "What kind of questions does ask?"

"Well, he did seem to ask about you a lot. What you are like, and where you came from? You know that sort of stuff." Someone asking any kind of questions about him, always hit Jason's radar.

"What did Stephany tell him about me?" he asked Kelsey. He wasn't sure he could remember much of the specifics of any of the conversations, but he did say that she told Patrick that Jason was from Belfast, and that he still had family there. Jason wasn't happy to hear that. She knew he had all of his papers showing he was born in the United States, and that story was never to change. Trying not to let Kelsey see it, Jason was very upset. Later he asked Stephany about telling the man he was from Belfast. She told him that it had been so long since anyone asked about him, she forgot about his cover story. He was going to have to check this guy out, and quickly.

"Do you know what his last name is, or where he is from?" Jason asked.

"No, that's one other thing about him. He doesn't seem to like to talk about himself very much."

"Maybe Lucy has more information about him. I think I would feel better knowing a little something about this guy if he's going to be playing around with my wife and best friends," Jason told Kelsey. Kelsey seemed to agree that they should try to find out more about him. He said that the guy seemed to get a bit 'off', when you try to ask anything about him. That was not a good sign to Jason; he would get busy checking him out that night. Later that evening, after Kelsey went home, Jason and Stephany got very much re-acquainted with each other. After the fun was done, Jason set about trying to do a little background search on Patrick. He tried several different ways of finding him, but nothing seemed to be showing up. Maybe he was going to need his last name, not just his first name and location. He would ask Lucy tomorrow what she knew about him.

The following day, Kelsey came back to the farm to help Jason finish the front of the house. When they were done, the house looked as if it was never wounded in a shootout Kelsey was indeed handy to have around! Jason invited both Kelsey and Stephany into town for dinner at the pub. He, of course, wanted answers about the new mystery guy. As the three of them settled in at a table in the pub, Timothy, the alternate barkeep, came over to them. "Where is Lucy?" Jason asked, sounding almost too upset.

"She has the night off. I'm filling in for her. What can I get you to drink?" he replied. As the night went on, Lucy and Patrick came into the pub. Simply waving to Jason's group, they sat at a table across the room. Jason immediately decided something was not right. He told Stephany that he was going to go over and introduce himself to Patrick. As he approached their table, Lucy looked a little sheepish and said, "I'm sorry we didn't come over to introduce Patrick to you." Jason held out his hand to shake hands with Patrick.

"Hello, I'm Jason, Stephany's husband. I understand that you have been to our house and joined our little 'play' group."

"Yes, I'm Patrick, hello, it's nice to finally meet you, I've heard a lot about you."

"Yes, and I've heard some about you, but not very much. What did you say your last name is?"

"I didn't, but it's Butterfield. I moved here from England a few months ago. I love it here. And I love the people here."

"It is beautiful here. And yes, some of the people here are very easy to love," Jason said looking at Lucy. He then went back to his own table and he, Stephany, and Kelsey continued to enjoy their evening at the pub. But Jason's mind was already at work, racing with all sorts of thought's and making mental notes about this Patrick Butterfield, from England. He had a feeling that if he entered 'Patrick Butterfield, England' into his system, he was not going to like what he saw. Later, at about 1:30 a.m., Jason was looking at exactly what he thought he would see. And it was not at all good. Patrick Butterfield, from England, was dead! Lucy's Patrick Butterfield, from England, was not who he said he was. He was in fact an American, with six aliases, one of which Jason recognised. This man was an American, thought to be living in England for the last two years. Jason knew him as a paid assassin. He also knew that most of his work was with Mexican drug Cartels. The following morning Jason…

To Be Continued

# Episode Eleven
## This Son-of-a-Bitch Has Got to Go!

The following morning Jason was on the phone with Shawn, "We have another rat in the house, here in Bruges. He is an American that I think has been living in England for the past couple of years. I have heard of him, or at least one of his aliases. He does most of his work for the Mexican drug Cartels. He's not fussy, he works for anyone of them that will pay him."

"Do you need help with him? Have you got any idea where to find this guy?" Shawn asked. Jason already had a plan and he told Shawn what he was going to do. He didn't want to alarm Stephany, so he didn't say anything to her about the issue. He knew that it was going to have to be taken care of very quickly, though. When he did the background check, he also got what was believed to be the man's current address. In the early afternoon of the same day, he told Stephany that he was running into town for some things he needed for the farm. He had already put one of his .45 cal. semi-automatic handguns in the car: One of the unregistered ones, one of his own makings.

Stephany said that she wanted to come with him. After a few moments, he told her that he may be a while, and he didn't think she should be hanging around town waiting for him all that time. For some reason Stephany's radar went up. "Okay, so I get the feeling this isn't just a normal trip to the farm supply store. What's going on, Jason?"

"I have some work that has to be taken care of, and I don't want you involved," he told her.

"What kind of work? Do you mean Tony work, here in Bruges?"

"Yeah, I'm afraid so."

"Who? How did you find out?" she asked.

"I'd really rather not get you involved. I think I should just handle this by myself. Maybe you can meet Kelsey at the pub or just visit with Lucy, just don't say anything about any of this to either one of them, okay? Today, I may just do a little watching, to make sure I have the right guy. After, I will meet you at the pub." After dropping Stephany at the pub, Jason headed off to where he believed he was going to find 'Patrick Butterfield', formerly of England. As he got close to his destination, Jason left the car, and walked over a small hill, to see a small farm style house sitting by the road. The house was a stand-alone house, no barn or other outbuildings on the property.

Jason laid on the top of the hill for a while just watching the house through his binoculars. Finally, a man appeared, coming out the front door. It was the man he had met with Lucy at the pub. And it was the man whose picture came up in his background check, under six different names. The name Jason knew him by was James Tully. As he watched, James was going back and forth between his car and the house. On one of the trips from the house, he was carrying a rifle, with a scope on it. And a silencer! He was preparing to make a visit to Jason's house. It was time for Jason to make a move.

When James went back into the house, Jason headed down off the hill in the direction of the little house. He was staying as low as he could and using the bushes and trees as cover. When he got to the hedgerow in front of the house, he waited for James to come back out of the house. As he waited, he began to get the feeling that James had been in the house too long. Just about that time, he also felt the barrel of a gun on the back of his head. "You know, I was on my way to pay you a visit, but it's awfully considerate of you to come to me old chap and save me the trip," James said.

"I've always tried to be a considerate kind of guy. Who sent you?"

"Oh, I don't think that's really important. It was just one of those Mexican underbosses you used to like to deal with. I don't think any of them liked you getting out of the business and leaving them without your help."

"Well, they obviously had you to fall back on."

"Yeah, good for me. Now if you would just stand up real slow, and hand over the gun, we'll be heading into the house."

"You going to do this in the house, you're going to make a mess in there," Jason said as he slowly stood up. Taking his gun out from under his belt, he handed it to James. With James behind him they headed for the house, the gun barrel still pressed against Jason's head. As they got to the front door Jason stopped.

"Go on in. The doors not locked," James told him. Turning the knob with his left hand, he pushed the door open. At the same time, he bent over at the waist, very quickly, and pulling a knife out of his boot with his right hand, he heard the gun fire. The bullet grazed most of the way up Jason's back. As it did that, he reached behind him, he drove his knife into James's right side. All the way up to the hilt. With both of them injured, they were then in hand-to-hand combat. They were both very well versed in that sort of thing. Jason had lost his grip on the knife and was trying to get it back. He was able to get his hand on the handle, but the knife must have hit bone when it went in. It was stuck!

James dropped the gun when he was stabbed, and he was trying more to get the gun back than fight with Jason. Finally, Jason gave up on the knife, and stepped back, and was able to kick James in the chest. The kick sent James back out the front door, and onto his back on the front walk. Jason grabbed the gun and, although he wanted to just shoot James, he resisted the urge. He needed information.

"Get up," he said to James. With the knife still in his side, James was not moving well at that point. Jason went out and grabbed him by the back of the collar and helped him up. "Put your hands behind you, with your wrists back-to-back," he told James. As he told James to do that, he pulled a zip-tie out of his back pocket. With his hands now zip-tied behind him, Jason pushed James into the house. When Jason told him to sit in a chair in the kitchen, James didn't seem to want to be very cooperative. A simple twist and wiggle of the knife seemed to help the situation. James fell into the chair, slumped over, and with his head slightly hung.

"Okay now, who exactly sent you?"

"I already told you, one of those Mexican underboss guys."

"I need to know which one it was, and you're going to tell me, you know you are, so why not save yourself a lot of pain, and me some time and just tell me?"

"It was one of Carlos's men, that one from San Carlos," James told him. Jason knew exactly who he was talking about.

"Any other people working with you?"

"You know better than that. I don't work with anybody else. I never have."

"Okay, so, tell me how you knew where to find me," Jason demanded.

"I been working on this a long time, I just found you." A little turn of the knife helped him to elaborate. "I followed some guys out of Belfast a little while ago. I know they went to your house, and they never left it. That's how I was sure it was you." Jason had the information he needed. Now all he had to do was get rid of James. Killing him at the house and leaving the body there was going to raise a lot of questions, especially after the shootout at Jason's house. Although, he thought, he had planted that little seed of those men being at the wrong house. And, the possibility that they were looking for some sort of gangland member. Maybe this could work after all.

Jason decided that he would try to make it look as if James was attacked in the same fashion he and Stephany were attacked. The trouble was, James was not going to stand out in front of the house and let Jason shoot him with an assault rifle. "Get up, and come with me," Jason said to James. At gunpoint, Jason brought James out to the front yard. Once there, Jason cut the zip-ties from James's wrists. Holding him at gunpoint, Jason slowly backed away from James as he stood at the front of the house. When he was about 18–20 feet from James, Jason shot him, with the entire clip of the semi-automatic .45 cal. handgun. He emptied the entire clip, before James fell to the ground. With James down, and dead, changing clips, Jason shot James twice at the stab wound to help disguise it. Then, going across the street, Jason emptied two clips into the front of the little house. When he was done, the scene looked very much like the one at the front of his own little house.

Jason left James lying on the ground, in front of his house. Before he left, he made sure that he had picked up every spent bullet casing from his gun. He walked back to his car, and then drove home where he called Kelsey to come over and help with the bullet wound running up his back. After caring for the minor flesh wound, just a scratch really, they both went to the pub, and enjoyed a late lunch with Stephany. The following morning a neighbouring farmer passing James's house noticed all of the bullet holes in it. He stopped to investigate further, and he found James lying dead, in a large pool of dried blood. The farmer turned around and went back to his house and called the police.

Within 30 minutes, James little farmhouse had several police officers, crime scene investigators, and detectives, crawling all over it. A local news reporter was also there, trying to get a story, but not much information was coming, yet. Some of the police officers at that scene were also at Jason's house, after the shootout there. They had been commenting on the similarities between the two scenes. One difference that was very noticeable was that there were no spent bullet casings at this location. They had found hundreds of spent casings from AR15 assault rifles at Jason's house. They also found several bullets in good enough condition to compare with the others at Jason's house. From that they were able to determine that there were, in fact, three different shooters at his house.

As they did their investigation here at James house, they found only one bullet in useable condition. The bullet, they thought, must have been one of the first to be fired. It apparently must have caused some minor flesh wound, as James came out his front door. After striking James, the bullet appeared to have hit the door at such an angle, that it ricocheted off the door, and imbedded itself into a piece of woodwork in the vestibule. Where it hit the door, there was a small trace of blood, at the time assumed to be from James. It would be tested at the lab anyway. The other odd thing about the bullet they found was that it was a .45 cal., probably from a handgun. As they dug bullets out of the front of James house, they too were smaller than those at Jason's house, also probably all .45 cal.

While this scene looked very much like the one at Jason's house, it had some very big and troubling differences. When news of the murder made its way to Jason and Stephany's farm, she looked at Jason and flatly asked, "Was that you?"

"He was hired by one of Carlos's underbosses to kill me. He followed the other three men here."

"How did you find out he was a hit-man, and that he was working for the Mexicans?" she asked him.

"The name 'James Butterfield' didn't sit right with me, so I did some background checking. James Butterfield, from England, is dead. So, I looked up American, James Butterfield, England, and this guy's picture came up, along with six aliases. I recognised one of the names, and right away I knew who he was."

"How did you know that he was sent here from one of the Mexicans to kill you?" Now she was very intrigued.

"I didn't until I was able to get a knife in his side, and a gun in his face. You'd be surprised at the information you can get from someone with a simple twist of a knife." Stephany had that worried and I'm thinking about something, look on her face. Jason let her think about whatever it was for a few minutes and then asked, "What are you thinking about? Are you concerned that James hit will bring the police back here?"

"Yes, I think that would be the most likely direction for their investigation to take. I hope you were very careful," she told him. And then after a few seconds, her face came to life as she asked almost in a panic, "What guns did you use?" Now Jason was a little offended at the question.

"Don't worry; I used one of my own guns. Even if they have bullets, and want to compare them to my gun, I will give them the registered one. The bullets won't line up." That seemed to settle her down a bit. She still, however, had some reservations about the whole thing. If he was planning on giving the police one of the guns Kelsey had given him that told her he used either a .38 cal. or a .45 cal. handgun. These were hardly the weapons of choice if he wanted the police to think the same men that attacked Jason and her, were the ones that killed James.

"Do you really think the cops are going to think the same guy's that attacked us, killed James?" she asked with a bit of Indignation in her voice.

Now he felt as if she was just mocking him. "No, I never said that. I just wanted it to look as if he was killed in the same manner as the way those guys tried to kill us. It doesn't necessarily mean that it has to be the same people," he tried to explain. Later that day, the police did indeed show up at the Bordeaux farm. The same officer that Jason dealt with about the shootout at his house, was now banging on his door once again. Jason answered the door, as if he knew nothing of the killing of James the day before.

"Officer, what can I do for you today?"

"Well good morning, Mr. Bordeaux. I am officer Pardue. It seems we have another 'gangland hit' on our hands, and I'm here to see if you can help me out with any of it." Jason immediately got the feeling that he was being accused of something.

"Who was killed, and what do you mean by, 'gangland hit'?" Jason asked.

"Oh, you know, like the one you suggested was tried here at your house. Nice job cleaning it up by the way."

"I didn't say it was a gangland type of hit. I was merely throwing it out there as an idea. So, you still haven't told me who was killed, and I have to assume that it was in the same way we were attacked," Jason said.

"The deceased was one, James Butterfield. Does that name mean anything to you?" Officer Pardue asked.

"Yes, I just met him the other day at the pub. I think he was a friend of Lucy's."

"So, you didn't really know him all that well?" the officer asked.

"No, as I said, I just met him the other day at the pub, and that was just to be introduced to him by Lucy. He seemed like a nice guy. Do you have any ideas about who would want to kill him like that?" asked Jason, with his best poker face.

"I really can't talk about it. You have a .45 cal. Handgun, don't you?"

"Yes, you know I do, I was just down at the station to register it. I think it was some time last week," Jason told him.

"Well, I'm going to need that gun. We have to do a ballistics' comparison with all of the known .45 cal. handguns in the area. This doesn't mean that you are a suspect at this point in time," the officer said. Jason agreed to turn over his handgun. Of course, it would be the gun Kelsey had given him, not the gun he used on James. Now he just had to hope that Kelsey was right, that the gun had never been used. Then the officer dropped a bombshell on Jason.

"I also need to get a sample of your DNA, for comparison." Stephany stood up from the table, "Are you saying that the shooter, or shooter's left their DNA at the scene?" She almost demanded, looking at the officer.

"We don't really know that for sure, ma'am, but there is that possibility," the officer replied.

"So, you think the shooting was done from up close then? That's not really like what happened here," Jason said.

"No, it's not exactly the same as here, but the manner of death and the way it was carried out, are very much the same. Now I'll take that gun if you don't mind, son. And are you going to give me the DNA sample, or are you going to make me go get a warrant?" The officer was now doing the demanding.

Jason gave him the DNA sample and the handgun. He had no idea there was any possibility of his blood being found at the scene. Now he was more than just a little worried, as was Stephany. As soon as the officer left, she turned to Jason and said, "Well, that's just great, leaving blood or some other DNA at a crime scene. You're getting sloppy in your old age."

"I can't think of how any of my DNA would be at that scene. You know how careful I have always been." He was trying to figure out how he could have left a sample of DNA at James's house. None of it was making any sense to him. Then it hit him, the bullet that grazed his back. He completely forgot to look for it when he was done. But then, it was nothing more than a minor little scratch. How could that have left enough DNA for them to do any kind of work-up on? After thinking about it for a few minutes, he began to feel better about it. He showed Stephany the scratch on his back, and she agreed, that couldn't have left enough DNA to be of any use to them.

One nerve wracking week later, in the mid-morning, officer Pardue was back at Jason and Stephany's front door yet again. Jason answered the door, "Officer Pardue, what brings you to our little house again on this fine morning?" The officer, not looking quite as chipper as Jason held out his handgun. Jason took it without saying anything.

"You know, the funny thing is, we couldn't match the bullet recovered at the scene with any of the guns retrieved from anybody in the area," the officer said.

"Why do you say it's a funny thing? It's possible that someone that wanted him dead, for some reason, may have followed him here from England," Jason replied. The officer had to agree with the logic of Jason's story, but both Jason and Stephany could tell, something wasn't sitting right with officer Pardue. He then told them that it would be another week or so for the DNA to come back. He also told them that the bullet found at the scene of James murder had been sent to Scotland Yard, to be run through their data base. That was just one more thing for both Jason and Stephany to worry about. All Jason was thinking was, *that gun better be as clean as Kelsey said it was.*

Meanwhile, back in Mexico, Juan Carlos Jesus' underbosses were all scrambling to take over the Cartel. They also had some competition from rival Menaloa Cartel leaders. It would turn out to be a very bloody and messy battle for power. The men that Shawn sent over to keep an eye on what was left of Carlos' Cartel were reporting back to Shawn. They reported that several of Carlos' underbosses had been killed, along with some from the other Menaloa Cartels. They also told Shawn that two of the other Menaloa Cartel heads had been killed.

"If you wanted to really get rid of Carlos' Cartel, and maybe some of the others, this would be the time to get over there and do it," Shawn told Jason.

"I'm not really interested in going to Mexico and fighting a war over drug Cartels," Jason replied. He really just wanted to be left alone, to live in peace. He knew the investigation into the murder of James Butterfield was not over, and that he was still a suspect. "Just keep your men in place over there. There's still a possibility of more of those damned Mexicans coming back at me."

"I know, my men will stay there until I tell them they can come back. They're good men. They will do their job as long as their still there," Shawn told Jason. Shawn's words were of some comfort to Jason, but he knew the Mexicans might send more Americans from airports in the States. Jason was also thinking a lot about Svetlana, and the Mexicans that took over her business. He didn't like what Annie did to her, but she was dead now, so he couldn't do anything about that. He really did want to just stay on the farm and live in peace, but he knew he couldn't let go of what happened to Svetlana.

A few days later, Jason said to Stephany, "I'm going to have to go to Russia. I can't let Svetlana down." Stephany knew at some point he was going to have to do that. "I know. I've just been waiting for you to tell me. I don't want you to go alone, though. I think it'll be too dangerous."

"I don't really have anybody around that I can take with me. You know that anyone that comes with me is going to have to be very good at what we do," he replied. She knew he was right but didn't want him going alone. She was worried that the Mexicans may have stepped up the security, knowing what Tony and Annie were able to do there.

"Call Shawn, he's probably the best one, other than me, to go with you. I would go, but I know you don't want me with you for something like that."

"Well, it's not that I don't want you with me, I think you would probably be the best choice, but we can't both put ourselves in a situation like that at the same time," Jason reminded her. "Maybe you're right. Maybe I should call Shawn. I'm sure he would be willing to come with me."

Jason and Stephany both had forgotten that there was still the DNA matter going on with the police. Officer Pardue would be reminding them shortly, though. Jason made his call to Shawn, and he said he was willing to go with Jason to Russia. They agreed on a day and time for Jason to pick him up with the jet, and head straight to Russia from Belfast.

Two days later, while Jason was in the hanger getting the jet ready for the flight to Belfast, and then Russia, officer Pardue came to the house for a visit. Stephany called Jason to tell him to come back to the house. The officer had news of the DNA report that he wanted to share with them. When Jason got to the house, they all sat at the kitchen table, the officer with some papers in front of him. Looking at both Jason and Stephany, he said, "The DNA report came back. It was inconclusive. However, there were several markers that suggest that had it been a better sample, it probably would have been a match to the sample you gave me." As he said that he was looking directly into Jason's eyes.

"If the report was inconclusive, how can you say that, with any amount of confidence at all?" Jason asked.

"Well, because there were several indicators that matched the indicators from your sample, just not enough to say that the sample at the crime scene came specifically from you," the officer said.

"If you can't say it was him, why say anything at all?" Stephany asked the officer. She was more than just a little upset about the accusation.

"Because I believe that it was you, Jason, at that house, and I believe it was you that killed James Butterfield. It may take me some time, but I will find a way to prove it. And while we're at it, let's talk some more about that gun you gave me to test. You say that was the same gun you used to defend yourself against those people that attacked your house?" Jason knew what the cop was getting at, but he had no choice but to keep going with what he had started.

"Yes, I told you that's the only .45 cal. handgun we have," he replied.

"And you say you ran what, maybe three full clips through it that night?" Pardue asked, maybe just a little too smugly.

"Yeah, I think that's what I told you at the time."

"Well, are you now saying you did, or you didn't, or you're not sure?" Jason looked at Stephany, and they both had the same thing running through their minds, *this son-of-a-bitch has got to go.*

"That's what I told you, and that's what I did," Jason said, trying not to let the cop know he was getting upset.

"Then maybe you can explain to me why my ballistics' guy is telling me that he thinks he's the first person to ever fire that gun?"

Looking Pardue dead in the eyes, and taking a few seconds to answer, Jason finally said, "I don't know, maybe he has an ego problem. I think we're done here today, officer." With that Jason, Stephany, and then finally officer Pardue stood up from the table.

"Yes, well we may be done here for today, son, but we are not done with this," Pardue said as he headed for the door. Stephany was the first one to say anything after Pardue's departure.

"You know that bastard is going to be a problem, don't you?"

"Yeah, I think I'm going to have to do something about him before I leave for Russia. I can't let him keep digging into this. But the thing is, if the DNA can't nail me, he really doesn't have anything other than a very clean gun," Jason mused. Thinking about that, Stephany had to agree. There really wasn't anything that put Jason at the scene other than Pardue's intuition. The fact that the ballistics tests showed the gun to be very clean, exceptionally clean, really wasn't a point of law, so much as just an observation. Maybe left alone, Pardue would run out of steam, and just go away.

Jason decided to go ahead with his planned trip to Russia. He called Shawn to tell him he was on his way, and after saying goodbye to Stephany, headed for Belfast. Somewhere over Eastern Europe, Stephany radioed Jason to tell him officer Pardue had been back to the house, looking for him. She said that there had been some new developments in the investigation, and he wanted Jason to go to the station with him. Stephany told Jason that when she told officer Pardue that he was away and wouldn't be back for a few days, the officer became very upset, to the point of threatening her if Jason didn't show up.

Jason said he would try to call that bastard to see what was happening, but he couldn't do that until he was back on the ground. About 30 minutes later, Jason placed a call to officer Pardue. "What the fuck do you think you're doing, threatening my wife over something between you and me?"

"I didn't threaten her, I simply told her that if you don't come in for questioning, we will bring her in as a material witness."

"Witness to what? Just what new developments do you think you have that would cause her to be a witness to anything?"

"Well now, Mr. Bordeaux, you know I can't discuss that over the phone with you. I need you to come to the station so we can have a nice little chat about certain aspects of your story regarding this .45 cal. Handgun you gave us to test, and just how much you actually know about our poor deceased Mr. Butterfield." Now Jason's mind was racing. *What could they have possibly found out?* He wondered.

"Well, right now I'm away, I'll be back in a couple of days, and I'll give you a call then," Jason told Pardue.

"Yes, your wife already told me that you were on some sort of business trip. And just what sort of business would that be, Mr. Bordeaux?"

"She didn't tell you? I'm checking out some different varieties of grapes to add to our vineyard," Jason said. Stephany had told officer Pardue that same story. It was the standard cover story they had worked out for just such occasions.

"Are you now? That sounds very exciting and all, but I suggest that you cut your trip a little short and get your ass into my station house to give me some answers in the next couple of days," officer Pardue said, sounding very angry as he said it.

"Don't worry, I'll be there," Jason told him, and then hung up the phone.

"Trouble with the local cops?" Shawn asked. Jason really didn't want to bring Shawn into the whole mess going on with officer Pardue. He decided to just give him the highlights of the story.

"This one cop has got his nose a little too far up my ass about the murder of that rat I told you about. He can't prove anything; he just thinks I'm the best one to put it on."

"Let's get this mess cleaned up, and then we can go take care of the cop," Shawn said. After stealing another car close by that same little airstrip Jason always used, they headed for the brothel. As they sat in the car and watched the building, Jason noticed that there were a couple of Mexicans milling around outside. One of them he recognised. It was the underboss that had worked for Carlos in San Carlos, Mexico. The one Jason did the unsanctioned hit for that started all the trouble with the Mexicans in the first place. Jason and Shawn worked out a plan.

Later that day, just as it was starting to get dark, Jason walked up to the underboss and said, "Hi, my name is Tony De Luca, and your number 63741. This brothel was the property of a very close friend of mine until you guys came and took it over. So, here's what's going to happen…"

To Be Continued

# Episode Twelve
## The Canals of Bruges

"So, here's what's going to happen." As Tony, (Jason) was saying that to number 63741 Shawn was busy slitting the throat of the other guard that they saw walking around outside the building. They both knew there were cameras, and that they have probably already been seen, but they were just going to have to deal with it. Jason continued, "We're all going inside, and you're going to take me to the security room. From there we're going to identify every fucking Mexican in the building and get them to the main lobby."

"Why do you think I would do that for you?"

"Remember what it was like when I shot that guy right next to you in San Carlos? Well, if you don't, I'm going to use one of those same bullets on your pecker. And then I'm going to drag you inside and put you on display for all of the girls to look at."

"You will be killed before you can get that far; there are probably five or six guns on you right now," the Mexican said with a bit of a smile on his face. Jason was sure there probably were some guns pointed at him, but he was counting on Shawn to help him with that issue.

"Do you think I would be stupid enough to come here by myself, you dumb ass piece of shit? Now let's get going to that security room."

Holding the Mexican by the back of the collar, with his gun pressed tightly against the back of his head, and Jason staying very close to the man, they entered the building. Just for this little trip, Jason had decided to dust off some of his own bullets, and he and Shawn were both using them, along with guns that Jason had made, so nothing would be traceable later. As they entered the building, Jason was happy to see Shawn had already been there. The guards just inside checking for weapons must have asked to see Shawn's, and well, he showed them.

"I see you have brought some friends with you," 63741 said.

"I told you I wasn't alone! Now the security room if you don't mind. Oh, and by the way, I have been here several times before, so I will know if you are trying to fuck with me."

As they went through the main lobby headed for the stairs, they saw two more Mexicans critically wounded, along with several of the women already gathered in the room. When they were approaching the top of the stairs, they saw four guards charging down the hallway at them. Suddenly all four fell to the floor, Shawn stood at the other end of the hall, with a smoking gun. He smiled at Jason, and then disappeared in the direction of the security room that Jason had told him about.

Jason pushed number 63741 down the hall toward the security room, Shawn suddenly appeared out of the room just across the hall from it. He raised his gun as if pointing it at Jason. Jason tripped the Mexican and they both fell to the floor, as guns were being fired from both ends of the hall, Jason turned and did some shooting of his own. Shawn and Jason took out six more guards. He got his captive up and they finally made it to the security room door.

"How many are in there?" Jason asked the Mexican. The man seemed to have lost his voice for some reason. Shawn suggested Jason help him find it again, and before he could do as Shawn suggested, 63741 told them there were usually three people in the room. Looking up at the cameras at the ceiling in the hall, Jason shot all of those that could see them. They moved back away from the door, and then he and Shawn spoke very quietly. Shawn removed the silencer from his gun and fired a couple of shots into the ceiling. Jason then threw his captive against the wall very hard, directly across from the security room door. Automatic weapons started sending dozens of bullets through the door, many of them, into number 63741.

As the man slumped to the floor, very much dead, the door started to open. Jason and Shawn then burst into the room, with their guns already issuing bullets in all directions. There were three men in the room, and all three went down before they got off any more shots of their own. Shawn very quickly sat at the security console and studied the camera views. As he panned from camera to camera, he was unable to find any more security guards left inside or outside the building. Jason and Shawn went from room to room, and very quickly gathered the women, and whatever little clothing they had.

With all of the women in the main lobby, and all of the patrons sent running, Jason told the women that they were going to be sent to a place where they would be free and safe. They were then led down the street to a bus that Jason had 'helped himself to' earlier in the day. While Shawn led the women to the bus, Jason took great pleasure in setting the building on fire. The brothel would be gone, once and for all.

Prior to running their raid on the brothel, Shawn had called his group in Belfast to make arrangements for two small planes to be sent to the little airstrip in Russia. Jason supplied coordinates and a flight path that would take them away from any known Russian ground patrols. He also had them drop below the radar screen one hundred miles before getting to the Russian border. It would be approximately another hour before the planes would be landing in Russia. The bus ride from the brothel to the airstrip would take about that long, so everything was just about on schedule.

When they arrived at the airstrip, the planes were not there. Sitting and waiting, feeling very much exposed, Jason turned to Shawn and said, "What do you think?"

"Let's not panic now, they're going to be here, trust me." Shortly after that, they began to hear the sounds of the small planes approaching. As soon as the planes had stopped, the women were split up and placed on the two planes, which then immediately headed back to Belfast. Jason and Shawn headed back in Jason's jet and would arrive quite a bit faster than the little planes would. That time was going to be used to make arrangements at the farm that Jason had grown up on, and his parents still owned.

Jason's parents no longer did much in the way of farming; they were too old. They kept a few chickens and goats for their own use and rented out the rest of the land to other farmers. Jason hadn't seen his family in several years. They knew he killed people for a living and weren't happy with him for that. It was, however, Jason's father that taught him to shoot the way he could. His father had been a sniper in the military, and he thought that Jason would follow in his footsteps. That, of course, didn't happen quite as planned. His parents knew and liked Shawn and helped the opposition cause whenever they could.

After getting back to Belfast, and going out to the farm, it was Shawn that first approached Jason's family with the idea of housing the sixteen women from Russia. They would be there until more suitable arrangements could be made. Jason's parents readily agreed to help, even knowing that Jason was involved. Once the deal had been struck, Jason came in to see his family. Both his mother and father were very happy to see him, and that he was alright. They were, however, more happy to see that he was actually helping all of those young ladies' get to a better place in life. They sat and talked for hours, Jason telling them about Stephany and the little farm in Belgium.

When the women from Russia arrived, Jason and Shawn stayed long enough to get everyone settled. Then Jason had to get back to Stephany and that pain in the ass, officer Pardue. Jason told Shawn to stay in Belfast; he would call him if he felt he was going to need his help. High above England, Jason radioed Stephany to tell her he was on his way home.

"That son-of-a-bitch, Pardue, has called or stopped here at the house at least twice every day since you left. He's really pissed off about something, but he won't tell me what he thinks he's got."

"Alright, well, I guess I'll have to go talk to him. I'd rather make him come to me at the house, though. I think I would feel better about it that way."

"Well, just don't go to the station. When he comes here, he is usually by himself, or with one other cop. Just wait for him to come back," Stephany suggested to Jason. He decided that's what he was going to do. He would just tell the cop that he just got home the next time he came to the house. Jason got home in the early evening of that same day. After putting away the jet, and storing all the weapons where they belong, he went to the house. After being very warmly greeted by Stephany, they sat down to a romantic dinner.

Mid-morning the following day, almost like clockwork, officer Pardue was again pounding on the little farmhouse door. Jason answered the door this time.

"Oh, I see you've been able to make your way back home, Mr. Bordeaux," the officer said.

"Yes, and a very good morning to you, too," Jason replied.

"So then, are you ready to come down to the station with me. I've some things that need to be cleared up."

"You're here now, why don't we just talk about whatever it is here?"

"Because like it or not, you're coming with me. You see I have a warrant for your arrest." Before Jason could react, Stephany jumped up from the kitchen table.

"On what charge?" She demanded. He had not said anything to her about that in any of his previous visits.

"Jason Bordeaux, I am hereby arresting you on suspicion of the murder of James Butterfield." As he said that, he was already getting his hand cuffs from his belt.

"On what evidence are you basing that charge? The DNA doesn't put me there, the bullet was not fired from my gun. So what else is there?" Now Jason was doing the demanding.

"Oh, and by the way, I also have a warrant to search the house and the barn," Pardue said as he handed the papers to Jason.

"Now turn around and put your hands behind you. Let's not make this any harder than it has to be."

"You still haven't said what you were able to get the warrant's based on," Stephany yelled at the cop.

"We're going to go over all of that down at the station, but for starters, we have your husband's fingerprints on the doorknob, and a footprint that I believe is going to match your husband's boots," Pardue yelled back at Stephany. A couple more police officers came into the house and started to execute the search warrant. They were doing it in the typical fashion that you might think, not being very neat about things. It was only serving to make both Jason and Stephany even madder.

At the police station, Jason was put into an interrogation room and left there by himself. Stephany had to wait out in the main lobby by herself. After about a half hour, a detective and officer Pardue came into the room with Jason. He was asked if he would be asking for an attorney. He declined reserving his right to one should he decide one would be needed.

"Okay then, let's start with the easy ones. You want to tell me how your fingerprints came to be on Mr. Butterfield's front doorknob?" the detective asked. Jason sat looking at officer Pardue, trying to think of what he was going to do to him.

"I have been to that house several times before Butterfield moved in. There's no telling how long those prints have been there."

"Well, I'm just going to tell you that they look pretty fresh to our latent print man. And the footprint outside the house; what can you tell me about that?"

"Again, if the footprint is even mine, it could have been left days or even weeks before the murder." Jason knew that wasn't going to fly, but he didn't have any other explanation for it.

"Recent rains would have washed it away, we all know that, so you want to try that one again?" the detective asked. Looking at Pardue, Jason could see a small smile coming to his face.

"I haven't been there recently, so whatever you have for a print can't be from me."

"Yeah, well we're going to check that out. Now we also did a little looking into your computer activity. Do you want to guess what we found in there?" the detective asked. Pardue was now smiling very brightly.

"I don't know. Why don't you tell me what you found in there?" Jason replied, not taking his eyes off officer Pardue.

"We found a background check that you did on the departed Mr. Butterfield. And it appears that you did it on the very day he was murdered. What have you got to say about that?"

"Yes, I did a background check on him. He was someone new, that was getting very friendly with some of our friends, and my wife said that she would like to get to know him better."

"And you do this type of background checking on all of the people your wife wants to get to know?"

"No. It's just that he was new to the area, and nobody knew anything about him, so I looked him up. The fact that I did that on the same day he was murdered is just an unfortunate coincidence," Jason replied. He was trying to stay as calm as possible, and not let them rattle him.

"The last time I checked anyone out, I don't think there was any law against it. I just like to be on the safe side. Especially after what happened at our house not so long ago."

"Let's talk a little bit about the gun you gave us. You say that was the gun you used on that night not so long ago, as you put it, at your house."

"Yes, that's the gun." Jason was going to have to wing this one too.

"Well then, how do explain that our ballistics expert says he believes that he was the first person ever to fire that gun?"

"That night at our house was the first time the gun had been fired. And I like to keep my gun very clean, so it doesn't surprise me that he would think that."

"Well, I must say, you certainly do keep your gun clean then." The detective was running out of stuff to throw at him, and Jason could feel it.

"It would seem to me that you really don't have enough to arrest a person on detective. Especially on a charge as serious as murder," Jason said as he looked at officer Pardue. The detective sat looking at the paperwork in front of him, looking for anything else that would stick even slightly better than what he had. Officer Pardue leaned over to whisper something in the detective's ear. He nodded and then looked at Jason and asked, "So, can you tell me just where you were, that morning, 19 days ago, when the murder took place?"

"Well, I'm not one hundred percent sure of the day, but I believe I was working on my farm, tending to the animals, as I always do in the morning. Later that day, I think I may have called my friend Kelsey to come over, and then we both went into town and had a late lunch with my wife at the pub."

After sitting at the table for another minute or so, the detective got up and had officer Pardue go out into the hall with him. The search of the property had gotten nothing more than the information on Jason's computer. They never found any boots, or shoes that matched the footprint at the murder scene. It would be very easy for any lawyer to explain the extremely clean gun to a jury, just the way Jason had explained it to him. The fingerprints on the doorknob didn't really prove anything other than the fact that Jason had been to the house at some time. There were no witnesses; the bullet didn't match Jason's gun, and Jason probably had any number of people that could put him somewhere other than the Butterfield house at the presumed time of the murder.

The detective was beginning to feel like a fool. Officer Pardue had convinced him to get those warrants, and he really didn't have the evidence that he led the detective to believe he had. He had to make a choice: Keep Jason detained and bring him before the judge with the crap he had for evidence or drop all of the charges now and let him go. It wasn't a hard decision for the detective to make. Over the objections of officer Pardue, all of the charges were dropped, and Jason was set free. As Jason walked past officer Pardue, the cop grabbed him by the arm, and very softly said, "I know you did this, and I'm going to find a way to get you."

Jason didn't say anything. He simply smiled at the officer, pulled his arm free, and walked away. Jason, of course, was thinking, *not if I get you first!* Which was exactly what he was planning to do. After leaving the police station Jason and Stephany went to the pub for dinner. Sitting at a table off to the side of the pub, they sat and watched the small boats on the canal that ran through the centre of town. Jason was trying to think about how he was going to take care of officer Pardue, without raising suspicion on himself. Stephany was eager to help.

"Do we know if Pardue is a drinker?" Jason asked Stephany. After thinking about that she realised that she really didn't know.

"I'm not really sure. Why? What are you thinking?"

"Well, these canals that the town is built around, they come in from the North Sea, don't they?"

"I think they were originally part of the river, Reie, but yes they were eventually connected to the North Sea. Again, what are you thinking?"

"I've been sitting here watching the flow of the current, and I think from here it looks like it heads out in the direction of the North Sea."

"I know Pardue lives at the north end of town. If he's a drinker, we could pay him a visit, fill him full of his favourite beverage until he passes out. Then we could drag him out the canal to the river. By the time we get him to the river, he probably would be drowned. We could let him go, and the current would take him out toward the sea." Jason was trying hard to think of anything they could do to get rid of this guy, which would look like an accident.

"There are a lot of questions that come up with that. Is he even a drinker? Does he live alone? And even if he is a drinker, how are we going to get that much alcohol in him?" Stephany asked Jason.

"Oh, I know how to get alcohol into a person. I came up with the perfect system when I was in Mexico with Annie. It shouldn't be too hard to get answers to the other questions. The bigger question is, are people going to believe he got drunk and fell in the canal?" Even as Jason was saying all of that, Stephany was looking at him with a dubious look on her face. The whole idea seemed too simple, and the timing of something like that happening seemed too unlikely. She loved the canals going through town, and all of the quaint little bridges over them, but never thought of them as a means of body disposal.

As time went by, the whole murder of James Butterfield sort of dropped off. But Jason still did the research into officer Pardue that he needed to do. He found that he was married, no children. His wife was not in good health but didn't seem to be critical either. Officer Pardue was indeed a drinker. It would appear that whisky was the drink of choice for him. And, he had been known to have a bit too much from time to time. Officer Pardue had still not given up his crusade on Jason either. He was keeping a very close eye on everything Jason did, and everywhere he went. This of course, only kept Jason thinking of more ways to get rid of him.

About five months later, the canals in the inner part of town were starting to ice over. If Jason was going to use them as a means of disposing of officer Pardue, it would have to be soon. And then, luck being with Jason, officer Pardue's wife died, suddenly, and unexpectedly. The officer seemed to be very distraught. He had been seen at the pub on a few occasions drinking more than he should have. This was perfect for Jason. On a Saturday night, the officer was at the pub, drinking with some of the other off duty officers. They were all drinking heavily. At a table in the corner of the pub, Jason and Stephany sat and watched them. When officer Pardue got up to go home, they followed him. What they didn't realise, was so did one of the other officers.

In the very early hours of Sunday morning, Jason and Stephany paid the officer a visit at his home. He was passed out in a chair in the living room. A bottle of whisky was on the floor next to the chair. It was lying on its side. They had come prepared. They had duct tape, zip-ties, a twelve-inch piece of plastic tubing, and a small funnel. It would appear, they wouldn't be needing any of those items. Officer Pardue was well past the point of putting up any kind of resistance to anything. Without wasting any time, they grabbed Pardue, and brought him outside his house. From the side of the yard at the rear of his house, the street entered one of those quaint little bridges that go over the canals that ran through town. It was a simple matter to lower the officer down to a small boat at the side of the canal.

Once in the boat, Jason began to row the boat in the direction following the current out to the North Sea. He didn't have to go very far before being beyond the limits of the town, and into the deeper, newer part of the canal flowing into the sea. From a second-floor window, too drunk to respond, was Pardue's drinking buddy, the other officer, watching and trying to understand what was going on. Dumping Pardue over the side of the boat, Jason held his head under to make sure that he would drown. The icy water had a slightly sobering effect on the officer, and he began to struggle. He was, however, too drunk to fight the inevitable very hard, or for very long. With officer Pardue now dead, Jason and Stephany brought the boat back and left it as they had found it.

Being cold out, they were both wearing gloves, so fingerprints would never be an issue. Going back up to Pardue's house, they spilled some of the whisky on the chair and the floor. When they left the house, they made sure to leave the door open, as if the man had just wandered drunkenly out into the night. The other officer at Pardue's house had, by that time, passed out. The following morning, he would awake to an empty, cold house. The previous night being somewhat fuzzy, he began to look for his friend. Not being able to find him, he finally reported officer Pardue missing. Over the next few weeks however, his memory would start to clear up.

It didn't take long for the news of the missing officer to make its way around town. A collection of police officers, and volunteers, Jason and Stephany being among them, searched the town. Having not found the missing man and having been told that he was very drunk the night before, the search was expanded to the canals. Boats were sent up and down the various canals that ran through the town. At some point, a police boat made its way out toward the sea, in the same canal Pardue's body was dumped. There, not far from the mouth of the sea, they found the body of officer Pardue.

Later that day, sitting at home and feeling some relief at the loss of officer Pardue, sipping some of Jason's wine, Stephany looked at him and said, "Do you realise that in all the time we've been working together, that was the first time we actually WORKED together?" Giving that some thought, he had to admit that he couldn't think of another time that they made a hit with each other.

"You know, I think you're right, I don't think we ever have gone out on a job with each other. It feels pretty good," he told her.

"So…are you saying you want to do more work together?" she asked playfully. She was hoping that he knew she was just playing.

"Well, no, I really would rather just tend to the farm, but if a situation came up, that required going out to do a job, I think it's nice to know that we can work together." It was true. He really didn't want to do anything other than be a farmer at this point in his life. She was good with that. There would, of course, be an investigation into the death of officer Pardue, but it would have no impact on Jason or Stephany. The officers that he had been seen drinking with that night all gave their accounts of that night, and that was just about all that was needed. The rest of the story of officer Pardue's demise was considered, as Jason thought it would be, and that was the end of it.

With officer Pardue out of the way, there were no more bothersome visits to the farm by the police. No more accusations or harassment. Life on the little farm went back to normal. Lucy and some of the other play time friends began to spend more time there again. Jason did try to integrate other varieties of grapes into his little vineyard, with moderate success. Jason and Shawn kept in touch from time to time, just to stay up to date on what might be going on in Mexico. Stephany was quite happy to play the part of the housewife for now. She would go to town and do some shopping every few days. Maybe, she would stop at the pub and visit with Kelsey or other friends. Kelsey did spend a fair amount of time at the farm, helping Jason, or helping himself to Jason and Stephany.

For the next several months, life was as it should be for the Bordeauxs': A happy and peaceful farming family in the little town of Bruges, in Belgium. Jason seemed to be very content, Stephany was wondering, could it really be this way now? Was all of the shit done? She never voiced her concerns to Jason. She put it down to her own small bit of paranoia and left it at that. As time passed, her little bit of paranoia began to fade, and she eased a little more into that feeling of contentment that Jason had been trying to share with her.

A storm was brewing, though! Jason and Stephany were unaware of it. Shawn and all of his men, placed in all the right places, were all unaware of it. But it was coming. And it was coming from somewhere nobody would ever have expected it. The storm had been months in the making and involved only a few people. But it would be one of great magnitude. And it would be a real test of the stability of the Bordeaux family. There would be no warning, no signs of impending doom. When this storm hit, with its great surprise, it would shake the ground beneath Jason and Stephany's feet, quite literally!

As summer was winding into fall, and Jason was finishing his grape harvest, the wine making was well under way. The grapes had been pressed; the skins left with some. Spices and citrus added to others. All being placed in oak barrels for aging, the barn was full, and had the sweet smell of the fruit in the air. It had been a good year, Jason thought, for the grapes. Just the right amount of rain and sun and enough cool nights and warm days to coddle the grapes just the way they liked it. He was going to have some very fine wine next year.

The storm was brewing, and it was getting closer. Still, nobody had any idea that it was out there. But it was there, and it was on its way. It was on its way to the Bordeaux farm and picking up speed as it came. The timing of this storm had been very well thought out. Still completely unaware of anything coming their way, the Bordeaux's feeling of contentment was going to play a very big part. The storm, like most bad storms, would hit sometime deep in the dark, and the quiet, of the night. That would be the best time to create confusion, and general chaos among the Bordeauxs' when it hit. The storm would be fast; it would be devastating; it would be potentially deadly…and it would be tonight.

To Be Continued

# Episode Thirteen
## No Wine for You

Usually when a storm hits, the people in its path know it's coming and have some idea of the intensity of it. The storm that hit the Bordeaux farm in the very dark and quiet hours of that night was of a different kind. That storm was completely unpredicted by the people in its path. That storm consisted of three rocket propelled grenades, borrowed, sort of, from the Belgian Armed Forces, Land Component. All fired at the same time, at the same target. One was fired from the top of the hill, above the airplane hangar, one from the street, at the end of the drive leading to the little farmhouse, and the last, fired from the back of the vineyard. All three of the grenades were fired by police offices of the town of Bruges, with one of them, also being a reserve member of the Belgian Land Component.

One of those officers was at the home of officer Pardue, the night Jason and Stephany took him for his little boat ride. He never said anything about what he saw for two reasons. The first, because he was so drunk that night, that it took a few weeks for his memory of that night to clear, and the second, because he had seen the way Jason seemed to be able to slip away from anything. He and his two fellow officers had been planning this for a very long time. They wanted both Jason and Stephany to get caught completely off guard. They certainly did that. The target of the grenades was the barn. The barn, now full of oak barrels filled with aging wine, was only about 30 yards from the little farmhouse.

Jason and Stephany were fast asleep, in the master bedroom. That bedroom was in the rear corner of the house, on the first floor. On the side of the bedroom, were two windows that looked out to the barn, and part of the fields beyond it. The rear wall of the bedroom had two windows that looked out over the vineyard. The force and concussion of the blast shattered windows in the house, caused things to fall off shelves, and other items to fall over. The blast sent pieces of the barn flying in all directions, including into the bedroom where they were sleeping. It also caused the entire house to shake violently.

Fortunately, neither one of them were hit with anything, but the floor was a mine field of burning bits of wine barrels, burning bits of the barn itself, and other sharp, broken pieces of wood and glass. Forcing both Jason and Stephany wide awake, the concussion also caused the desired effect of confusion for which the police officers were hoping. After the rain of small, and some large, chunks of the barn had settled down, the men began their assault on the house. Their intension was to be able to catch the occupants still stunned by the blast. Maybe, with luck, they had been hit with flying barn parts, and were either already dead, or at least disabled. If none of that had happened, then maybe they could at least catch them, without weapons to defend themselves. All of them coming from the distance they were gave Jason and Stephany time to shake off the shock, and dig the assault rifles out in preparation for an armed assault on the house.

They ran up to the second floor of the house. Not knowing exactly what was happening made preparing a little more difficult. Jason went to the front of the house, and Stephany to the rear. Hitting a switch, Jason lit the property for several yards around the house, with very bright light. He saw a man running up the driveway, and he was a very easy target for Jason. Stephany saw the man in the vineyard. Even though he had grape vines to help cover him, she was able to take him out easily. Not knowing how many people were out there, they both held their positions for a short time. Not seeing anyone else in the front of the house, Jason started to look out the side windows. What was left of the barn was still burning brightly. He couldn't see anything beyond that. As he was looking at the fire, shots rang out and bullets sprayed the window where he was standing.

As Stephany was running past the open door to that room, she heard the gunfire, and saw Jason fall to the floor. She also saw bullets tear through the wall just in front of her. She stopped and ran into the room to Jason. He had been hit, twice. He told her to get the man in the yard before he got to the house. Looking out and seeing the fire and little else, she heard the gunfire once again. Out of the corner of her eye, she was able to see the muzzle flash, just before ducking to the floor. When the man stopped shooting, she got up to the lower corner of the window and shot him.

Going back to tend to Jason, she found that one of the wounds was just a graze and would be easily cared for whereas the other was going to be a bit more involved. After about ten minutes, without hearing any more gun shots, Stephany ran from window to window and not seeing any movement in the yard, she called Kelsey. While she waited for him to get to the house, she tried to keep pressure on the wound that Jason had suffered to his right shoulder. He was bleeding badly and was losing consciousness. She was getting worried.

When Kelsey, their veterinarian friend, finally got to the house, Jason was unconscious and still bleeding quite a bit. He told Stephany he was going to need some clean sheets, torn into strips, to use as bandages. As she was taking care of that, Kelsey first rolled Jason over to see if the bullet had gone all the way through, it had not. Kelsey didn't like the look of that. He was going to have to try to fine it, and remove it, without the use of an x-ray. He didn't want to do any more damage than had already been done. So, after cleaning the wound as best he could, he began to poke around a bit for the bullet. He couldn't seem to find it, but he knew it had to be there, not too far from the entrance wound.

The sound of the explosion brought unexpected company. A farmer from down the road, about a mile or maybe a little more, was awakened by the sound. He had apparently been able to see the flames of the burning barn from his property and called the police and fire companies. Both were now beginning to arrive at the Bordeaux property. As the flashing lights and sirens began to come up the drive to the little farmhouse, Stephany began to panic. She had to get rid of the automatic assault rifles they had used. Kelsey told her not to worry about the firemen just yet, and he would stall the police. That would give her enough time to put the guns away in their hiding places.

As the firemen began to tend to the barn fire, some of the police officers began checking the scene outside. One of the officer's came to the house. Kelsey called him to the second-floor bedroom where Jason was. After immediately calling for an ambulance for Jason, the police officer began to talk to Kelsey.

"So, you want to tell me what the hell happened here?" the officer asked.

"Well, I'm not a hundred percent sure. I don't live here, I'm the vet for the farm. I Got a call from Stephany, Mrs. Bordeaux, that her husband had been shot. She said that someone blew up the barn, and then started to shoot at the house. She told me that she was pretty sure they were dead or gone, and she wanted me come over to take a look at Jason here."

"Why would someone blow up their barn?"

"Well, I guess I don't know the answer to that either," Kelsey told the officer. About that time another officer radioed the one talking to Kelsey and told him he better come and take a look at what they found outside. The police officer headed downstairs, followed closely by Kelsey. Stephany had finished stashing the guns and pulled out the semi-automatic handguns. She knew the police were going to be wanting to see them again. After installing silencers, she fired a couple of rounds from each gun. That was just so the police would see that the guns had been fired that night. As the ambulance was coming up the drive, three police officers along with Kelsey, were standing next to the drive looking down at a dead off duty police officer.

From the base of the hill, above the airplane hangar, came a call from another officer, and another from about the middle of the vineyard. Going to look at all of the dead men in the yard, all were immediately identified as off duty police officers of the Bruges' police department. Further investigation of the grounds turned up the three grenade launchers that had been 'borrowed' from the Belgian Land Component. Now thoroughly confused as to why three off duty police officers would attack the Bordeauxs' with rocket propelled grenades, and then automatic assault rifles, the investigation was going to get difficult.

As the ambulance crew brought Jason out to the ambulance, Stephany came with them. The lead officer stopped her before she could get to the ambulance.

"Mrs. Bordeaux, you have got to help me out here. Why would three of our off-duty officers attack you and your husband like this?" He sounded as confused as he looked.

"What! Those men were off duty police officers? We had no idea who they were. And why would they do this to us?" She wanted answers as much as he did.

"Can you think of any reason anybody would do this to you?" the officer asked her. As she looked at the three dead men, now lined up, side by side on the ground, she began to recognise them. She realised they were the one's drinking in the pub with Pardue, the night he went missing. That was almost a year ago. Could they know Jason and Stephany had something to do with that? How could they know? And if they did know, why did it take them so long to come after them for it? And why this? Why not arrest them for it, if they knew what happened?

To answer the police officer's question she simply said,

"No, I thought we were pretty well liked here in town."

"Looking at three dead bodies, all off duty police officers from my department, has got to mean something, wouldn't you say?"

"Well, it tells me that you should keep a better eye on what the men in your department are up to, on and off duty," Stephany replied. She was trying to make sure the officer understood that she was as confused about the officers being there as he was. With that having been said, she jumped into the back of the ambulance as it was leaving. Kelsey was now left to deal with the police by himself. The lead officer apparently didn't feel that Kelsey was going to be of much help. As the police were getting ready to leave, one of them spotted something scrawled on the side of Jason's truck. It was a message, written with a spray can of bright orange paint. The message simply read, 'we know what you did'.

When asked about the message on the truck, Kelsey seemed to be just as surprised as the police officer.

"I have no idea why that is there, or when it got there," Kelsey replied to the officer.

"So, you really don't know anything about what happened here tonight?" The officer came back with again.

"Like I told you, I am just the vet they use here at the farm. I don't live here," Kelsey repeated to the officer.

Kelsey really didn't know. Neither Jason nor Stephany had ever told him about their little adventure with officer Pardue. Not knowing why three off duty police officers would do that was driving him crazy. The barn fire was out, and a few firemen were just soaking the ashes. While they were doing that, a couple more were in the house, putting out the small fires created by the burning barn bits that had come into the bedroom. The police wanted to get a look inside the house but were going to need a warrant for that. They didn't really have any good reason to give to the judge to get a search warrant, so they would have to be creative.

Later that day, as Stephany sat at the hospital with Jason, the police chief was in front of a judge. He was asking for that search warrant. He told the judge that they wanted to get in and search the house for drugs. He said that he believed they were smuggling drugs through their little town. He told the judge that he knew Jason had his own private jet, that, by the way, was not registered anywhere in the country. He found out about the jet while doing the investigation. No one else knew about it, not even Kelsey. He also told the judge, that because of the multiple gun shots in the victims, both last time, and this time, he believed the Bordeauxs' might possess some unregistered assault rifles as well. The judge granted the search warrant, and the police went back to the little farmhouse. Kelsey was still there, cleaning up the mess in the bedroom. He would also fix the broken windows as he got the time. When the police got back to the house, Kelsey was handed the search warrant papers, and ordered out of the house. Standing in the yard, he called Stephany to let her know what was happening.

"Can you stay at least until their done?" she asked him.

"Yes, of course I'll stay. I'll keep you up to date on what's happening here too," he replied. Through the course of the search, the police really didn't find anything of any use to them. As the policemen were preparing to leave the house, the lead officer went up to Kelsey and said, "So, I guess we're just supposed to believe that the Bordeauxs' were able to get six or seven shots into all of those officers', using the two little handguns we were given?"

"As I told you, I wasn't here, so I can't help you with any of your questions." Kelsey shot back at the officer. He was really getting tired of talking to that guy about things that he already told him he didn't know. He was, though, a little surprised at the number of bullets they were apparently able to hit those guys with. As the police left the property, Kelsey called Stephany.

"The cops are gone now. They apparently didn't find anything. At least I didn't see them take anything from the house."

"Did they ask you any questions about what happened?" Stephany asked him.

"The only thing the lead officer asked, was how you were able to get so many bullets into his officers with those little handguns? You know, Stephany, when they test those guns against the bullets in those men, they are going to have some questions."

"I know, but what else could I do? I couldn't give them two unregistered assault rifles." She knew the handguns were going to be a problem, but at the time, she was just concerned about Jason. She knew at some point, the autopsy of the three men would yield several .223 cal. bullets. The handguns she gave the police were one .38 cal. and one .45 cal. It was definitely going to raise some questions. Maybe Jason would have some answers to that problem. The second day that Jason was in the hospital just one police officer arrived, the one that had questioned Stephany at the house the night of the attack. He wanted to talk to Jason about the incident. Stephany was still there, and Jason, not feeling too well, was a little cranky.

"Mr. Bordeaux, how are you feeling today?" The officer started with.

"I feel like someone that's been shot. How do you think I feel?" Jason growled back at him.

"Well, I know you can't be feeling too good, but I have some questions I have to ask you."

"What is it? Can't it wait?" Stephany asked a little sharply.

"I don't want to take up too much of your time, so really for now I just have one question that I really would like an answer to. If you were using the handguns that you gave us, Mrs. Bordeaux, how did those men come to have all of those .223 cal. bullets in them?" The officer seemed just a bit smug when he asked the question.

"We have two AR15's. They were given to me by a friend from Ireland to try out. I have been thinking of getting something like that for protection at the farm," Jason told the officer. Hearing the explanation, the officer just stood and looked blankly at Jason.

"Then why didn't we find them in the search of your house?"

"Because they don't belong to us, we didn't want you to take them, we have to give them back to the guy that owns them," Jason said.

"Well, I'm afraid that I'm going to have to see those guns, regardless of who owns them."

"Are you just going to test them to see if the bullets match, and then give them back to us?" Stephany asked.

"I'm going to test them, yes. But I am also going to have to check ownership, and registration of them." The officer looked at both Jason and Stephany with a very hard and serious face. Both of them were trying to think of some way around the issue. Jason told the officer that he was tired and wasn't going to answer any more questions at the moment. He was just trying to politely tell the officer to get out of his room. After he left, Jason told Stephany to call Shawn.

"Tell him we need two registered AR15's as quick as he can get them to us. In the meantime, we're going to have to figure some way of stalling the police." Stephany looked out the window, to see if the officer had left yet. When she saw that the police car was gone, she told Jason she would go down and call Shawn from the parking lot. When she came back up, she said, "I told Shawn about the guns. He said he could get them to us in a couple of days." Stephany was worried that was going to be too long. Jason told her it was going to have to do, and they were going to have to stall until they got the guns. He figured if the police already searched the house, and didn't find them, as long as nobody was home, they would be okay. Shawn called Stephany's cell phone back a few minutes later.

"Hey, Stephany, is Jason around? Why did you call me and not him?" he asked.

"Hi Shawn, Jason is right here; I'll put him on, and he can talk to you about it." She gave the phone to Jason.

"Hi Shawn! What's up?" he asked.

"I wanted to tell you what's going on in Mexico, but I also wanted to know why Stephany called me for the guns, and not you?"

"Well, we had a bit of excitement at our house a couple of nights ago. Three guys blew up our barn, and then shot up our house. We got the bastards, but I took one in the shoulder, so I'm in the hospital for now."

"Wow! That really sucks. Do you know who the guys were?" Shawn asked with a hint of shock in his voice.

"Yeah, they were actually three off duty cops from town here. Somehow, they got their hands on three grenade launchers and blew up the barn. Then they started to charge on the house with automatic rifles, so we had to us ours to stop them." Shawn was starting to get the picture and understand why they needed the guns.

"Alright, well the guns will be there soon. But listen, the battles for the leadership of the Cartels are over. All three Menaloa Cartels have new people running them. And so far from what I've been told, I think they're all crazy. They're running around raping, and killing people in the towns around them, and they're grabbing little kids, and forcing drugs on them to get them hooked." That got Jason thinking.

"Do you think any of them are going to try to start anything over here with me?" he asked Shawn.

"I don't know, but I wouldn't put it past any of them. I don't think any of my men have heard anything about that yet. I'm surprised there wasn't any fallout from Russia, after burning down the brothel."

"Yeah, I know, I really thought there would be something from that. How are the girls doing?" Jason asked. He was also wondering how his parents were doing, maybe he would ask. Shawn told him the girls were fine. Several of them had already been placed and seemed happy. He then told Jason that just in case he was wondering his parents also were doing fine. Shawn must have read his mind.

The following morning the doctors told Jason that he was going to be able to go home that day. Jason thought that wasn't good because the guns wouldn't be there until tomorrow. He decided he had to stall the doctors for one more day. Stephany was staying away from the house, too. She was staying at Kelsey's house, and he was running over to the farm to tend to the animals each morning. If the police showed up at the farm looking for the assault rifles, Kelsey would simply tell them he had no idea where they were.

Very late that afternoon Stephany got a call. The guns from Ireland had arrived. Stephany was at the hospital with Jason. He had found a way to stall his release for one day. After getting the call, Stephany left the hospital, and went to pick up Kelsey. The two of them went to the farm to get the guns. The timing was almost too good. As they were at the house taking delivery of the guns, the police showed up looking for the guns. Stephany had the Irishmen hide upstairs while the police were there.

"Well, I see we finally caught you at home, Mrs. Bordeaux," the officer said. There were only two of them: The one she had spoken to at the hospital, and the other she had never met.

"Yes, I just came to get the house ready for Jason to come home. I suppose you want those assault rifles," she said to him.

"Yes, I certainly would like to see them. If everything checks out okay with them, you should get them back in a couple of days. Here are the handguns you gave me," the officer said as he handed the guns to Stephany.

"You know, these guns are important, but still, why the hell would three off duty police officers do that to you guys? I think that's the more important question, and we haven't been able to come up with anything on that yet. I don't suppose you can help shed some light on that for me, can you?" Stephany could tell him exactly why, but she wasn't saying anything to anybody, not even Kelsey. Two days after giving the rifles to the police, Jason was home. He stood looking at the burned down barn, and thought, there'll be no wine for you next year. The following morning that same officer was banging on their front door again.

"Good morning officer, how are you this fine day?" Jason greeted him.

"The bullets that killed those men did not come from the guns your wife gave me," the officer said cutting right to the chase.

"Well, those are the only two assault rifles that were in the house at the time. I don't know what to tell you. Maybe whoever did the testing got it wrong."

"You know that's bullshit. Those are not the guns you used that night. Now where are they?" Jason could see the officer's blood pressure was rising. He was thinking the man's head was going to pop.

"Really, those are the guns we used. We don't have any others. I was told you searched the house. I would have thought you would have found them if we had them." Jason could see the officer really starting to heat up.

"If you don't produce the guns that fired those bullets, I'm going to cuff you and run you in," he said, his face maybe just a little too close to Jason's.

"How is that going to help you get those mysterious guns?" Jason asked.

"I'll keep you there until your wife brings the right guns in, and I don't give a shit how long you have to sit in there." Jason knew he was serious and didn't want to be spending time sitting in the town jail. He was going to have to think of something that would fix the mess once and for all. Jason looked at Stephany, who to that point, hadn't said a word. Then he looked back at the officer.

"Alright officer, those are not the guns we used. Those are the guns that belong to our friend, the one's he lent to us to try out. We do have two of our own, but they are not registered yet because we got them the same day those guys blew up our barn. We just didn't have time to get to the station to register them."

"Now we're getting somewhere. I knew you were trying to pull some sort of shit here. Get me those guns right now." Jason went upstairs to the hiding place and retrieved the guns. He brought them down and gave them to the officer.

"Are we going to get the other one's back, so we can return them to the guy that owns them?" Stephany asked.

"You'll get them back when we're done checking them out. And that's only if they check out to be legitimate," the officer growled.

"What about these guns?" Jason asked. The officer told them that they would be checked against the bullets from the victims, and then the numbers would be checked to make sure they weren't stolen. If everything was good, they would have to come to the station and register the guns, and then they could get them back.

"But we're going to have to have a very serious conversation as to why three off duty police officers would come and blow up your place and then try to kill you," the officer said as he headed for the door. Jason didn't like the way he said that, or the way it sounded. He knew it was not going to be a conversation that was going to go well. Stephany looked at Jason. She was obviously concerned about something.

"Are those guns going to check out okay?" she asked, referring to the one's they used to kill the three men.

"Yes and no," Jason said, and then paused a bit.

"They are basically legitimate. The only thing is, I can't produce papers for them if they want to see some." Stephany's face seemed to darken just a bit. He knew she was afraid that the police probably would want some kind of papers on them. And how were they going to register them if they didn't have anything showing they own the guns? Jason was a step ahead of her on that. He picked up the phone and called Shawn.

"Hey Shawn, I guess we're done with the rifles you sent over, but now I'm going to need some help with paperwork for two other rifles."

"Okay, I'm sure I can get you whatever you need. Are you going to be able to come pick them up, or do you want me to send them?"

"I think I better come pick them up. I'm in a bit of a bind for them," Jason told his friend. Shawn told him he would have the papers in about an hour after Jason gave him the information needed for the paperwork. He also told Jason that he had more news from Mexico, and they could talk about that while waiting for the papers. Jason really didn't want to hear anything more about Mexico, but Shawn sounded as if the news was something he should hear. Stephany wanted to go with him to Belfast, and Jason thought maybe that would be alright.

"Yeah, I think maybe you can meet my family while we're there, I believe they will like you, and I know you're going to like them," he told her.

"Oh…I'm not sure I'm ready for that kind of pressure," she replied with a playful smile.

"But I do have a question about the guns, but more, or at least, along with the men we killed." Again, Stephany looked worried.

"Do you think that the police will also test our rifles against the first group of men that we shot in the yard, as well as the last three? And do you suppose those policemen told anybody else what and why they were going to do what they did?" she asked, with a very concerned look on her face. Jason had to admit to himself, he had never given that a thought. Was what she said about him getting sloppy, really a truth?

"I don't know, but you make a very good point here. How are we going to explain the same bullets in both groups of men?" As far as the three of those men telling anyone what they were up to, Jason thought the chances were slim. After talking about it for a little while, Jason, trying to ease some of Stephany's concerns, went out to get the jet ready for the trip to Belfast. While he was out doing that, the phone rang, and Stephany picked it up.

"Hello," she greeted.

"Mrs. Bordeaux, this is officer Leblanc. I think I would like to see both you and your husband at the station. This afternoon would be good."

"Oh, well we're just getting ready to go to Belfast to meet with some people, can this wait until we return?" she asked hm.

"No, I think I would really like to see you before you leave the country," the officer replied. Stephany felt a very large knot growing inside her.

"Well, I'm going to have to talk to Jason. He isn't here right now."

"And when do you expect him back?" *The officer was not going to give up easily,* she thought.

"I don't know, sometime within the next three or four hours I suppose." She wasn't sure how long they were going to be able to stall this guy. He seemed a bit more aggressive about his job than officer Pardue was.

"Well, you just make sure you're both in my office before the end of the day. Goodbye." He hung up, not waiting for her to say anything more. She went out to the hanger to tell Jason about the call. As she already knew, he was not happy with the message. Not looking at Stephany, and talking more to himself than to her, he wondered out loud, "Are we going to have to wipe out that entire police force?" Stephany, knowing he wasn't really asking a question, suggested, "You know, gas leaks have been known to happen, and they can be devastating, and even better, deadly."

"I knew I married you for some reason. Do you really think we could pull something like that off, and get away with it?"

"I'm not really sure, but one thing I am sure of, is that I think it's time for you to start getting a bit of your 'Tony' back on," she said, dead seriously. Jason stood leaning on the side of the jet, legs crossed, and arms folded in front of him. He was just looking at the floor. He was wondering, was she right? Did Tony have to live again? He didn't want that, but maybe she was right. It seemed as if just being Jason the farmer was not going to work as he had planned. Looking at Stephany, he finally said, "Maybe you're right. Things just seem to have a way of catching up with us." Jason had no idea, just how much of his past was about to catch up with them. They would, however, soon find out.

To be Continued

# Episode Fourteen
## Hello Again, and a Sad Farwell

The cars came up the drive, maybe just a little faster than they should have been going. It was about nine a.m. and there were three of them: All marked police cars. Kelsey stood leaning against the fence by the drive and watched calmly, having been told to expect them. As the cars all came to a stop not far from him, Officer Leblanc threw open the front door on the passenger side of the lead car. He was out of the car almost before it had stopped. Walking, almost running up to Kelsey, he growled, "Where the fuck are they?"

"Good morning officer, I don't know if we've met. I'm Kelsey. I'm here tending to the farm while the Bordeauxs' are away," Kelsey said smiling, and holding his hand out to shake the officer's hand.

"I know who the fuck you are. Where the fuck are the Bordeauxs'?" The officer did not take Kelsey's hand.

"They had to go to a friend's funeral, I was told that they may have mentioned that to you when last you spoke. They'll be back in a couple of days."

"Where is this funeral, which, by the way, they never mentioned? Mrs. Bordeaux just told me they were going to Belfast to meet some friends."

"Yes, that's the funeral they went to," Kelsey told him. The officer's face began to redden.

"They were told to be in my office before they went anywhere. Apparently, they feel that the investigation of three of my officers being found dead out here is not very important," Officer Leblanc replied, now moving in a little too close to Kelsey. Kelsey, a large man held his ground.

"May I remind you, officer, those three dead officers of yours were all killed in self-defence, after they blew up the Bordeaux's barn. With, if you'll remember, grenade launchers that were somehow stolen from the Belgian Land Component. After that they made an assault on the house, shooting at the Bordeauxs' with automatic weapons." It was Kelsey's face that was starting to redden now. Officer Leblanc just turned and surveyed what was left of the burned down barn, and at the bullet holes, and broken windows in the house. He turned to Kelsey and told him to get in touch with the Bordeauxs' and tell them that if they did not present themselves in his office within the next few days, he would have a warrant drawn for their arrests. The charges would be obstruction of justice and possession of illegal firearms.

Kelsey simply nodded, and bid the officer, 'Good day'. Officer Leblanc made no reply, just got into his car and they all left the property. Kelsey never did get in touch with Jason or Stephany. He knew when they would be home, and there was no changing that. He spent much of his time at the farm, cleaning, and making more repairs, inside and out, as he had done after the first attack on his friends. The Bordeauxs' were very busy in Belfast, doing apparently what they did best. Bringing 'Tony' back to life. There were, of course, some things that were going to have to go along with that.

While in Belfast, Jason also wanted to take a little time to introduce Stephany to his family. The meeting went well, and his parents seemed to approve of her, and take her in freely. She also liked them as soon as they met. Everyone got along very well. Nothing was mentioned as to the real reason for the trip, and nobody dared to ask. Shawn came around for a short visit, and they all had a bit of a typical Irish get together.

When they returned home, Jason and Stephany spent some time with Kelsey, thanking him for tending to the animals, and doing more repairs to their house. Kelsey told them about the somewhat unpleasant visit from Officer Leblanc. The only reply he got was from Stephany,

"What an asshole that one is," she said, not really looking at anyone as she said it. Kelsey had to leave; he had some things to tend to at his own house. Jason and Stephany decided to pay Officer Leblanc a visit before his blood pressure popped his head. Upon arriving at the police station, they were both immediately brought to separate interrogation rooms. After being left alone in the rooms for about a half hour each, a detective, along with Officer Leblanc entered the room with Jason. A detective along with a female officer entered the room with Stephany.

"So, Mr. Bordeaux, I suppose we should start with why you have been avoiding this meeting."

"I can't really say that I have been avoiding the meeting, it's just that we've had a lot of shit to deal with in the past few days. I think you guys all know that.

And then we had the funeral of one of my best friends to go to. We weren't going to miss that."

"Well, I can understand all of that, but we do have some serious questions that need to be addressed here. Let's go back a bit, and start with the first assault on your house, the one by the three men that seem to have disappeared, along with their car. You remember that one, don't you, Mr. Bordeaux?"

"Yes, of course I remember it. What about it? I thought we were done with that," Jason replied.

"Well, we were, sort of, I mean the file was never officially closed because we never found the perpetrators. What we did find, however, was that the bullets from the assault rifles you said you just purchased, matched some bullets found at the scene of the first attack, as well as the bullets found at the second attack. How do you account for that, Mr. Bordeaux? I mean you can see my dilemma here, can't you?" The detective was a bit too sure of himself, and Officer Leblanc had that same stupid smile Jason remembered on Pardue's face.

Reaching into his coat pocket, Jason pulled out some neatly folded papers. He handed them to the detective. As the detective opened the papers, Officer Leblanc leaned over his shoulder to see what he had. The papers were registration documents for the two assault rifles that Jason had given the officer at his house. They were also transfer of ownership, sales documents, to Jason. The original registration was dated over three years ago, and the transfer of ownership was dated the day before the blowing up of the barn.

All of the papers were signed and notarised in Belfast and were very legitimate looking. They were, of course, all forgeries. With the papers accepted as proof of current ownership, the detective still wanted an explanation for the bullets found at the first scene.

"We had the guns at the house at that time. We couldn't tell you that, because we were afraid you would have confiscated them," Jason told him. The explanation sounded plausible to the detective. The smile on Officer Leblanc's face disappeared. Meanwhile, in the other room, Stephany was being asked the same questions, and was giving the same answers. After the two detectives got together and compared notes, Stephany was released. The detective still had more questions for Jason.

"Okay, Mr. Bordeaux, so I want you to tell me why you might think three off duty police officers from this department, might want to blow up your barn, and then attack you and your wife in the middle of the night?" he asked straight out.

"If I had any idea about that, I would be more than happy to share it with you. The truth is, I haven't a clue."

"Well, let me venture a guess here. Do you think that those men might have thought that you had anything to do with the demise of Officer Pardue?" the detective asked, looking Jason square in the eyes. Now it was Jason that was wondering what evidence they had about that night.

"I don't see how they could. Why would we do anything to Officer Pardue? I was under the impression he got drunk and fell into the canal behind his house."

"Yes, well that was the official story. It now appears that there might have been a little more to it than that," replied the detective. As the detective continued, Jason wasn't saying anything.

"In going through the files left behind by the three deceased officers, we found notes by one of them that would seem to indicate that he saw a man and a woman putting Officer Pardue into a small boat in the canal. Later that same night, the notes indicate, those two people came back in that same boat, without the officer. Everyone knows there was some bad blood between you and Pardue. I think that man and woman could have been you and your wife."

"That's an awfully strong accusation to make about someone, based on some notes you found in a file that was never brought to anyone's attention, or even investigated." Jason was a little surprised at the existence of the notes. He now realised that they had been watched that whole night. He was feeling as if he was getting sloppy; that had to stop.

"At this point, all we have are the notes in that file, but I want you to be very sure that we are going to be investigating them completely," the detective said. "For now, you are free to go. Just don't go too far; we may want to talk to you about this again."

Jason left the station with Stephany. On the way home he told her what the detective told him about the notes they had. She was as surprised as he was. She never saw anyone in the area that night either. Were they both out of practice and getting sloppy?

"So, what are we going to do if they come back with stronger evidence?" she asked Jason. He didn't say anything for several minutes, just sat thinking about it.

"I'm not sure that we can take the chance that they can do that," he said looking more like 'Tony' by the minute. Stephany smiled just a bit, glad to see the man she knew, coming back to life. That night, the two of them sat at the kitchen table and, over several hours, discussed, organised, and put their plans for the next few days, and nights, in order. The sleepy little town of Bruges would be a little less sleepy for a bit. Jason was comfortable with the plan; Stephany could hardly contain herself. She was so very happy and proud to see her man back.

The building that housed the police department was just off the centre of town and backed up to the central canal. There was a beautifully arched foot bridge spanning the canal, connecting the walkway next to the building to the opposite walk on the other side of the canal. Underneath the bridge, on each side of the canal, was an outlet for the street drain system, with a light steel grate at the opening of the drain. Sitting in a very small boat, with nothing more than an adjustable wrench, Jason was able to remove the grate below the walk by the police station.

The street drain was small, too small for Jason to fit in. It was now Stephany's turn. She was able to crawl into the drain, to a point next to the police station, where, without much trouble, she was able to gain access to the underground services feeding the building. Along with water, sewer, and electric power, she found the natural gas line. It was then a simple matter of attaching the pre-made explosive device to the already heavily corroded pipe, running only about a foot below the floor of the building. The bomb was fitted with a remote-control detonation system that would completely destroy itself when detonated. There would be no trace of the bomb.

With Stephany back out of the drain, the little boat was sunk, and the two of them swam, underwater, with the use of very long snorkels, into another canal. In an area that was mostly vacant buildings, they made their way back to the surface, and out of the water. Being very careful not to be seen this time, they made their way back to the farm.

Jason knew from his dealings with Officer Pardue, and later, Officer Leblanc, that the morning shift-change was at 7:30 a.m. He and Stephany would be working at the farm at that time, tending to the animals. Stephany had called Kelsey and Lucy to come over for breakfast, as a sort of thank you for their help with things that had been going on at the farm. At about 7:45, Jason got up to use the bathroom. A few minutes later he came back and sat at the table and continued as if nothing had changed. But something had most certainly changed.

As news of the explosion began to make its way around town, it finally made it to the little farmhouse. Both Kelsey and Lucy were still there. Reports of a massive and devastating explosion at the police station were heard. The reports were saying that the damage was extensive, and that there were many casualties. The entire building had, in fact, collapsed, and it was thought that there may not be any survivors. As the news came to the little farmhouse, all four of them made their way to the centre of town, as very shocked and concerned citizens. It was true. There was nothing left standing where the police station stood just the day before.

"Does anyone know what happened, or if anyone was killed?" Jason asked someone standing near him.

"They say that the cause of the explosion is unknown but might have been a natural gas leak that got up into the building, and then a spark set it off. So far, I've heard of at least twelve dead," the bystander replied. As Jason stood looking at the destruction, not just to the police station, but several buildings around it, Stephany was almost giddy with what they had done. The building was gone, and a very large crater was left where it once stood. The blast had taken part of the canal wall out as well. That, along with the beautiful little arched foot bridge, was now in the canal.

Buildings around the police station had holes in some of the exterior walls that looked as if they had been attacked by cannon balls. Windows had been shattered in buildings blocks away from the blast. Jason finally turned to Stephany, and with just a hint of a smile on his face, he whispered in her ear, "That'll teach those fucking cops for blowing up all my wine."

As the two of them tried to move away from other people so they could talk, Stephany looked around at the destruction.

"Do you think that wonderful Officer Leblanc was in the building?" she asked, trying not to look overly happy with herself.

"I don't know, but it was shift-change, so I'm thinking he was," Jason replied, and then added, "Isn't that just awful?"

"I don't know about you, but I can't help it, I feel alive again, I mean really alive!" Stephany said looking at Jason. He had to agree with her. That old feeling, he used to get when he was in the prime of 'Tony' was coming back, and he liked it.

"You were right; I need to be Tony. I thought I was ready for this quiet farming life shit, but clearly, I'm not. I've got to get back out there," he told her.

"We've got to get back out there." She immediately corrected him. He nodded, and the two of them continued walking around the devastated area, holding hands, as if they were walking in the park. Kelsey finally caught up to them, with Lucy tagging along. He told them that he had heard all but three of the town's police officers had been killed in the blast. He had also heard someone say that the blast might have been the result of a bomb.

"Are you sure they think it was a bomb?" Jason asked his friend. He thought he may have sounded a little too anxious as soon as he said it.

"I don't think there's anything official yet. It was just something I heard someone say," Kelsey answered. Lucy told them that it was time for her to get to the pub and left the group. After surveying the damage, and trying to get what information they could, the three of them also headed for the pub for lunch. After spending a couple of hours at the pub, eating, drinking, and talking about the morning's events among themselves and with others, Jason and Stephany headed back to the farm. Kelsey made his way back to his own house.

In the days and weeks that followed, a very intense investigation into that morning's event was conducted by Scotland Yard, at the request of the Belgian government. Members of the Belgian Land Component were brought in to act as interim police officers, along with the few officers that were not killed in the blast. In the end, twelve of the fifteen police officers had been killed. All of the police records filed over the last ten years had been destroyed. And the official finding of that very intense investigation into the blast came down to a very corroded gas line, that had started leaking into the building, and was set off by a spark of some kind. And yes, Officer Leblanc was among the dead.

Jason had been in contact with Shawn on a regular basis. No real news had been reported from any of Shawn's people watching the new Mexican Cartels. Shawn was still trying to get Jason to go to Mexico and help him take out some of the new leaders of the Cartels. Jason was beginning to give it more thought. He knew they were still raiding the towns, raping women and girls, and killing people just for the fun of it, and nobody was doing anything to try to stop them. In the back of his mind, he knew Tony would stop them. He knew that Shawn knew that too.

Finally getting the mess at the little farm cleaned up, the house repairs completed, and a new barn built, the farm began to return to normal again. Jason was looking forward to a new grape harvest, coming up soon. He had rationed what wine he had left after the season of no wine. He and Stephany had done most of the repairs at the farm themselves, with some help from Kelsey and a few other friends. More wine had gone into that effort than he had anticipated, so he was running low by now.

One evening over dinner, as Jason looked at Stephany, she appeared to be lost in some very deep thoughts.

"What are you so lost in thought about?"

"What if we were to go to Mexico with Shawn and his men? We could help put a stop to the raids by the Cartels, and it might help get us back out there doing what we do best," she replied. Jason didn't say anything for a few minutes.

"We could do that, but what about the farm? And don't you think it might draw some unwanted attention to us?"

"I don't see how that would draw attention to us. We could have Kelsey and Lucy live here while were gone. We could tell them that we're going on a vacation after all of the shit that's been happening. I think that would be reasonable," she told him. He thought about that for a minute or two and agreed that it might work. He told her that he would call Shawn and talk to him about the details. He knew Shawn would be very happy with the news.

A few days later, a letter came in the post. It was from the newly formed police department. The letter looked like a simple form letter that had probably been sent to every home in the town. The letter was asking people to voluntarily bring any weapons they owned into the new police station and register them with the police department for their records. Jason knew the only guns they could register were the two handguns they had already registered. He wondered, was there still some question about them having automatic weapons at the farm? Did one or more of the surviving original police officers have some idea about the weapons?

Jason and Stephany went to the new police station as good citizens of the town to register their handguns. While they were there doing that, although Jason felt as if a thousand eyes were on him, nobody said anything about the automatic rifles, or the matching bullets from two different shootings. He found himself feeling a bit paranoid, and maybe a little too skittish. He knew that he would have to get over such feelings if Tony was coming back. Tony would never approve of such feelings, and neither would Stephany. So, he didn't mention it to her.

It had taken Shawn a few weeks to get all of his men and the supplies they would need coordinated. Once he was ready at his end, he called Jason to tell him, and to set a date for their Mexican adventure to commence.

"Alright! I just have to get Kelsey and Lucy here and put together what we're going to bring to the party, and we can get started," Jason told him. Stephany had been preparing for the last several days and was ready to go. Jason just had to load the guns and his 'mystery bullets' in the jet, and he would be ready. After talking it over with Stephany, they had both decided to bring back Tony's signature exploding bullets for the Mexican party.

Kelsey and Lucy had both been asked about staying at the farm while Jason and Stephany went on vacation. They both said they were happy to do it for them. Stephany called them both and told each of them what day they would be leaving. As the day was approaching, Kelsey got into a small accident with his car. It wasn't a bad accident, but he was going to be in the hospital for a few days, maybe a little longer. Jason called Shawn to let him know about the delay. Shawn told him he had his men all set up in Mexico, and it was going to be a small problem, but they would work it out.

"If Kelsey's not out of the hospital in a week, we'll come anyway, Lucy can stay here and when Kelsey is better, he can join her," Jason told Shawn.

"Okay but try not to let it go any longer than that. My men are sitting and waiting for us," Shawn said. Jason knew the timing had to be right for something like this to work, and he understood Shawn's anxiety. He would move things along as best he could at his end. Stephany was feeling a bit edgy, too. She was ready and wanted to get going. Jason was showing Tony's patience, it was something that made him very good at what he did. Stephany knew that and had a great deal of respect for it. She was trying to gain his level of patience, for she knew it could only help her be better at what she wanted to do.

With another week to wait, life at the farm continued. The Bordeauxs' went about their days trying not to show any signs that anything was different. They went to the pub a couple of times to meet with friends. They visited Kelsey in the hospital. He was doing well, but still had some time before they would release him. They even stopped by the new police station to see how the newly formed police department was coming along. None of the remaining original officers had ever been involved in any of the investigations into the Bordeauxs', and they felt safe knowing that.

Kelsey was finally released from the hospital. He was moved into the little farmhouse under the very capable and watchful eyes and hands of Lucy. The Bordeauxs' were now ready to head to Belfast to meet with Shawn and get their new Mexican adventure under way. As Jason was pulling his jet out of the hanger, he noticed a small hole in the canopy that had not been there before. Then, to his surprise, another small hole appeared just above the instrument panel. Someone was shooting at him!

Jason hit full power and the jet shot down the runway. Getting up into the air, he then began to circle the farm, trying to see if he could find who was doing the shooting. He called Stephany and told her what was happening. She and Lucy both grabbed the AR15s that were always kept ready in the house. On the fourth or fifth pass over the hills to the West of the house, Jason saw a car parked under some trees. It was a small red car. He didn't see anyone around and couldn't find the shooter. Taking a chance, he slowed the jet and made a very low, slow pass over the trees covering the car.

Passing over the car, Jason didn't recognise it. Circling around, he saw the car take off, headed in the direction of the hills to the North, and the Netherlands. From the air, Jason was able to pick a spot on the road that would allow him to get the jet down very close to the ground, in front of the car. As the car approached the area, Jason brought down his jet, face to face with the car, almost hitting it as he flew over it. The driver panicked and drove off the road. The car got stuck in a ditch next to the road, and while the driver was trying to free the car, Jason was landing the jet.

As Jason ran toward the car, he was carrying one of the AR15s from the jet. He was hoping he wouldn't have to use it. He wanted to know who this person was, and why he was shooting at him. He got within about fifteen yards of the car, and it bolted forward, out of the ditch and into the field beyond the ditch. With no other choice, Jason opened fire on the car. He sprayed the car with the full extended clip of bullets from his gun. The car began to slow, and finally stop, in the high brush and grass of the unkept field. He couldn't see any movement inside the car.

Closing in on the driver's side of the car, Jason replaced the clip in his gun. Finding a thick bush about fifteen yards from the car, he got down on the ground behind it.

"You, in the car, get out with your hands empty and where I can see them," he ordered. There was no response, verbal or otherwise.

"I'm only going to tell you one more time, get out of the car. If you don't, I'll be forced to shoot again." Still no response! He got up and approached the car very carefully. As he watched the driver, he could see only a slight bit of movement. The driver was slumped over with his head lying on the steering wheel. When Jason pulled the door open, he could see that the driver had been shot at least four times, through the back of the seat. When he grabbed the hair, which was pulled back in a short ponytail, he pulled the driver upright, to find that it was a woman.

"Who are you, and why were you shooting at me?" He demanded of the badly wounded woman. She gave no response.

"Did someone send you after me?" He tried again. Still no response. The woman turned her head to look at him, smiled, just a bit, and died. When he looked around inside the car, he didn't see any weapons. He expected to find a silenced sniper rifle. It was not there.

Did that mean she left it at her perch site, or was there someone still out there, that she left behind? He had no way of knowing.

Before leaving the car, Jason checked the trunk, still hoping to find the sniper's rifle. He found nothing but a couple of old semi-automatic rifles. He called Stephany as he was walking back to the jet. Lucy answered the phone.

"Hey Lucy, where's Stephany?" he asked.

"She's upstairs, somebody has been shooting at us ever since you left," Lucy told him. She sounded frantic.

"Are they still shooting?"

"Yeah, Stephany's been up there taking shots, but I don't know if she can really see who it is that's doing the shooting," Lucy replied.

"Okay, well I'm on my way back now, I'll be there in just a couple of minutes. Tell Stephany I'll do some fly-bys. If I spot anyone, tell her I'll tip my wings over the shooter," Jason was just hoping to be able to see who was out there. He knew flying over too slow, or too low, would give the shooter too much of a target. He was going to have to be very careful. About a minute after Jason hung up, Stephany came down the stairs. She told Lucy that she found and shot the bastard but wasn't sure if he was dead.

"I'm going out to check on him. If he's not dead maybe I can find out who he is and why he's out there shooting at us," she told Lucy.

"Well, I'm going out with you, just in case you need some back-up," Lucy replied. They both headed for the door.

"I'm not sure that's such a good idea. Why don't you wait until Jason gets back? Maybe he can check the guy from the air," Kelsey begged. But they were already out the door. They headed for the small hills just to the west of the farm. As they got into the first group of small hills, they found a man lying on the ground, dead.

"Shit, I was hoping to be able to talk to him before I actually killed him," Stephany said in a rather dejected tone. She picked up his rifle, and the two of them headed back to the house. As they were walking back to the house, Lucy saw Jason's jet on the runway. It was just pulling up to the hanger. Jason got out and was walking over to the two of them as they both waved. Stephany called out to him that she had killed the guy that was shooting at them. Like Stephany, Jason was hoping to be able to talk to the man first. But at least the shooting was once again over.

"Is everyone okay here?" Jason asked when he caught up to the women. Stephany told him everything was fine there, and then gave him a very big hug. After Stephany, Lucy smiled at Jason, and she too gave him a very big hug. Stephany gave the sniper's rifle to Jason. As he was looking it over, and realising it was old, and of Russian origin, his mind began racing with all sorts of possibilities.

"Did the guy look Mexican, American, or maybe Russian?" he asked Stephany. As the two of them were face to face, Stephany began to answer him, and then simply fell to the ground. Jason and Lucy exchanged a very quick glance and then both went to their knees to inspect Stephany. There was no gun shot heard; Jason didn't see any blood, or marks on her body. But as Jason and Lucy each looked at Stephany's face, they knew in their devastated hearts…Stephany was dead.

To Be Continued

# Episode Fifteen
## It's All About Erin

Jason and Lucy both knelt and looked into her face, and they knew in their devastated hearts, that Stephany was dead. Forgetting that there was still someone out there with a high-powered rifle and scope shooting at them, Jason rolled Stephany's body over. There he found the mark. One bullet through her back, and into her heart. She died instantly. As they each held one of Stephany's hands in theirs, Lucy let out a small scream, and fell over on her back. Reality finally came rushing back to Jason.

Without Jason realising it, Kelsey had come from the farmhouse and scooped up Lucy in his arms. He was yelling at Jason to pick up Stephany and get back in the house. Jason placed Stephany's body on their bed. Kelsey had pushed everything off the kitchen table and placed Lucy on it. She was still alive. Lucy had been shot in the upper left thigh. The bullet entered the back of the leg making a small entry hole. When it came out the front of her leg, however, it took with it, a very large piece of flesh. Kelsey was working frantically to stop the bleeding. As Jason ran by, on his way to the second floor, he stopped to check on Lucy. Through his tears, he told Kelsey to do whatever he could for her, and then made his way up the stairs.

From a window in the back of the house, Jason panned the area at the back of the vineyard through binoculars. He searched the area for several minutes, and then he saw a flash. Sunlight reflecting off the lens of a rifle scope. Re-focusing his binoculars and concentrating on that area he saw something. A person, lying on their stomach, looking directly at him through the scope of a snipers rifle. After backing quickly out of the window, he realised he knew that person. That person was a woman he had seen only in photos. But she was familiar to him. She was Shawn's youngest sister, Erin. *What the fuck?* He thought. He decided he had to chance another look, just to be sure. As he stuck his head into the window, a large chunk of the window frame was blown out, just above his head.

Jason called Shawn. He had to know what was going on.

"Shawn, why the fuck is your sister, Erin here shooting up my house? That fucking little bitch killed Stephany!"

"What are you talking about? Stephany's dead? How, and what do you mean, Erin's shooting up your house?" Shawn was shocked, confused, dumfounded by what Jason had just said.

"You heard me, your fucking little sister just shot and killed Stephany, right in front of me. She shot Lucy in the leg and took a shot at my head as I looked out a window at her. You know what has to happen here, right?"

"Christ, Jason, let me try to get in touch with her first. I have to find out what the fuck is going on."

"Yeah, well you better do it right fucking quick, cause the little fuck is going to start suffering in about two minutes."

"Let me talk to her first, please, Jason. I have to know why she's doing that."

"Before she dies, I definitely intend to find out why she's doing this. You can be sure of that." Jason hung up the phone and made his way to the basement of the house. The foundation of the house, as most in the area, was constructed of field stone and mortar. Below the stairs there was a small spring-operated panel. When opened it produced a hole in the wall approximately 22 inches by 30 inches in size. It was opened by pressing on a particular stone that was not associated with the opening, or even that wall. When closed, it was impossible to find. On the other side of that opening was a concrete hall, or tunnel. The hall leads directly to the secret room behind the workshop, under the hanger.

The concrete hall was built using wooden forms, each two feet wide, to form the concrete walls. About halfway between the house and the hanger, one of those two-feet-wide concrete panels was actually a door. That door lead to another room, approximately twelve feet by fourteen feet in size. That door was opened by pulling on one of what looked like hundreds of other concrete wall tie stubs, on the wall, opposite the door. The room was empty, except for several metal hooks bolted to one wall. The hooks all had chains and shackles hanging from them. The room had never been used for anything. But, if things went right for Jason, it was about to!

Jason went down the concrete hall to the secret room under the hanger. He made his way up to the hanger floor, and went out the side door, away from the vineyard. He then followed the low hills, around the back of the vineyard, and came up behind Erin. She was still lying on the ground, looking through the rifle scope at the house. He very quietly came up to her, and before she knew what was happening, had given her a hard, and shocking, whack to the back of the head. Stunned from the blow to the head, it was a simple matter for Jason to zip-tie her hands behind her back before she could recover.

Jason roughly grabbed a handful of hair on the back of Erin's head and brought her to her feet. He turned her to face him, and after looking in her eyes for a few seconds, not really knowing why he took the time for that, he punched her square in the face. Erin went down. She was out and would be for a few minutes. While she was still out, he grabbed her feet, and began to drag her, face down, to the hanger. She was going to the empty concrete room for a visit. Even though she was Shawn's little sister, she had killed Stephany, and Jason was not going to show much mercy to anyone who did that.

When Jason got Erin to the hanger, he simply rolled her down the stairs to the workshop below. She was awake at the time, but her face and head were already scraped and bloody from being dragged by her feet from the vineyard. He went down the stairs, again brought her to her feet by a handful of hair, and then walked her into the secret room, through the concealed passage to the concrete hall, and into the empty concrete room. In all of the time that took, neither one of them said a word to the other. Jason slammed Erin's head against the concrete stunning her, almost knocking her unconscious again. That gave him time to cut the zip-ties and secure her wrists in the wall shackles.

As Erin was working to regain her senses, Jason was working on preparing a table of tools he might be using to help Erin tell her story to him. The one thing constantly in the back of Jason's mind the entire time was, *Shawn is on his way here.* He knew he had to get whatever he was going to get from her before Shawn got there. His plan was, get what he wanted to know from her, kill her, and get rid of the body before Shawn got there. He could always tell Shawn she got away before he could get to her. Jason's table of implements was ready, and Erin was looking a bit more bright eyed. He walked up to face her, ready to start his interrogation, and she drove her right knee into his balls, VERY hard.

After he recovered, Jason decided he was going to take it all the way with her. He grabbed each of her feet and shackled them, spread eagle to the wall. With that done, he then cut off all of her clothes, telling her she was never going to need them again. He then moved the table of implements close to her and began to show each item to her. He had an impressive list of torture devises on that table and made sure she knew what each item was. The interrogation began.

"You know who I am?" Jason wanted to be sure she knew he was Shawn's friend.

"Yes, I know who the fuck you are. You're the one that got my brother, Liam, killed."

"I had nothing to do with the death of Liam, you know who did that."

"Yeah, it was those fucking Mexicans, but they never would have been in Belfast if they weren't looking for you." She had tears in her eyes now.

"That entire setup was Shawn's idea, and I told him I would be there if he wanted me to be. But he said he had it under control and didn't want me to go to Belfast. Why did you kill my wife?"

"So, you could feel what I was feeling, you fucking bastard."

"She had nothing to do with any of that. You picked the wrong one to go after, bitch." Jason then turned to the table and picked up a set of battery jumper cables. He connected one end to a car battery on the table, and then turned to Erin, and clamped them, one on each nipple. As she screamed in pain, he slowly turned to the table, and disconnected the positive cable. The smell of brunt flesh was in the air. He turned back to Erin and said, "Shawn's on his way here for you, but he's never going to find you."

He disconnected the positive cable from her nipple and clamped it onto a steel bar. The bar was about two inches in diameter, and ten inches to twelve inches long. One end was slightly rounded. He stuck that end into a can of axle grease and then he stuck it inside her pussy, all the way up to the end where the positive battery cable was clamped. Erin began to squirm, trying to get the bar to fall back out of her. Jason placed a length of two-by-four on the floor up to the bottom of the bar. It wasn't going anywhere. She began to scream as loud as she could. He connected the positive cable.

Jason stood and watched as Erin's body convulsed violently against the concrete wall. He could see small billows of smoke coming from any part of her body that had metal touching it. Yes, she most definitely brought the 'Tony' out in him, and he liked the way it made him feel. The smell of burnt flesh was very heavy in the air, and he wanted her alive, at least for a bit longer. He turned to the battery and disconnected the cables from it. Erin just hung on the wall from her wrists. The nipple the negative cable was connected to was all but gone, melted. Smoke still flowed from her crotch; the smell was horrible. He disconnected the cable from her nipple, but left the steel bar where it was, he wasn't quite done with that yet.

"Erin? Erin, are you still with me?" He slapped her face a couple of times. She opened her eyes about halfway, then, she mumbled a few unintelligible words. Satisfied that she was still with him, he turned the lights out, and left the room. He went back down the concrete hall to the basement of the house, and back up to the main floor. Before going back to Stephany's body, he went in to check on how Kelsey was doing with Lucy. He had her leg patched up and had her resting in a reclining chair. They were both having a drink.

"Where have you been?" Kelsey asked Jason when he came in.

"I found the shooter, I was just out taking care of that," Jason replied.

"I wish you brought that bastard back here. There are a few things I'd like to do to him. I still can't believe Stephany's gone. It's still not real for me yet," Kelsey told Jason.

"Well believe me, that fucking little bitch wished she was never born."

"It was a woman?" both Kelsey and Lucy said in perfect, loud harmony.

"Yeah, it was, but I don't want to talk about it right now," Jason said as he headed back to be with Stephany's body. As he sat with her, he realised that he didn't know anything about her past, at least not before they had gotten together. He didn't know if there was anyone he should call, or if there was even anyone that would want to say goodbye to her, or care if she was alive or dead. He remembered that she said she wanted to be cremated when the time came. But he couldn't remember what she wanted done with the ashes. He decided he would have her cremated and hold on to the ashes until he could decide what he wanted to do with them. It would have to be something that would honour the life they had together.

The police were called, and again, lots of questions were asked. While Jason, Kelsey and Lucy were being interrogated, Stephany's body was taken away by the coroner's office.

"Why would anyone want to do this to you? Who were they? How many were there, and where are they now?" Both Jason and Kelsey had heard them all before. After the first round of questions at the little farmhouse, Lucy was sent to the hospital by ambulance, and Jason and Kelsey were asked to make an appearance at the police station the following morning.

After Kelsey went home that night, Jason paid Erin another visit. He brought her a little water, and a donut that had been hanging around for a couple of days. He knew he couldn't stay very long; Shawn was on his way to the house. He force-fed her the donut, and then a little water. Then he told her to have a good night. He would be back later tomorrow.

"Oh, and by the way, your brother Shawn is here. He knows you killed Stephany, but he doesn't know I have you down here. The two of you will never see each other again, dead or alive," Jason said with that special 'Tony' look in his eyes. As he turned to leave her again, he stopped and turned to face her. Looking her in the eyes once again, he gave her a hard right hook to the side of her face. Blood began to pour from her mouth, along with two teeth. He looked at her and said, "Well, that's okay, you aren't going to be needing them anymore."

Jason turned the lights off and left the room again. Back up in the house, he sat and thought about his life with Stephany, and waited for Shawn. About an hour and a half later, just before it began to get dark, Shawn was at Jason's door. When Jason answered the door, Shawn gave him a big hug and told him how sorry he was about Stephany. They went into the kitchen and sat at the table to talk about her, and Shawn's sister, Erin. Irish whiskey was brought out to help the conversation along.

"Are you sure it was Erin that was doing the shooting?" Shawn asked.

"I'm one hundred percent sure. I was looking right at her through binoculars. She was lying on the ground on a small hill at the back of the vineyard."

"Where is she now, did you shoot her?"

"No, I went out to try to grab her. I wanted to know why she was shooting at us, but she got away."

"She just ran off, and you couldn't catch her?" Shawn sounded a bit doubtful of Jason's story.

"She took one shot at me while I was looking at her from a second-floor window. I think she must have gotten up and ran right after taking the shot. I left the window to go after her, but she was already gone. I have no idea where she went. Did you talk to her at all?"

"No, I tried to call her several times, but her phone was turned off, and she never returned any of my messages."

"Where do you think she might have gone?" Jason asked, trying to keep Shawn thinking she got away.

"In this area, I don't know. I didn't think she knew anyone around here."

"Why would she kill Stephany, and try to kill Lucy and me?"

"That's a good question. She never said anything to me about planning anything like this. I thought she liked you guys." Shawn sounded very puzzled by the whole thing. Jason wanted to get off the subject.

"So…what are you going to do about Mexico? I won't be able to go for another week or more, now," Jason asked.

"I don't know. I think we can wait if you still want to go. I just wasn't sure you would."

"Well, I have to go to the police station in the morning to make a statement, and then I have to take care of Stephany. That's going to take about a week, and after that, I really don't know what I want to do."

Jason liked the way he felt morphing back to 'Tony', but did he really want to start doing that again? He was going to have to think about that, long and hard, before making a decision.

Shawn spent the night at Jason's house, and in the morning, Jason and Kelsey went to the police station to make their statements. When they arrived at the station, Jason was again put into an interrogation room by himself, and Kelsey in another. Detectives, along with an officer that had been at the house, went into each room. All of the same questions were asked over again, and all of the same answers given. They both wrote out their statements and after being there for about two hours, they left to go back to the farmhouse. Shawn was still there, and on his cell phone to someone back in Belfast. He was trying to find out if Erin had shown up back there yet.

"Have you found your sister yet?" Jason asked him.

"No, nobody has seen or heard from her. That's really not like her, I'm a little worried that something might have happened to her."

"You think she might have run into someone here, in Belgium?"

"I don't know what to think. If she got away from here, I would think she would go back to Belfast, or at least call me and tell me where she went. She never goes anywhere without checking in with me."

"That almost sounds like you think she didn't leave here," Kelsey said. Jason was thinking the same thing, and glad that Kelsey said it.

"Well, I do find it hard to believe that my little sister could get away from someone with Jason's background. But if he says she got away, then I guess that's what happened."

"Now I'm starting to think you have some doubts about that. Why would I lie about something like that?" Jason was a little upset at the thinly veiled accusation.

"I'm just trying to put myself in your place. If I were you, and someone shot my wife, I would do everything I could to catch the bastard. And I'm willing to bet that you've got five different ways of getting from this house to anywhere on the back of the property. So…if you did catch her, and you've killed her, just tell me, so at least I'll know where she is or what happened to her."

"I swear that I haven't killed your sister, Shawn." It was true, she was still alive, and would be for a while longer. She wasn't done suffering for what she had done to 'Tony'.

"Alright, well I guess there's not much point in my hanging around here. I'm going back to Belfast. I'll try to keep the Mexican thing on the line as long as I can, if you really still want to do it," Shawn told Jason. Then added, "I'm going to keep looking for Erin, if you hear anything would you please let me know? And if you do grab her, please, before you go all 'Tony' on her, let me know about that, too."

"You know I will, Shawn. I wouldn't leave you hanging about something like that." Shawn left, headed for Belfast, or so Jason thought. Shawn, however, was in no rush to leave the area. He was sure that his sister was still around, maybe even still on the property. He was also about 70% sure that it was not her choice to still be around. Jason, he thought, wasn't being completely honest with him. He had to know if his friend had his sister, or if he already killed her. He wasn't leaving until he got the answers he needed.

Shawn left the yard, but he didn't go far. He drove into the little hills just behind the hanger and hid the car under some low hanging trees. From the top of one of the hills he would be able to watch the little farmhouse without being seen. Kelsey was still in the house with Jason.

"So, did she really get away from you?" Kelsey asked, maybe a bit tentatively.

"Yeah, all I found when I got out there was the rifle she was using. That reminds me, the gun is still there, I better go get it before she comes back and decides to start shooting again." Jason wasn't going to tell anyone about Erin. He wanted to be sure it didn't get back to Shawn. When Jason said he was going out to pick up to gun, Kelsey said he would go with him. The two of them went out the back door of the house, unaware that Shawn was watching them. At the back of the vineyard, where Jason had grabbed Erin, there was no rifle! He knew they were in the right spot. There were still a couple of spent bullet casings that hadn't been picked up.

He had Erin, so where did the fucking gun go?

"Are you sure this is the right spot?" Kelsey asked.

"Yeah, look at the bullet casings. Somebody came and took the gun," Jason said with maybe a bit of panic in his voice.

"Maybe Erin came back and took the gun and left," Kelsey replied. He was sure that was the only answer.

"Yeah, that must be what happened. Or maybe Shawn came out here and picked it up before he left." Jason was more talking to himself at that point than Kelsey. He knew Erin didn't have the gun, and nobody else knew about it. He was sure Shawn came out and grabbed it before he left.

"I'm going to call Shawn to see if he grabbed the gun," Jason said.

"Yeah, but I still don't see why he would have done that."

Jason called Shawn while they were still out at the back of the vineyard. Shawn was only about one hundred yards from them at the time. He answered the phone but was trying to be as quiet as possible at the same time.

"Hey Shawn, did you go out to the back of the vineyard and grab the gun Erin was using before you left?"

"No, I didn't know where the gun was."

"Well, somebody came out here and grabbed it, it's gone."

"Nope, it wasn't me. Maybe Erin came back for it," Shawn suggested. He was watching Jason through the scope on the rifle while talking to him.

"Yeah, that must be it. Where are you? You sound like you're trying not to be heard by anybody?" Jason was a little suspicious at that point.

"Yeah, there's just some people around, and I don't want them to hear me. Listen, I gotta go. I'll talk to you later."

The line went dead, and Jason's 'Tony' radar went up. Something wasn't right about Shawn. He had the feeling that Shawn wasn't really on his way back to Belfast. Jason was going to have to do a sweep of the property. He had a feeling that Shawn was still there, somewhere, watching him. He and Kelsey went back to the house with Jason, doing his best to act as if nothing was wrong. After having a couple of pints together, Kelsey went home.

Jason went back down to the concrete room to visit with Erin. He didn't want to stay long. He was sure Shawn was still out there and might come back to the house. Erin looked as if she was either unconscious or sleeping. He kicked the two-by-four under the steel rod, driving it harder into her. She let out a weak cry of pain.

"Ah, there you are," he said. Not wanting to waste any time, he unhooked the chain on her right hand and foot, from the concrete wall. He then grabbed her, and rather harshly spun her around so that she was facing the wall, instead of backed up to it. He reconnected her hand to another shackle, that one, hanging from the ceiling, but left her foot un-tethered. Then he freed the other hand and foot from the wall shackles. Erin was too weak to put up any resistance at all. He connected her free hand to another shackle hanging from the ceiling. Jason made a bit of a show of selecting his next item from the table. He, of course, knew exactly what he was going to use.

He selected a very large wooden rod and made sure she got a good look at it. One end was thicker and heavier than the other. He made this one years ago, specifically for the purpose it was about to be used. He then removed the steel rod from inside of her.

"As long as you're going to be hanging around for a little while longer, you might as well, be hanging around," he said. Then without any hesitation he hoisted her off the floor. She was now just hanging about eighteen inches off the floor, by her wrists. Erin again let out a small weak cry of pain. She was at that point aware she could feel the pain but wasn't quite sure where it was coming from. She was, however, about to become sure. Then, starting at her feet, he broke all of her toes by hitting them very hard with the wooden rod. After the toes, he broke all of the bones in her feet. He continued, slowly working his way up each leg, breaking each bone at least twice. With her pelvis shattered, both hips broken, and every bone below that point broken, he stopped.

Erin had at some point during the beating stopped responding. She was unconscious. The pain must have been excruciating. But it was going to get worse. Before continuing, Jason placed smelling salts under her nose, and taped them there. He didn't want her sleeping through the rest of the beating. Once he was sure she was awake, he started the beating again. He started with her ribs, front and then back. He then broke both of her shoulders. Erin was extremely weak, but awake and feeling the blows of the rod, and the bones breaking. She was trying to scream and cry, but very little sound would come out at that point. Jason continued. He broke all of the bones in both of her arms. Her body was just hanging, misshapen, swollen, and discoloured. Jason left her there like that and went back to the house.

When he came back to the room Jason placed a heavy plastic tarp under her body, planning for the inevitable. Jason poked at her a few times but got no response. He had to smile; she was dead. He walked around her body as it hung there from the ceiling. Poking her a few more times here and there with his wooden rod, just to make sure she was gone. After satisfying himself that she was really dead, he released the chains holding her suspended above the tarp.

Erin's body slammed to the floor with an ugly sound of broken bones, and flesh torn from the bones. She landed perfectly on the plastic tarp. Blood was pouring out of her, and Jason was sure she was dead. When he checked, however, the girl was still alive! So, not one to miss an opportunity, he grabbed his wooden rod and, while she lay in a heap of flesh on the tarp, he broke her back.

"Have a pleasant afternoon, Erin." Then in his best 'Arnold' voice, he added, "I'll be back." He turned the lights off and went back to the main floor of the house. He had to do a sweep of the yard before it started to get dark. He was sure he would find Shawn out there somewhere.

From two windows in the rear corner of the house that faced the barn, Jason was able to see about 98% of the property. Keeping away from the windows, and not moving, he stood looking through binoculars. As he panned the vineyard, and the hills beyond he didn't see anything that caught his attention. He then panned the runway and hills above and beyond it. There he caught a small flash of light. Refocusing on that spot, he saw that the flash was a reflection of sunlight. It came from the sunglasses Shawn had placed on top of his head as he looked through the rifle scope. *Amateur!* Jason thought.

Jason sat at his kitchen table and wondered what to do. He could just go out and tell Shawn that he knew he was still there and try to get him to leave. He didn't think that was going to work, though. He could go back out through the tunnel and come up behind him. But then he was probably going to have to kill him. Maybe, he thought, that was where the whole thing was going anyway. Was Shawn going to force him to kill his friend? Jason truly didn't want that. He was still hoping that Shawn would accept that Erin got away and had gone somewhere else.

Finally, he decided to call Shawn.

"Shawn, I know you're still out there on the hill past the runway. Why don't you come back to the house and have a pint? It's going to start getting cold out there soon," he said when Shawn answered the call.

"What are you talking about?"

"Oh, come on Shawn, I can see you looking through the rifle scope that you don't have, on the gun you didn't pick up. I don't know where Erin is, honestly. So come back to the house if you're not leaving just yet," Jason told him.

A few minutes later, Shawn came to the door. He was carrying the rifle that Erin had killed Stephany with.

"You really don't have her?" he asked. Jason just sighed, and waved a hand to beckon his friend in.

"How long have we known each other? You really think I could do something like that to you?"

"No, not normally, but this is Stephany we're talking about here. I would think the rules would change, somehow."

"The rules for Erin are different. If I catch her, you know I'll have to kill her. But you are still my friend, and regardless of what happens, I will always consider you my friend," Jason told him. A few minutes later there was a knock at the door.

Jason looked out the window, then turned to Shawn and told him the police were back.

"Hello, officer. What can I do for you?" Jason greeted the officer as he opened the door.

"Hello, Mr. Bordeaux, we're just here trying to carry on the investigation into your wife's murder. Oh, is that the gun, we've been looking for that?" the officer asked. Quickly realising that it was against the law for him to have the rifle, Jason told him it was. He said he found it at the back of the vineyard after the shooting. The officer quickly grabbed the gun and said it would be placed into evidence.

"So, have you given any more thought as to who might have wanted your wife dead?"

"As I said before, I don't think she was the target. I was the target, she just got in the way as the shot was fired," Jason replied.

"Well, then, who would want you dead?"

"There are some people from my distant past that might want me dead, but I'm not going to go into that, ever," Jason said with absolute defiance in his voice.

"Okay, so you don't think that's relevant to the murder of your wife. Well, I'm going to take the rifle, and have it run for fingerprints DNA, and ballistics. I'll be back when I have the results." The officer said his goodbyes, took the rifle and left. Jason felt better knowing that Shawn no longer had the rifle. After having a couple of pints, Shawn left the house, and did, this time, head back to Belfast. He wasn't, however, done looking for Erin. And he wasn't done looking for her at the little farmhouse in Bruges, Belgium!

To Be Continued

# Episode Sixteen
## The Ghost Has Returned

Jason was finally alone. He ran back down to the concrete room, and Erin. Thinking of more things he wanted to do to her, he still wasn't quite done with her, for she really had to pay for killing Stephany. But when he got back to her, she really was dead. *Fuck*, he thought to himself. He had so many more things he wanted to do to her. He released her from the hanging shackles and let her body flop completely to the floor on the plastic tarp. After he rolled her up in it, he carried her body to the airplane hangar. She would remain there until he had a hole dug and was ready to dump her body.

He knew he was going to have to be very careful about digging the hole. He felt as if there were a thousand eyes on him all of the time. Jason went back to the house, and after having done another full sweep of the property, decided it would be safe to dig. He took his backhoe to an area between a couple of the small hills behind the hanger. There, he dug his hole for Erin's body. Jason had done the whole process so many times before that he had gotten very efficient at it. In less than ten minutes, the hole was dug, the body was in it, and the hole was filled.

Back in the house, at the kitchen table, Jason sat with a glass of wine, and his thoughts. Stephany's ashes would be ready in the next few days. He still didn't know what to do with them. The police investigation, with nothing more than the gun, was going nowhere. As he sat and drank his wine, his thoughts began to run to the farm. The little house, on the property that once seemed so perfect for Stephany and him, just seemed sad and lonely now. He did love the house. The barn and hanger were perfect for him. The vineyard, something he wasn't sure he would do much with, he actually found to be one of the best parts. But would he be able to stay there?

Then, of course, there was Shawn. Should he go to Mexico with him? Jason wasn't sure that he could fully trust his friend. He knew Shawn still had his ideas about Erin never leaving Jason's property. At least not alive. But, then again, maybe 'Tony' was just what Jason needed. Jason thought that maybe by going to Mexico, and doing what he and Shawn had talked about, they might start to bond and mend the relationship. He decided he would call Shawn in the morning and talk to him about the Mexican thing.

"Hey, Shawn, how are you doing this morning?" Jason wanted to start off a bit slow and test the Shawn waters.

"I'm okay. How are things there?"

"I'm doing okay. Have you heard from Erin yet?" Jason asked, testing Shawn's reaction.

"No, and I don't really expect to." Shawn sounded almost as if he were still accusing Jason. He didn't like the tone of the answer.

"Well, I'm sorry to hear that. Listen, Stephany's ashes will be ready in a couple of days. After that, I'm free and up for the Mexican thing if you are."

"I'll have to talk to my guys. I don't know. This might not be the right time," Shawn replied.

"Okay, well I'm up for it, whenever you are. Give me a call and let me know about that, and if you hear anything from Erin," Jason told him. He wasn't comfortable with the feeling he was getting from Shawn. He felt as if the Shawn he knew wasn't the one he was just talking to. Jason decides to give him a couple of days, and then try him again; he hoped he would get a better feeling then. In the meantime, Jason had made a decision about another part of his future life. As sad as it made him to admit it, he knew he wasn't going to be able to stay at the little farm much longer. Too many people had been able to find him there. He had to leave.

Shawn called back a couple of days later and told Jason that he didn't think he was going to be able to do the Mexican thing as they had planned. At least not at the time, or in the very near future. He told Jason that he didn't feel that the timing was right; and that his men were telling him that things in Mexico were too unstable to make an organised hit possible. Jason was reading between the lines and decided the decision was more about Erin than it was about Mexico. He also got a call from the funeral home. Stephany's ashes were ready. He went and picked them up.

The feeling he got from his conversation with Shawn gave him an incentive to step up his move into the next phase of his life. He began the search for a new base of operation. After several days of internet searches, he thought he had found a place that looked interesting. After doing a little more in-depth research on one particular spot, he dusted off the jet and headed east. He was headed for the island of Corsica.

The island of Corsica is located in the Mediterranean Sea, off the West coast of Italy, and the East coast of France. He was looking more specifically at the town of Saint-Florent, in the North-West region. When he arrived there, landing on a small strip of land next to the sea, he was able to walk into town. As he walked around the centre of town, he had a very good, easy, laidback feeling about the place. The language, a mix of French and Italian, was easy for him to pick up since he was fluent in French. After visiting a local pub, he stopped by a real estate office.

Knowing what he was looking for when he went in, he didn't waste any time.

"Hello, my name is Anthony, Tony, really, Tony Alberto. I'm moving over from Naples, Italy and I'm looking for a small working vineyard or maybe a small farm with a vineyard on it. Do you have any listings that you think might interest me?"

"Hi, my name is Yvette. Why don't you have a seat, and we can take a look at what's available." The realtor was young, very pretty, and Jason thought, *quite sexy*.

"Okay, we do have a couple of properties that might interest you. How large of a farm or vineyard were you looking for?" she asked.

"Well, I don't really know. It would have to be small enough to be manageable by just two or three people, but big enough to yield enough wine to make it worth having," he told her.

"Okay, well, I have this one just outside of town. It backs up to the sea and is 230 hectares. I also have another one that is much farther from town and is 116 hectares." After looking at the photos she gave him of each property, he decided to take a look at the one closest to town. As soon as he saw the place, he knew it was the right place for him. It was very much like the property he was leaving in Belgium. He loved it. The house was a typical Mediterranean style, with white stucco walls, and a red clay tile roof. The front entry had a six foot-deep porch running between two bumped out rooms. There were four Doric columns supporting a second-floor porch with four matching columns, and a heavy masonry balustrade.

The house was slightly larger than the one in Bruges, but most of it was on the first-floor level. The master suit was on the second floor, in the rear of the house, with a six foot-deep covered porch looking out over the vineyard in the back yard. Below the porch was a stone deck, off the living room, with stone steps leading down to the back yard. While the property was 230 hectares, the vineyard only covered about ninety of them. There was a barn, in very good condition, also near the house, similar to the set up in Bruges. There was a second barn, for wine storage and aging, with a tasting room off the back of it, overlooking the vineyard.

The land not covered by the vineyard was full of low rolling hills. Most of it was open pasture and grazing land. The farm included a few cows and several goats and sheep. He really wasn't looking for the animals. He would sell them off if he bought the property. Walking out into the vineyard, he found it to be in very good shape, with well-tended grapes and vines. The vineyard had two varieties of grape, Caracole Nero and Carcajolo Bianco, producing one red, and one white wine. He was allowed to taste a sample of each and was impressed with both.

After being on the farm for a while, he realised that his jet was on a strip of land that was a part of the property. He left it just beyond a range of low rolling hills between the main property and the sea. Standing and surveying the lay of the land, he felt that a landing strip and hanger could be built just beyond the barn, maybe a little closer to the house than it was in Bruges. He immediately told the realtor that he would take the property.

He wanted to close right away, and get moved in, but was told it would be at least three weeks to get the closing ready. When he left Bruges, he had no intensions of ever returning to the area again. He was going to need a place to stay until he could move into his new home. Taking another walk around the beautiful old town, he found the Hotel Bellevue, just across the street from the small Harbour. He decided he would stay there until he could move into his house.

Once he was settled into a room at the hotel, he again set out to study the town, visit the pub for dinner, and start trying to make some new friends. He never said anything to anybody in Bruges about the move. He felt bad about not saying goodbye to Kelsey and Lucy, but he couldn't let anyone know about the move. He was going to need to be that old ghost-like person if a new 'Tony' was on his way. And yes, a new 'Tony' was definitely on his way. He did, of course, bring Stephany's ashes with him.

When he left the little farm in Bruges, he only brought with him, the tools of his trade: The Assassin Trade. He knew he could buy whatever else he was going to need once he was settled into a new place. Over the course of the following three weeks, he had made a couple of new friends, and become very friendly with Yvette, the realtor. He also remembered to move his jet off the property. It couldn't be seen by anyone connected to the new property, or to him. He knew he had to start being much more careful than he was in Bruges.

As soon as the closing was complete, he moved into the house, and brought the jet back to the property. He immediately started work on the runway and hanger. The farm had an old backhoe, but it was still in pretty good working condition, so Jason, (Tony) was able to use it for the work. He also, as soon as he moved in, began selling off whatever the farm had for animals. He was done with the farm life. The wine life, however, was going to stick with him. He really enjoyed that.

Tony built the new hanger by himself. That way, he could build the workshop and secret room below it without anyone knowing about them. He had learned a lot about building from Kelsey. Doing the work made him think about Kelsey a lot, which made him think about Lucy just as much. He did miss both of them, but he knew he would never be able to go back. At least, not once the ghost had been re-born. Tony was already working on that, as he was working on the new building.

Having dusted off the cell phone scrambler he used when he was 'Tony', he made a call to an old contact in Russia.

"28119, this is 1001. How have you been?" Tony asked when he got him on the line.

"1001, I thought you were out of the business."

"Yeah, well I'm back and ready for anything as before," Tony replied.

"Well, I had someone else that I was using, but I haven't been able to reach him for a while now. Maybe we can get back to our old working arrangement. I don't have anything for you right now, but I think some things are about to happen, I might need your help then."

"You know how to reach me when you need me. All of the other details are the same as they were." They ended the call and Tony felt good with the conversation. He would call his best client in Colombia next.

"77910, this is 1001. How have you been?" Tony said.

"I heard that 1001 was dead. Who the fuck is this?" the Colombian growled.

"Yeah, a lot of people heard that I was dead. Well, here I am, alive and back in business just as before," Tony told him.

"How do I know you are who you say you are?"

"Remember that thing you had me do, I think it was back about five years ago now. You needed me to get together with the Minister of the Central Government Law Enforcement Agency for you. And I took care of your problem with him, do you remember that?"

"I remember, so you are back. That is very good to hear, I have missed your service." Number 77910 sounded happy to hear that it was really Tony. Their business relationship would return to what it was. Number 77910 even had a job for Tony to do right away. He told Tony he would call back with all of the information in the next day or two. Tony was feeling good getting back to work again. And he knew that Stephany would be very proud of him for doing it. He had calls to make to contacts in the United States, Brazil, Venezuela, Germany, and France. He also made another couple of calls to other contacts in Russia. He conspicuously made no calls to Mexico. All of the contacts were glad to hear from him.

Tony was back in business. He began buying the materials needed to make his signature 'Exploding Bullets', which he was even going to use again. He started to get his workshop set up to make the bullets, and to work on his guns, silencers and scopes. He felt more alive than he had in years. With the property being as large as it was, he was even able to set up a rifle range, to test his rifles before going on a job.

Meanwhile back in Bruges, Kelsey and Lucy were looking for Jason. They hadn't heard from in about a month, and nobody had seen him around town. The police were still working on Stephany's murder and had more questions for Jason. Kelsey had been taking care of the animals thinking Jason would be back soon. The police went to the little farmhouse and found the door unlocked. When they went in to check on Jason, they found him gone, but all of his belongings were still there. His clothes, wallet, with driver's license and a few credit cards, were still there. Jason's truck was still in the yard; the keys were on the little table by the front door.

Kelsey and Lucy had provided statements about Stephany's murder that cleared Jason as a suspect. But the police were looking for him not as a suspect, but as a missing person, or possible abduction. Both Kelsey and Lucy were very upset about their friend and tried to give the police all the information they could that would help them in their investigation. In a search of the property, the airplane hangar was discovered. Nobody there knew about the jet, not even Kelsey. So, the hanger was thought to be just another storage building. The workshop below the hanger, set up as a machine shop would be, was thought to be used to repair farm equipment, and maybe some hobby tinkering. Kelsey knew what the shop was really used for.

Jason would never be found, and never be heard from by anyone in Bruges again. He had, in his life as Tony, perfected the art of walking away from one life to start another. In his new life as Tony, he was back in the business he loved, and was on his way to his first job. Number 77910 had called him back with details of the job he had mentioned in the earlier call. The job, the removal of a high-ranking officer in the Colombian Army, excited Tony. The details given to him by his contact, gave him all the information he needed. He couldn't wait to get things started again.

He landed at the same little airport he used before, near Cartagena. Walking around the area, he found a car convenient and easy to steal. The job was an easy one: A good one to get started with he thought. Take out the general, during the activities of the National Celebration Day of the Colombian Military Guard. The celebration was to take place the day after Tony arrived in the city. Most of the activities would be held in the main square of the city centre, and Tony could pick his time for the hit. Tony had himself set up in an empty apartment, well outside the centre of the city, about four hundred yards from the square.

The following morning, as the festivities began, Tony watched, first through binoculars, to get a wider view of the area. As a parade got started, which was really nothing more than a show of military might mean to impress the natives, Tony found the general. He was sitting, with other high-ranking military men, in raised seats next to the street. He would occasionally turn to look in Tony's direction, but for the most part, he sat looking in profile to Tony. Other heads were more of a problem than Tony had anticipated. The general was sitting behind other men, and Tony didn't really have a clear shot at him, from where he was.

Tony thought about moving but didn't want to take the chance of being seen. He was going to have to make it work from where he was. After patiently waiting, looking through his rifle scope at the general for more than an hour, he got his chance. He squeezed the trigger. He couldn't help himself; he knew he had to get out of there, but he just wanted to watch for a few seconds. A small hole appeared on the side of the general's head. Then both of his eyes popped out, followed by that grey brain soup, created by the lead pellets in his bullet. The general's body didn't move for a few seconds, and then, just fell to one side, ever so slightly.

The men next to the general immediately got up and started looking in Tony's direction, not at him, but in his direction. It was time for him to move. He got up, and very quickly made his way to the street, and the stolen car. He drove very calmly back to the jet, and left Colombia. While he was on his way back to Corsica, he got a call. As he made the connection, he heard number 77910 come on the line.

"It has been a long time since I have seen such a thing happen. It's good to have you back my friend," he told Tony.

"Thank you! I rather enjoyed it myself, and it is good to be back. You know what to do about the rest of the payment. Use the same numbers I gave you before."

"The money will be on its way very soon. If I need you again, I'll let you know." And the call was ended.

When Tony got back to his vineyard, after putting away the jet, and storing his weapons, he just wanted to relax with a nice glass of wine. He decided he would take a walk into town and visit the pub where he had already stopped. He wasn't really looking to pick up any 'close' friends, at least not yet. But maybe he could just sit and talk to some of the locals for a while, just to pass some time. He sat at a small cafe style table out in front of the pub, just watching the people go about their day.

"May I join you?" he heard someone say. It was the realtor that sold him the vineyard.

"Yes, please have a seat. Can I get you a glass of wine, or something else to drink?" he asked as she sat.

"A glass of whatever you're having would be fine," she said.

"So…how do you like our little town so far?"

"You know, I think I'm going to be very happy here," he told her as he was getting up to get her wine.

"Have you had time to see very much of the town yet? There are some beautiful old buildings and quaint little cobblestone streets here."

"Yeah, while I was waiting to close on the property, I had lots of time to wander around town. It is a beautiful old town, and I do love some of the old architecture."

"What's it like where you came from, Naples, was it?" she asked. Tony froze, ever so slightly.

"Naples has really gone to the dogs in recent years; it was definitely time to get out." He had never actually been to Naples and was hoping she hadn't either.

"I've never been to Italy. Can you imagine that, living so close, and never going there?"

"Well, if you get the chance to go, I suggest that you focus your visit on Tuscany, and the Northern regions. It is so much more beautiful there than in the South."

"I'll have to remember that. Maybe someday, if we both have the time, you can go with me and be my tour guide."

"We might be able to work that out, sometime." Tony knew she was trying to pick him up, but he just was not ready. He wasn't sure he was ever going to want to get close to anyone again. He remembered what happened when he let the ghost go away before. He didn't want that to happen again. He still thought about Annie, as much as he did Stephany. He stood up to leave, saying that he had to get back to the vineyard. She stood up to give him a hug, (he wasn't going to), so he hugged her back. She then closed in for a kiss. Being a good foot taller than Yvette, he kissed her on the forehead, and then left.

Back at the vineyard, Tony wandered through the grape vines, checking and occasionally tasting one here and there. It was getting close to harvest time, and he couldn't wait. He had several oak barrels in the barn just waiting to be filled. While he spent most of his days coddling the grapes along, he got a call from Russia. The person that called didn't have a code number, and didn't have a referral code to give him, but said that he was a friend of Padlov, Svetlana's brother. Being very cautious, Tony asked a few questions that only someone that close to either of them would know the answers to. Convinced the person was telling the truth, he let the call come through.

"What can I do for you?"

"There will be a meeting, on a very large yacht off Monaco. There are going to be some very bad people at that meeting. Russian drug lords will be meeting with some men from South America. They are going to hire them to kill several small-time drug runners here in Russia, so they can take over all of their businesses. One of the small dealers is a brother of mine."

"How did you find out about this meeting?"

"I overheard a conversation in the back of a bar, so I did some checking. The yacht is already there waiting for the men from Russia."

"When is the meeting supposed to take place?" Tony knew killing someone on a yacht anchored in a bay such as Monaco Bay, was not going to be easy. Getting away with it was going to be even harder.

"The meeting is supposed to be sometime next week, but I'm not sure of the day. I think they're going to be on the boat for at least a week."

"That doesn't really give me much time to set something up. Do you know the name of the yacht?"

"Yes, it's called De Senhors, (The Lords) in Portuguese," he told Tony.

"Okay, from now on, you will be code number 62561. Use that number when you call me. You can call me 1001. Payment terms are half up front, and the rest when the job is finished. Here are the numbers to send your payments to." Tony gave him his payment instructions, along with the cost of the hit. The man agreed to everything, and the call was ended. Tony had some work to do to get ready for the job. He already knew what he was going to do, and how he was going to do it. The job would take some modifications to his jet. Tony was sure he could have the modifications competed in a few days.

As the jet rested in the hanger, Tony set about cutting two slots in the bottom of each wing. The slots were fit with electric covers and made to accommodate one, AMG-114R Hellfire air to ground missile in each of them. The missiles were seven inches in diameter, and about five feet–four inches long, with fragmentation warheads. He installed a cradle in each slot, which could be controlled from the cockpit to release each missile. The missiles, purchased on the black market, did not come cheap, but they did come. The only way Tony could test his new toy, was to install mock missiles, the same size and weight as the real ones, and fly out over the ocean and drop them. The system worked perfectly.

In testing the new system, Tony found that because the jet had variable sweep wings, he had to be sure they were in the right position before dropping the missiles. As the meeting time approached, Tony called number 62561.

"I'm ready to take care of that thing. Are we still going with it?" he asked.

"Yes, I'll send the money today. The Russian group left here yesterday."

"Okay! Then I'll plan on seeing them two days from now. I'll let you know how our meeting goes." And the call was ended.

When the time came for Tony to make his move on the yacht, he didn't have a photo of it, so he was just looking for a name. He arrived over Monaco Bay at about 3:00 p.m. He didn't want to draw attention to his jet, so he continued on, looking for someplace close by to land. There was a small strip of land that looked good enough for a quick landing about a half mile from the Bay. After landing, he headed straight for the bay on foot. In the hills overlooking Monaco Bay, Tony had a perfect view of the entire Bay. He sat and scanned the water looking for the yacht called De Senhors. He was pretty sure the 'Lords' it was referring to, was the drug lords that owned it.

It didn't take long to find the one he was looking for. It was a 103-foot white and blue yacht. It looked very new, with nice sleek lines. There was a helicopter pad above part of the rear deck. The rest of the deck was open. A large hot tub was built into a section of the foredeck. The bridge, above the main salon, had a small, enclosed side-deck bumped out on each side to assist in docking the large vessel. The main salon had glass all the way around it, including sliding doors to the rear deck. All of the windows on the yacht had very dark privacy glass in them.

After noting what the ship looked like and where it was moored, Tony went to town and settled in for a nice dinner and a couple glasses of wine. He then walked around town, just looking at the place. He had never been there before and wanted to see if he had been missing anything. He decided he had not! Later, after it got dark, he went back to the jet and waited. He was going to hit the yacht at around 3:30 a.m. hoping everyone that should be on board would be by then. As the time approached, he got airborne.

Using the night vision system displayed on the canopy in front of him, it was almost as if he were flying in the day light. Out over the Bay, he headed for the yacht. It wasn't there! He made a few passes over the entire bay and did not find the yacht. Over the Bay, he was only a few hundred feet up. He decided to go up to eight hundred feet, and head out over the open ocean. *That fucking tub had to be somewhere close by,* he thought. About fifteen miles out, he found the yacht. It was not under power, but at anchor either. There were no lights on, not even the required marker lights.

After circling the yacht, a couple of times, each time lower than the last, he made a very wide turn, and came in for the hit. From about five hundred feet up, and a half mile away, he fired two of the Hellfire missiles. Both of them hit their intended mark. There was a massive explosion, followed by a large but brief fire. And then nothing more than several small bits of flaming boat parts, spread out in a very large debris field. Tony did a couple of fly-bys just to get a good look at his work. He decided that he liked his new missile toys.

Back in Bruges, the police were convinced that Jason had been abducted, and maybe even killed. They had intensified their search and were starting to look in England and Ireland. Scotland Yard had been asked to get involved. Kelsey was doing his own search as well. He had walked every inch of the farm looking for any sign of a fresh hole. He didn't find one. He was also checking on the internet and talking to Shawn. He knew that Shawn was upset with Jason about something, but he didn't know what that was about. The police were thinking of expanding their search to the continent.

Tony was back at his vineyard. He put away the jet and went to the house for a few hours of sleep before calling number 62561 to let him know the job was done. Shortly after going to bed, the phone rang.

"Hello?" he said in a slightly groggy voice.

"Hey, this is 62561. I heard about the yacht. That must have been something to see. I wish I could have been there."

"How did you hear about it so soon?" Tony asked, much more clear headed.

"It's all over the news, you should turn on your television," the man told him.

"Okay, maybe I will. Did you send the rest of the money?"

"Yes, it should be in your account by now."

"Alright, I'm going to take a look at the news, give me a call if there is anything else I can do for you."

Tony turned on the television to a news channel. What he saw was not what he had expected to see. The reporter on the scene in Monaco was talking about a yacht that had exploded off the coast. The yacht, she was saying, had several diplomats on board, from around the world. They were there in an attempt to form a peace accord between their countries. Tony was not happy! He was back on the phone with number 62561.

"You lied to me about who was on the boat."

"If I told you the truth, would you have taken the job?"

"You know I wouldn't have; I don't do that sort of work. But I will be very happy to show you exactly what kind of work I do," Tony replied, and then got off the phone. He was very upset that he was tricked into that job. He was, however, very happy that his call scrambler tracked every incoming call. Number 62561 was going to get a visit from Tony. It wasn't going to be the kind of visit the man would be glad to get. It was going to be more of what you might think of as a 'Tony' visit. Yes, Tony was absolutely back, and the ghost was coming with him. Tony went back to bed for a couple hours of sleep. When he got up, Tony began his internet search for the location of number 62561. As he was doing that, a missing person alert from Scotland Yard popped up. Tony sat staring at Jason. "Oh shit!"

## The End